Bret Harte

A Phyllis of the Sierras, and a Drift from Redwood Camp

Bret Harte

A Phyllis of the Sierras, and a Drift from Redwood Camp

ISBN/EAN: 9783337422875

Printed in Europe, USA, Canada, Australia, Japan

Cover: Foto ©Andreas Hilbeck / pixelio.de

More available books at **www.hansebooks.com**

AND

A DRIFT FROM REDWOOD CAMP

BY

BRET HARTE

London

CHATTO & WINDUS, PICCADILLY

1888

CONTENTS.

A

PHYLLIS OF THE SIERRAS.

Part I.

CHAPTER I.

WHERE the great highway of the Sierras nears the summit, and the pines begin to show sterile reaches of rock and waste in their drawn-up files, there are signs of occasional departures from the main road, as if the weary traveller had at times succumbed to the long ascent, and turned aside for rest and breath again. The tired eyes of many a dusty passenger on the old overland coach have gazed wistfully on those sylvan openings, and imagined recesses of primeval shade and virgin wilderness in their dim perspectives. Had he descended, however, and followed one of these diverging paths, he would have come upon some rude waggon track, or "log-slide," leading from a clearing on the slope, or the ominous saw-mill, half hidden in the forest it was slowly decimating. The woodland hush might have been broken by the sound of water passing over some unseen dam in the hollow, or the hiss of escaping steam and throb of an invisible engine in the covert.

Such, at least, was the experience of a young fellow of five-and-twenty, who, knapsack on back and stick in hand, had turned aside from the highway and entered the woods one pleasant afternoon in July. But he was evidently a deliberate pedestrian, and not a recent deposit of the proceeding stage-coach; and, although his stout walking-shoes were covered with dust, he had neither the habitual slouch and slovenliness of the tramp, nor the hurried fatigue and growing negligence of an involuntary wayfarer. His clothes, which were strong and serviceable, were better fitted for their present usage than the ordinary garments of the Californian travellers, which were too apt to be either above or below their requirements. But perhaps the stranger's greatest claim to originality was the absence of any weapon in his equipment. He carried neither rifle nor gun in his hand, and his narrow leathern belt was empty of either knife or revolver.

A half-mile from the main road, which seemed to him to have dropped out of sight the moment he had left it, he came upon a half-cleared area, where the hastily cut stumps of pines, of irregular height, bore an odd resemblance to the broken columns of some vast and ruined temple. A few fallen shafts, denuded of their bark and tessellated branches, sawn into symmetrical cylinders, lay beside the stumps, and lent themselves to the illusion. But the freshly cut chips, so damp that they still clung in

layers to each other as they had fallen from
the axe, and the stumps themselves, still
wet and viscous from their drained life-
blood, were redolent of an odour of youth
and freshness.

The young man seated himself on one
of the logs and deeply inhaled the sharp
balsamic fragrance—albeit with a slight
cough and a later hurried respiration. This,
and a certain drawn look about his upper
lip, seemed to indicate, in spite of his
strength and colour, some pulmonary weakness. He, however, rose after a moment's
rest with undiminished energy and cheerfulness, readjusted his knapsack, and began
to lightly pick his way across the fallen
timber. A few paces on, the muffled whirr
of machinery became more audible, with
the lazy, monotonous command of "Gee
thar," from some unseen ox-driver. Presently, the slow, deliberately swaying heads
of a team of oxen emerged from the bushes,
followed by the clanking chain of the

"skids" of sawn planks, which they were
ponderously dragging, with that ostentatious
submissiveness peculiar to their species.
They had nearly passed him when there
was a sudden hitch in the procession. From
where he stood he could see that a project-
ing plank had struck a pile of chips and
become partly imbedded in it. To run to
the obstruction and, with a few dexterous
strokes and the leverage of his stout stick,
dislodge the plank was the work, not only
of the moment, but of an evidently energetic hand. The teamster looked back and
merely nodded his appreciation, and with a
"Gee up! Out of that, now!" the skids
moved on.

"Much obliged, there!" said a hearty
voice, as if supplementing the teamster's
imperfect acknowledgment.

The stranger looked up. The voice came
from the open, sashless, shutterless window
of a rude building—a mere shell of boards
and beams half hidden in the still leafy

covert before him. He had completely
overlooked it in his approach, even as he
had ignored the nearer throbbing of the
machinery, which was so violent as to im-
part a decided tremor to the slight edifice,
and to shake the speaker so strongly that
he was obliged while speaking to steady
himself by the sashless frame of the window
at which he stood. He had a face of good-
natured and alert intelligence, a master's
independence and authority of manner, in
spite of his blue jean overalls and flannel
shirt.

"Don't mention it," said the traveller,
smiling with equal but more deliberate
good-humour. Then, seeing that his inter-
locutor still lingered a hospitable moment
in spite of his quick eyes and the jarring
impatience of the machinery, he added
hesitatingly, "I fancy I've wandered off the
track a bit. Do you know a Mr. Bradley
—somewhere here?"

His hesitation seemed to be more from

some habitual conscientiousness of statement than awkwardness. The man in the
window replied, " I'm Bradley."

" Ah! Thank you : I've a letter for you
—somewhere. Here it is." He produced
a note from his breast-pocket. Bradley
stooped to a sitting posture in the window.
" Pitch it up." It was thrown and caught
cleverly. Bradley opened it, read it
hastily, smiled and nodded, glanced behind
him as if to implore further delay from the
impatient machinery, leaned perilously from
the window, and said :

" Look here ! Do you see that silver-fir
straight ahead ?"

" Yes."

" A little to the left there's a trail.
Follow it and skirt along the edge of the
canyon until you see my house. Ask for
my wife—that's Mrs. Bradley—and give
her your letter. Stop !" He drew a car-
penter's pencil from his pocket, scrawled
two or three words across the open sheet,

and tossed it back to the stranger. "See you at tea! Excuse me, Mr. Mainwaring;— we're short-handed—and—the engine——" But here he disappeared suddenly.

Without glancing at the note again, the stranger quietly replaced it in his pocket, and struck out across the fallen trunks towards the silver-fir. He quickly found the trail indicated by Bradley, although it was faint and apparently worn by a single pair of feet as a shorter and private cut from some more travelled path. It was well for the stranger that he had a keen eye or he would have lost it; it was equally fortunate that he had a mountaineering instinct, for a sudden profound deepening of the blue mist seen dimly through the leaves before him caused him to slacken his steps. The trail bent abruptly to the right; a gulf fully two thousand feet deep was at his feet! It was the Great Canyon.

At the first glance it seemed so narrow that a rifle-shot could have crossed its tranquil depths; but a second look at the comparative size of the trees on the opposite mountain convinced him of his error. A nearer survey of the abyss also showed him that, instead of its walls being perpendicular, they were made of successive ledges or terraces to the valley below. Yet the air was so still, and the outlines so clearly cut, that they might have been only the reflections of the mountains around him cast upon the placid mirror of a lake. The spectacle arrested him, as it arrested all men, by some occult power beyond the mere attraction of beauty or magnitude; even the teamster never passed it without the tribute of a stone or broken twig tossed into its immeasurable profundity.

Reluctantly leaving the spot, the stranger turned with the trail that now began to skirt its edge. This was no easy matter, as the undergrowth was very thick, and the foliage dense, to the perilous brink of the precipice. He walked on, however, wondering why Bradley had chosen so circuitous and dangerous a route to his house, which naturally would be some distance back from the canyon. At the end of ten minutes' struggling through the "brush," the trail became vague, and, to all appearance, ended. Had he arrived? The thicket was as dense as before; through the interstices of leaf and spray he could see the blue void of the canyon at his side, and he even fancied that the foliage ahead of him was more symmetrical and less irregular, and was touched here and there with faint bits of colour. To complete his utter mystification, a woman's voice, very fresh, very youthful, and by no means unmusical, rose apparently from the circumambient air. He looked hurriedly to the right and left, and even hopelessly into the trees above him.

"Yes," said the voice, as if renewing a suspended conversation; "it was too

funny for anything. There were the two
Missouri girls from Skinner's, with their
auburn hair ringleted, my dear, like the
old 'Books of Beauty'—in white frocks
and sashes of an unripe greenish yellow,
that puckered up your mouth like per-
simmons. One of them was speechless
from good behaviour, and the other—well!
the other was so energetic she called out
the figures before the fiddler did, and
shrieked to my *vis-à-vis* to dance up to
the entire stranger—meaning *me*, if you
please."

The voice appeared to come from the
foliage that overhung the canyon, and the
stranger even fancied he could detect
through the shimmering leafy veil something that moved monotonously to and
fro. Mystified and impatient, he made a
hurried stride forward, his foot struck a
wooden step, and the next moment the
mystery was made clear. He had almost
stumbled upon the end of a long veranda

that projected over the abyss, before a
low, modern dwelling, till then invisible,
nestling on its very brink. The symmetrically trimmed foliage he had noticed
were the luxuriant Madeira vines that hid
the rude pillars of the veranda; the
moving object was a rocking-chair, with its
back towards the intruder, that disclosed
only the brown hair above, and the white
skirts and small slippered feet below, of
a seated female figure. In the meantime, a second voice from the interior
of the house had replied to the figure
in the chair, who was evidently the first
speaker:

"It must have been very funny; but as
long as Jim is always bringing somebody
over from the mill, I don't see how *I* can
go to those places. You were lucky, my
dear, to escape from the new Division
Superintendent last night. He was in-
sufferable to Jim, with his talk of his
friend the San Francisco millionaire, and

to me with his cheap society airs. I do
hate a provincial fine gentleman."

The situation was becoming embarrassing
to the intruder. At the apparition of the
woman, the unaffected and simple directness he had previously shown in his equally
abrupt contact with Bradley had fled
utterly. Confused by the awkwardness of
his arrival, and shocked at the idea of
overhearing a private conversation, he
stepped hurriedly on the veranda.

" Well ? Go on ! " said the second voice
impatiently. " Well, who else was there ?
What did you say ? I don't hear you.
What's the matter ? "

The seated figure had risen from her
chair, and turned a young and pretty
face somewhat superciliously towards the
stranger, as she said in a low tone to her
unseen auditor, " Hush ! there is somebody
here ! "

The young man came forward with
an awkwardness that was more boyish

than rustic. His embarrassment was not lessened by the simultaneous entrance from the open door of a second woman, apparently as young as and prettier than the first.

"I trust you'll excuse me for—for—being so wretchedly stupid," he stammered, "but I really thought, you know, that—that—I was following the trail to—to—the front of the house, when I stumbled in—in here."

Long before he had finished both women, by some simple feminine intuition, were relieved, and even prepossessed, by his voice and manner. They smiled graciously. The later comer pointed to the empty chair. But, with his habit of pertinacious conscientiousness, the stranger continued : " It was regularly stupid, wasn't it ?—and I ought to have known better. I should have turned back and gone away when I found out what an ass I was likely to be ; but I was—afraid—you know, of alarming you by the noise."

" Won't you sit down ? " said the second
lady pleasantly.

" Oh, thanks. I've a letter here—I——"
He transferred his stick and hat to his left
hand as he felt in his breast-pocket with
his right. But the action was so awkward
that the stick dropped on the veranda.
Both women made a movement to restore
it to its embarrassed owner, who, however,
quickly anticipated them. " Pray don't
mind it," he continued, with accelerated
breath and heightened colour. " Ah, here's
the letter!" He produced the letter
Bradley had returned to him. " It's
mine, in fact—that is, I brought it to
Mr. Bradley. He said I was to give it
to—to—to—Mrs. Bradley." He paused,
glancing embarrassedly from the one to
the other.

" I'm Mrs. Bradley," said the prettiest
one, with a laugh. He handed her the
letter. It ran as follows :

C

"DEAR BRADLEY,—Put Mr. Mainwaring through as far as he wants to go, or hang him up at The Lookout, just as he likes. The Bank's behind him, and his hat's chalked all over the Road. But he don't care much about being on velvet. That ain't his style—and you'll like him. He's somebody's son in England.

"B."

Mrs. Bradley glanced simply at the first sentence. "Pray sit down, Mr. Mainwaring," she said gently; "or, rather, let me first introduce my cousin—Miss Macy."

"Thanks," said Mainwaring, with a bow to Miss Macy, "but I—I—I—think," he added conscientiously, "you did not notice that your husband had written something across the paper."

Mrs. Bradley smiled, and glanced at her husband's endorsement—"All right. Wade in." "It's nothing but Jim's slang," she said, with a laugh and a slightly heightened

colour. "He ought not to have sent you
by that short cut; it's a bother, and even
dangerous for a stranger. If you had come
directly to *us* by the road, without making
your first call at the mill," she added, with
a touch of coquetry, "you would have had
a pleasanter walk, and seen *us* sooner. I
suppose, however, you got off the stage at
the mill?"

"I was not on the coach," said Mainwaring, unfastening the strap of his knapsack. "I walked over from Lone Pine
Flat."

"Walked!" echoed both women in simultaneous astonishment.

"Yes," returned Mainwaring simply, laying aside his burden and taking the proffered
seat. "It's a very fine bit of country."

"Why, it's fifteen miles," said Mrs.
Bradley, glancing horror-stricken at her
cousin. "How dreadful! And to think
Jim could have sent you a horse to Lone
Pine. Why, you must be dead!"

"Thanks, I'm all right! I rather enjoyed it, you know."

"But," said Miss Macy, glancing wonderingly at his knapsack, "you must want something, a change—or some refreshment—after fifteen miles."

"Pray don't disturb yourself," said Mainwaring, rising hastily, but not quickly enough to prevent the young girl from slipping past him into the house, whence she rapidly returned with a decanter and glasses.

"Perhaps Mr. Mainwaring would prefer to go into Jim's room and wash his hands and put on a pair of slippers?" said Mrs. Bradley, with gentle concern.

"Thanks, no. I really am not tired. I sent some luggage yesterday by the coach to the Summit Hotel," he said, observing the women's eyes still fixed upon his knapsack. "I dare say I can get them if I want them. I've got a change here," he continued, lifting the knapsack as if with a sudden sense of its incongruity with its surroundings, and depositing it on the end of the veranda.

" Do let it remain where it is," said Mrs. Bradley, greatly amused, "and pray sit still and take some refreshment. You'll make yourself ill after your exertions," she added, with a charming assumption of matronly solicitude.

" But I'm not at all deserving of your sympathy," said Mainwaring, with a laugh. " I'm awfully fond of walking, and my usual constitutional isn't much under this."

" Perhaps you were stronger than you are now," said Mrs. Bradley, gazing at him with a frank curiosity that, however, brought a faint deepening of colour to his cheek.

"I dare say you're right," he said suddenly, with an apologetic smile. " I quite forgot that I'm a sort of an invalid, you know, travelling for my health. I'm not very strong here," he added, lightly tapping his chest, that now, relieved of the bands of his knapsack, appeared somewhat thin and hollow in spite of his broad shoulders. His voice, too, had become less clear and distinct.

Mrs. Bradley, who was still watching him, here rose potentially. " You ought to take more care of yourself," she said. " You should begin by eating this biscuit, drinking that glass of whisky, and making yourself more comfortable in Jim's room until we can get the spare room fixed a little."

" But I am not to be sent to bed—am I ? " asked Mainwaring, in half-real, half-amused consternation.

" I'm not so sure of that," said Mrs. Bradley, with playful precision. " But for the present we'll let you off with a good wash and a nap afterwards in that rocking-chair, while my cousin and I make some little domestic preparations. You see," she added with a certain proud humility, "we've got only one servant—a Chinaman, and there are many things we can't leave to him."

The colour again rose in Mainwaring's cheek, but he had tact enough to reflect that any protest or hesitation on his part at that moment would only increase the difficulties of his gentle entertainers. He allowed himself to be ushered into the house by Mrs. Bradley, and shown to her husband's room, without perceiving that Miss Macy had availed herself of his absence to run to the end of the veranda, mischievously try to lift the discarded knapsack to her own pretty shoulder, but, failing, heroically stagger with it into the passage and softly deposit it at his door. This done, she pantingly rejoined her cousin in the kitchen.

"Well," said Mrs. Bradley emphatically. "*Did* you ever? Walking fifteen miles for pleasure—and with such lungs!"

"And that knapsack!" added Louise Macy, pointing to the mark in her little palm where the strap had imbedded itself in the soft flesh.

"He's nice, though; isn't he?" said Mrs. Bradley tentatively.

"Yes," said Miss Macy; "he isn't, certainly, one of those provincial fine gentlemen you object to. But *did* you see his shoes? I suppose they make the miles go quickly, or seem to measure less by comparison."

"They're probably more serviceable than those high-heeled things that Captain Greyson hops about in."

"But the Captain always rides—and rides very well—you know," said Louise reflectively. There was a moment's pause.

"I suppose Jim will tell us all about him," said Mrs. Bradley, dismissing the subject, as she turned her sleeves back over her white arms, preparatory to grappling certain culinary difficulties.

"Jim," observed Miss Macy shortly, "in

my opinion, knows nothing more than his note says. That's like Jim."

" There's nothing more to know, really," said Mrs. Bradley, with a superior air. " He's undoubtedly the son of some Englishman of fortune, sent out here for his health."

" Hush ! "

Miss Macy had heard a step in the passage. It halted at last, half irresolutely, before the open door of the kitchen, and the stranger appeared with an embarrassed air. But in his brief absence he seemed to have completely groomed himself, and stood there, the impersonation of close - cropped, clean, and wholesome English young manhood. The two women appreciated it with cat-like fastidiousness.

" I beg your pardon ; but really you're going to let a fellow do something for you," he said, " just to keep him from looking like a fool. I really can do no end of things, you know, if you'll try me. I've

done some camping-out, and can cook as
well as the next man."

The two women made a movement of
smiling remonstrance, half coquettish, and
half superior, until Mrs. Bradley, becoming
conscious of her bare arms and the
stranger's wandering eyes, coloured faintly,
and said with more decision:

"Certainly not. You'd only be in the
way. Besides, you need rest more than
we do. Put yourself in the rocking-chair,
in the veranda, and go to sleep until Mr.
Bradley comes."

Mainwaring saw that she was serious,
and withdrew, a little ashamed at the
familiarity into which his boyishness had
betrayed him. But he had scarcely seated
himself in the rocking-chair before Miss
Macy appeared, carrying with both hands
a large tin basin of unshelled peas.

"There," she said pantingly, placing her
burden in his lap, "if you really want to
help, there's something to do that isn't

very fatiguing. You may shell these
peas."

"*Shell* them—I beg pardon, but how?"
he asked, with smiling earnestness.

"How? Why, I'll show you—look."

She frankly stepped beside him, so close
that her full-skirted dress half encompassed
him and the basin in a delicious confusion,
and, leaning over his lap, with her left hand
picked up a pea-cod, which, with a single
movement of her charming little right
thumb, she broke at the end, and
stripped the green shallow of its tiny
treasures.

He watched her with smiling eyes; her
own, looking down on him, were very
bright and luminous. "There; that's easy
enough," she said, and turned away.

"But—one moment, Miss—Miss—— ?"

"Macy," said Louise.

"Where am I to put the shells?"

"Oh! throw them down there—there's
room enough."

She was pointing to the canyon below. The veranda actually projected over its brink, and seemed to hang in mid-air above it. Mainwaring almost mechanically threw his arm out to catch the incautious girl, who had stepped heedlessly to its extreme edge.

"How odd! Don't you find it rather dangerous here?" he could not help saying. "I mean—you might have had a railing that wouldn't intercept the view and yet be safe?"

"It's a fancy of Mr. Bradley's," returned the young girl carelessly. "It's all like this. The house was built on a ledge against the side of the precipice, and the road suddenly drops down to it."

"It's tremendously pretty, all the same, you know," said the young man thoughtfully, gazing, however, at the girl's rounded chin above him.

"Yes," she replied curtly. "But this isn't working. I must go back to Jenny.

You can shell the peas until Mr. Bradley comes home.   He won't be long."

She turned away, and re-entered the house.   Without knowing why, he thought her withdrawal abrupt, and he was again feeling his ready colour rise with the suspicion of either having been betrayed by the young girl's innocent fearlessness into some unpardonable familiarity, which she had quietly resented, or of feeling an ease and freedom in the company of these two women that were inconsistent with respect, and should be restrained.

He, however, began to apply himself to the task given to him with his usual conscientiousness of duty, and presently acquired a certain manual dexterity in the operation.   It was "good fun" to throw the cast-off husks into the mighty unfathomable void before him and watch them linger with suspended gravity in mid-air for a moment —apparently motionless—until they either lost themselves, a mere vanishing black

spot in the thin ether, or slid suddenly at a
sharp angle into unknown shadow. How
deuced odd for him to be sitting here in
this fashion! It would be something to
talk of hereafter, and yet—he stopped—it
was not at all in the line of that characteristic adventure, uncivilized novelty, and
barbarous freedom which for the last month
he had sought and experienced. It was not
at all like his meeting with the grizzly last
week while wandering in a lonely canyon;
not a bit in the line of his chance acquaintance with that notorious ruffian,
Spanish Jack, or his witnessing with his
own eyes that actual lynching affair at
Angels. No! Nor was it at all characteristic, according to his previous ideas of frontier rural seclusion—as for instance the Pike
County cabin of the family where he stayed
one night, and where the handsome daughter
asked him what his Christian name was.
No! These two young women were very
unlike her; they seemed really quite the

equals of his family and friends in England
—perhaps more attractive—and yet, yes it
was this very attractiveness that alarmed
his inbred social conservatism regarding
women.   With a man it was very different ;
that alert, active, intelligent husband, instinct with the throbbing life of his saw-
mill, creator and worker in one, chal-
lenged his unqualified trust and admiration.

He had become conscious for the last
minute or two of thinking rapidly and
becoming feverishly excited ; of breathing
with greater difficulty, and a renewed tendency to cough.   The tendency increased
until he instinctively put aside the pan
from his lap and half rose.   But even that
slight exertion brought on an accession of
coughing.   He put his handkerchief to his
lips, partly to keep the sound from disturbing the women in the kitchen, partly because
of a certain significant taste in his mouth
which he unpleasantly remembered.   When

he removed the handkerchief it was, as he
expected, spotted with blood.   He turned
quickly and re-entered the house softly, regaining the bedroom without attracting
attention.   An increasing faintness here
obliged him to lie down on the bed until it
should pass.

Everything was quiet.   He hoped they
would not discover his absence from the
veranda until he was better;   it was
deucedly awkward that he should have had
this attack just now—and after he had made
so light of his previous exertions.   They
would think him an effeminate fraud, these
two bright, active women and that alert,
energetic man.   A faint colour came into his
cheek at the idea, and an uneasy sense that
he had been in some way foolishly im-
prudent about his health.   Again, they
might be alarmed at missing him from the
veranda;   perhaps he had better have remained there;   perhaps he ought to tell
them that he had concluded to take their

advice and lie down. He tried to rise, but the deep blue chasm before the window seemed to be swelling up to meet him, the bed slowly sinking into its oblivious profundity. He knew no more.

He came to with the smell and taste of some powerful volatile spirit, and the vague vision of Mr. Bradley still standing at the window of the mill and vibrating with the machinery; this changed presently to a pleasant lassitude and lazy curiosity as he perceived Mr. Bradley smile and apparently slip from the window of the mill to his bedside.

"You're all right now," said Bradley cheerfully.

He was feeling Mainwaring's pulse. Had he really been ill, and was Bradley a doctor?

Bradley evidently saw what was passing in his mind. "Don't be alarmed," he said gaily. "I'm not a doctor, but I practise a little medicine and surgery on account of

D

the men at the mill, and accidents, you
know. You're all right now; you've lost
a little blood ; but in a couple of weeks in
this air we'll have that tubercle healed,
and you'll be as right as a trivet."

"In a couple of weeks!" echoed Mainwaring, in faint astonishment. "Why, I
leave here to-morrow."

"You'll do nothing of the kind," said
Mrs. Bradley, with smiling peremptoriness,
suddenly slipping out from behind her
husband. "Everything is all perfectly
arranged. Jim has sent off messengers to
your friends, so that if you can't come to
them they can come to you. You see, you
can't help yourself! If you *will* walk
fifteen miles with such lungs, and then
frighten people to death, you must abide
by the consequences."

"You see, the old lady has fixed you,"
said Bradley, smiling, "and she's the
master here. Come, Mainwaring, you can
send any other message you like, and have

who and what you want here; but *here* you must stop for awhile."

"But did I frighten you really?" stammered Mainwaring faintly, to Mrs. Bradley.

"Frighten us!" said Mrs. Bradley. "Well, look there!"

She pointed to the window which commanded a view of the veranda. Miss Macy had dropped into the vacant chair, with her little feet stretched out before her, her cheeks burning with heat and fire, her eyes partly closed, her straw hat hanging by a ribbon round her neck, her brown hair clinging to her ears and forehead in damp tendrils, and an enormous palm-leaf fan in each hand violently playing upon this charming picture of exhaustion and abandonment.

"She came tearing down to the mill, barebacked on our half-broken mustang, about half an hour ago, to call me 'to help you,'" explained Bradley. "Heaven knows how she managed to do it!"

CHAPTER II.

THE medication of the woods was not over-estimated by Bradley. There was surely some occult healing property in that vast reservoir of balmy and resinous odours over which The Lookout beetled and clung, and from which at times the pure exhalations of the terraced valley seemed to rise. Under its remedial influence and a conscientious adherence to the rules of absolute rest and repose laid down for him, Mainwaring had no return of the hæmorrhage. The nearest professional medical authority, hastily summoned, saw no reason for changing or for supplementing Bradley's intelligent and simple treatment, although astounded that the patient had been under no more radical or systematic cure than travel and exercise. The women especially were amazed that Mainwaring had taken "nothing for it," in their habitual experience of an unfettered pill-and-elixir consuming democracy. In their knowledge of the thousand "panaceas" that filled the shelves of the General Store, this singular abstention of their guest seemed to indicate a national peculiarity.

His bed was moved beside the low window, from which he could not only view the veranda, but converse at times with its occupants, and even listen to the book which Miss Macy, seated without, read aloud to him. In the evening, Bradley would linger by his couch until late, beguiling the tedium of his convalescence with characteristic stories and information which he thought might please the invalid. For Mainwaring, who had been early struck with Bradley's ready and cultivated intelligence, ended by shyly avoiding the discussion of more serious

topics, partly because Bradley impressed
him with a suspicion of his own inferiority,
and partly because Mainwaring questioned
the taste of Bradley's apparent exhibition
of his manifest superiority. He learned
accidentally that this millowner and backwoodsman was a college-bred man ; but
the practical application of that education
to the ordinary affairs of life was new to
the young Englishman's traditions, and
grated a little harshly on his feelings. He
would have been quite content if Bradley
had, like himself and fellows he knew,
undervalued his training, and kept his
gifts conservatively impractical. The
knowledge also that his host's education
naturally came from some provincial institution unlike Oxford and Cambridge,
may have unconsciously affected his general estimate. I say unconsciously, for his
strict conscientiousness would have rejected any such formal proposition.

Another trifle annoyed him. He could

not help noticing also that, although
Bradley's manner and sympathy were confidential and almost brotherly, he never
made any allusion to Mainwaring's own
family or connections, and, in fact, gave no
indication of what he believed was the
national curiosity in regard to strangers.
Somewhat embarrassed by this indifference,
Mainwaring made the occasion of writing
some letters home an opportunity for
laughingly alluding to the fact that he
had made his mother and his sisters fully
aware of the great debt they owed the
household of The Lookout.

"They'll probably all send you a round
robin of thanks, except, perhaps, my next
brother, Bob." Bradley contented himself
with a gesture of general deprecation, and
did not ask *why* Mainwaring's young
brother should contemplate his death with
satisfaction. Nevertheless, some time afterwards Miss Macy remarked that it seemed
hard that the happiness of one member of

a family should depend upon a calamity to
another. "As for instance?" asked Mainwaring, who had already forgotten the
circumstance. "Why, if you had died,
and your younger brother succeeded to
the baronetcy, and become Sir Robert
Mainwaring," responded Miss Macy, with
precision. This was the first and only
allusion to his family and prospective rank.
On the other hand he had—through naïve
and boyish inquiries, which seemed to
amuse his entertainers—acquired, as he
believed, a full knowledge of the history
and antecedents of the Bradley household.
He knew how Bradley had brought his
young wife and her cousin to California,
and abandoned a lucrative law practice
in San Francisco to take possession of
this mountain mill and woodland, which
he had acquired through some professional
service.

"Then you are a barrister really?" said
Mainwaring gravely.

Bradley laughed. " I'm afraid I've had more practice—though not as lucrative a one—as surgeon or doctor."

" But you're regularly on the rolls, you know; you're entered as counsel, and all that sort of thing?" continued Mainwaring, with great seriousness.

" Well, yes," replied Bradley, much amused. " I'm afraid I must plead guilty to that."

" It's not a bad sort of thing," said Mainwaring naïvely, ignoring Bradley's amusement. " I've got a cousin who's gone in for the law. Got out of the army to do it—too. He's a sharp fellow."

" Then you *do* allow a man to try many trades—over there," said Miss Macy demurely.

" Yes, sometimes," said Mainwaring graciously, but by no means certain that the case was at all analogous.

Nevertheless, as if relieved of certain doubts of the conventional quality of his host's attainments, he now gave himself up to a very hearty and honest admiration of Bradley. "You know it's awfully kind of him to talk to a fellow like me, who just pulled through, and never got any prizes at Oxford, and don't understand the half of these things," he remarked confidentially to Mrs. Bradley. "He knows more about the things we used to go in for at Oxford than lots of our men, and he's never been there. He's uncommonly clever."

"Jim was always very brilliant," returned Mrs. Bradley indifferently, and with more than even conventionally polite wifely deprecation; "I wish he were more practical."

"Practical! Oh, I say, Mrs. Bradley! Why, a fellow that can go in among a lot of workmen and tell them just what to do —an all-round chap that can be independent of his valet, his doctor, and his—banker! By Jove—*that's* practical!"

"I mean," said Mrs. Bradley coldly,

" that there are some things that a gentleman ought not to be practical about nor
independent of. Mr. Bradley would have
done better to have used his talents in
some more legitimate and established
way."

Mainwaring looked at her in genuine
surprise. To his inexperienced observation
Bradley's intelligent energy and, above all,
his originality, ought to have been priceless
in the eyes of his wife—the American female
of his species. He felt that slight shock
which most loyal or logical men feel when
first brought face to face with the easy dis-
loyalty and incomprehensible logic of the
feminine affections. Here was a fellow, by
Jove, that any woman ought to be proud
of, and—and—he stopped blankly. He
wondered if Miss Macy sympathized with
her cousin.

Howbeit, this did not affect the charm
of their idyllic life at The Lookout. The
precipice over which they hung was as

charming as ever in its poetic illusions of
space and depth and colour; the isolation
of their comfortable existence in the taste-
ful yet audacious habitation, the pleasant
routine of daily tasks and amusements, all
tended to make the enforced quiet and
inaction of his convalescence a lazy recreation.   He was really improving; more than
that, he was conscious of a certain satisfaction in this passive observation of novelty
that was healthier and perhaps *truer* than
his previous passion for adventure and that
febrile desire for change and excitement
which he now felt was a part of his disease.
Nor were incident and variety entirely
absent from this tranquil experience.   He
was one day astonished at being presented
by Bradley with copies of the latest English
newspapers, procured from Sacramento, and
he equally astonished his host, after profusely thanking him, by only listlessly
glancing at their columns.   He estopped a
proposed visit from one of his influential

countrymen; in the absence of his fair
entertainers at their domestic duties, he
extracted infinite satisfaction from Foo-Yup,
the Chinese servant, who was particularly
detached for his service. From his invalid
coign of vantage at the window he was
observant of all that passed upon the
veranda, that al fresco audience-room of
The Lookout, and he was good-humouredly
conscious that a great many eccentric and
peculiar visitors were invariably dragged
thither by Miss Macy, and goaded into
characteristic exhibition within sight and
hearing of her guest, with a too evident
view, under the ostentatious excuse of ex-
tending his knowledge of national character,
of mischievously shocking him. "When
you are strong enough to stand Captain
Gashweiler's opinions of the Established
Church and Chinamen," said Miss Macy,
after one of those revelations, "I'll get Jim
to bring him here, for really he swears so
outrageously that even in the broadest in-

terests of international understanding and
goodwill neither Mrs. Bradley nor myself
could be present."

On another occasion she provokingly
lingered before his window for a moment
with a rifle slung jauntily over her shoulder.
"If you hear a shot or two don't excite
yourself, and believe we're having a lynching case in the woods. It will be only me.
There's some creature—confess, you expected me to say 'critter'—hanging round
the barn. It may be a bear. Good-bye."
She missed the creature—which happened
to be really a bear—much to Mainwaring's
illogical satisfaction. "I wonder why," he
reflected, with vague uneasiness, "she
doesn't leave all that sort of thing to girls
like that tow-headed girl at the blacksmith's."

It chanced, however, that this blacksmith's tow-headed daughter, who, it may
be incidentally remarked, had the additional
eccentricities of large black eyes and large

white teeth, came to the fore in quite another fashion. It was when, Mainwaring being able to leave his room and join the family board, Mrs. Bradley found it necessary to enlarge her domestic service, and arranged with their nearest neighbour, the blacksmith, to allow his daughter to come to The Lookout for a few days to "do the chores" and assist in the house-keeping, as she had on previous occasions. The day of her advent Bradley entered Mainwaring's room, and, closing the door mysteriously, fixed his blue eyes, kindling with mischief, on the young Englishman.

"You are aware, my dear boy," he began with affected gravity, "that you are now living in a land of liberty, where mere arti-ficial distinctions are not known, and where Freedom from her mountain heights gene-rally levels all social positions. I think you have graciously admitted that fact."

"I know I've been taking a tremendous lot of freedom with you and yours, old man,

and it's a deuced shame," interrupted Mainwaring, with a faint smile.

"And that nowhere," continued Bradley,
with immovable features, "does equality
exist as perfectly as above yonder unfathomable abyss, where you have also,
doubtless, observed the American eagle
proudly soars and screams defiance."

"Then that was the fellow that kept me
awake this morning, and made me wonder
if I was strong enough to hold a gun
again."

"That wouldn't have settled the matter,"
continued Bradley imperturbably. "The
case is simply this : Miss Minty Sharpe,
that blacksmith's daughter, has once or
twice consented, for a slight emolument,
to assist in our domestic service for a day
or two, and she comes back again to-day.
Now, under the ægis of that noble bird
whom your national instincts tempt you to
destroy, she has on all previous occasions
taken her meals with us, at the same

table, on terms of perfect equality. She will naturally expect to do the same now. Mrs. Bradley thought it proper, therefore, to warn you, that, in case your health was not quite equal to this democratic simplicity, you could still dine in your room."

"It would be great fun—if Miss Sharpe won't object to my presence."

"But it must not be 'great fun,'" returned Bradley, more seriously; "for Miss Minty's perception of humour is probably as keen as yours, and she would be quick to notice it. And, so far from having any objection to you, I am inclined to think that we owe her consent to come to her desire of making your acquaintance."

"She will find my conduct most exemplary," said Mainwaring earnestly.

"Let us hope so," concluded Bradley, with unabated gravity. "And, now that you have consented, let me add, from my own experience, that Miss Minty's lemon-pies alone are worthy of any concession."

E

The dinner-hour came. Mainwaring, a little pale and interesting, leaning on the arm of Bradley, crossed the hall, and for the first time entered the dining-room of the house where he had lodged for three weeks. It was a bright, cheerful apartment, giving upon the laurels of the rocky hill-side, and permeated, like the rest of the house, with the wholesome spice of the valley—an odour that, in its pure desiccating property, seemed to obliterate all flavour of alien human habitation, and even to dominate and etherealize the appetizing smell of the viands before them. The bare, shining, planed, boarded walls appeared to resent any decoration that might have savoured of dust, decay, or moisture. The four large windows and long, open door, set in scanty strips of the plainest, spotless muslin, framed in themselves pictures of woods and rock and sky of limitless depth, colour, and distance, that made all other adornment impertinent. Nature, invading the room at

every opening, had banished Art from those
neutral walls.

"It's like a picnic, with comfort," said
Mainwaring, glancing round him with boyish
appreciation. Miss Minty was not yet there;
the Chinaman was alone in attendance.
Mainwaring could not help whispering, half
mischievously, to Louise, "You draw the
line at Chinamen, I suppose?"

"*We* don't, but *he* does," answered the
young girl. "He considers us his social
inferiors. But—hush!"

Minty Sharpe had just entered the room,
and was advancing with smiling confidence
towards the table. Mainwaring was a little
startled; he had seen Minty in a holland
sun-bonnet and turned-up skirt crossing the
veranda only a moment before; in the
brief instant between the dishing-up of
dinner and its actual announcement she
had managed to change her dress, put on
a clean collar, cuffs, and a large jet brooch,
and apply some odorous unguent to her re-

bellious hair. Her face, guiltless of powder
or cold cream, was still shining with the
healthy perspiration of her last labours as
she promptly took the vacant chair beside
Mainwaring.

"Don't mind me, folks," she said cheerfully, resting her plump elbow on the table,
and addressing the company generally, but
gazing with frank curiosity into the face of
the young man at her side. "It was a
keen jump, I tell yer, to get out of my old
duds inter these, and look decent inside o'
five minutes. But I reckon I aint kept
yer waitin' long—least of all this yer sick
stranger. But you're looking pearter than
you did. You're wonderin' like ez not
where I ever saw ye before?" she continued, laughing. "Well, I'll tell you.
Last week! I'd kem over yer on a chance
of seein' Jenny Bradley, and while I was
meanderin' down the veranda I saw you
lyin' back in your chair by the window
drowned in sleep, like a baby. Lordy! I

mout hev won a pair o' gloves, but I reckoned you were Loo's game, and not mine."

The slightly constrained laugh which went round the table after Miss Minty's speech was due quite as much to the faint flush that had accented Mainwaring's own smile as to the embarrassing remark itself. Mrs. Bradley and Miss Macy exchanged rapid glances. Bradley, who alone retained his composure, with a slight flicker of amusement in the corner of his eye and nostril, said quickly : "You see, Mainwaring, how Nature stands ready to help your convalescence at every turn. If Miss Minty had only followed up her healing opportunity, your cure would have been complete."

"Ye mout hev left some o' that pretty talk for *him* to say," said Minty, taking up her knife and fork with a slight shrug, "and you needn't call me *Miss* Minty either, jest because there's kempeny present."

"I hope you won't look upon me as company, Minty, or I shall be obliged to call you 'Miss' too," said Mainwaring, unexpectedly regaining his usual frankness.

Bradley's face brightened; Miss Minty raised her black eyes from her plate with still broader appreciation.

"There's nothin' mean about that," she said, showing her white teeth. "Well, what's *your* first name?"

"Not as pretty as yours, I'm afraid. It's Frank."

"No, it aint, it's Francis! You reckon to be Sir Francis some day," she said gravely. "You can't play any Frank off on me; you wouldn't do it on *her*," she added, indicating Louise with her elbow.

A momentous silence followed. The particular form that Minty's vulgarity had taken had not been anticipated by the two other women. They had not unreasonably expected some original audacity or

gaucherie from the blacksmith's daughter,
which might astonish yet amuse their
guest, and condone for the situation forced
upon them. But they were not prepared
for a playfulness that involved themselves in a ridiculous indiscretion. Mrs.
Bradley's eyes sought her husband's mean-
ingly; Louise's pretty mouth hardened.
Luckily, the cheerful cause of it suddenly
jumped up from the table, and saying that
the stranger was starving, insisted upon
bringing a dish from the other side, and
helping him herself plentifully. Mainwaring rose gallantly to take the dish from
her hand, a slight scuffle ensued, which
ended in the young man being forced
down in his chair by the pressure of
Minty's strong plump hand on his shoulder.
"There," she said, "ye kin mind your
dinner now, and I reckon we'll give the
others a chance to chip into the conversation," and at once applied herself to the
plate before her.

The conversation presently became general, with the exception that Minty, more or less engrossed by professional anxiety in the quality of the dinner and occasional hurried visits to the kitchen, briefly answered the few polite remarks which Mainwaring felt called upon to address to her. Nevertheless he was conscious, *malgré* her rallying allusions to Miss Macy, that he felt none of the vague yet half-pleasant anxiety with which Louise was beginning to inspire him. He felt at ease in Minty's presence, and believed, rightly or wrongly, that she understood him as well as he understood her. And there were certainly points in common between his two hostesses and their humbler though proud dependent. The social evolution of Mrs. Bradley and Louise Macy from some previous Minty was neither remote nor complete; the self-sufficient independence, ease, and quiet self-assertion were alike in each. The superior position was

still too recent and accidental for either
to resent or criticize qualities that were
common to both. At least, this was what
he thought when not abandoning himself
to the gratification of a convalescent
appetite; to the presence of two pretty
women, the sympathy of a genial friend,
the healthy intoxication of the white
sunlight that glanced upon the pine
walls, the views that mirrored themselves
in the open windows, and the pure atmosphere in which The Lookout seemed
to swim. Wandering breezes of balm and
spice lightly stirred the flowers on the
table, and seemed to fan his hair and forehead with softly healing breath. Looking up
in an interval of silence, he caught Bradley's grey eyes fixed upon him with a sub-
dued light of amusement and affection, as
of an elder brother regarding a schoolboy's
boisterous appetite at some feast. Mainwaring laid down his knife and fork with a
laughing colour, touched equally by Brad-

ley's fraternal kindliness and the consciousness of his gastronomical powers.

"Hang it, Bradley, look here! I know
my appetite's disgraceful; but what can a
fellow do? In such air, with such viands
and such company! It's like the bees
getting drunk on Hybla and Hymettus,
you know. I'm not responsible!"

"It's the first square meal I believe
you've really eaten in six months," said
Bradley gravely. "I can't understand
why your doctor allowed you to run down
so dreadfully."

"I reckon you aint as keerful of yourself,
you Britishers, ez us," said Minty. "Lordy!
Why there's Pop invests in more patent
medicines in one day than you have in two
weeks, and he'd make two of you. Mebbe
your folks don't look after you enough."

"I'm a splendid advertisement of what
your care and your medicines have
done," said Mainwaring, gratefully, to Mrs.
Bradley; "and if you ever want to set up

a 'Cure' here, I'm ready with a ten-page
testimonial."

"Have a care, Mainwaring," said Bradley,
laughing, "that the ladies don't take you
at your word. Louise and Jenny have been
doing their best for the last year to get me
to accept a flattering offer from a Sacramento firm to put up an Hotel for Tourists
on the site of The Lookout. Why, I believe
that they have already secretly in their
hearts concocted a flaming prospectus of
'Unrivalled Scenery' and 'Health-giving
Air,' and are looking forward to Saturday
night hops on the piazza."

"Have you really though?" said Mainwaring, gazing from the one to the other.

"We should certainly see more company
than we do now, and feel a little less out
of the world," said Louise candidly. "There
are no neighbours here—I mean the people
at the Summit are not," she added, with a
slight glance towards Minty.

"And Mr. Bradley would find it more

profitable—not to say more suitable to a man of his position—than this wretched saw-mill and timber business," said Mrs. Bradley decidedly.

Mainwaring was astounded; was it possible they considered it more dignified for a lawyer to keep an hotel than a saw-mill? Bradley, as if answering what was passing in his mind, said mischievously, "I'm not sure, exactly, what my position is, my dear, and I'm afraid I've declined the hotel on business principles. But, by the way, Mainwaring, I found a letter at the mill this morning from Mr. Richardson. He is about to pay us the distinguished honour of visiting The Lookout, solely on your account, my dear fellow."

"But I wrote him that I was much better, and it wasn't necessary for him to come," said Mainwaring,

" He makes an excuse of some law business with me. I suppose he considers the mere fact of his taking the trouble to come

here, all the way from San Francisco, a
sufficient honour to justify any absence of
formal invitation," said Bradley, smiling.

" But he's only—I mean he's my father's
banker," said Mainwaring, correcting himself, " and—you don't keep an hotel."

" Not yet," returned Bradley, with a
mischievous glance at the two women, " but
The Lookout is elastic, and I dare say we
can manage to put him up."

A silence ensued. It seemed as if some
shadow, or momentary darkening of the
brilliant atmosphere ; some film across the
mirror-like expanse of the open windows,
or misty dimming of their wholesome light
had arisen to their elevation. Mainwaring
felt that he was looking forward with un-
reasoning indignation and uneasiness to this
impending interruption of their idyllic life ;
Mrs. Bradley and Louise, who had become
a little more constrained and formal under
Minty's freedom, were less sympathetic ;
even the irrepressible Minty appeared

absorbed in the responsibilities of the dinner.

Bradley alone preserved his usual patient good-humour. "We'll take our coffee on the veranda, and the ladies will join us by-and-by, Mainwaring; besides, I don't know that I can allow you, as an invalid, to go entirely through Minty's bountiful *menu* at present. You shall have the sweets another time."

When they were alone on the veranda, he said, between the puffs of his black briarwood pipe—a pet aversion of Mrs. Bradley—"I wonder how Richardson will accept Minty!"

"If *I* can, I think he *must*," returned Mainwaring drily. "By Jove, it will be great fun to see him; but"—he stopped and hesitated—"I don't know about the ladies. I don't think, you know, that they'll stand Minty again before another stranger."

Bradley glanced quickly at the young

man; their eyes met, and they both joined
in a superior and, I fear, disloyal smile.
After a pause Bradley, as if in a spirit of
further confidence, took his pipe from his
mouth and pointed to the blue abyss before
them.

"Look at that profundity, Mainwaring,
and think of it ever being bullied and over-
awed by a long veranda-load of gaping,
patronizing tourists, and the idiotic flirting
females of their species. Think of a lot of
over-dressed creatures flouting those severe
outlines and deep-toned distances with
frippery and garishness. You know how
you have been lulled to sleep by that
delicious indefinite far-off murmur of the
canyon at night—think of it being broken
by a crazy waltz or a monotonous German
—by the clatter of waiters and the pop of
champagne corks. And yet, by thunder,
those women are capable of liking both and
finding no discord in them!"

"Dancing aint half bad, you know," said

Mainwaring conscientiously, "if a chap's got the wind to do it; and all Americans, especially the women, dance better than we do. But I say, Bradley, to hear you talk, a fellow wouldn't suspect you were as big a Vandal as anybody, with a beastly, howling saw-mill in the heart of the primeval forest. By Jove, you quite bowled me over that first day we met, when you popped your head out of that delirium tremens shaking mill, like the very genius of destructive improvement."

"But that was *fighting* Nature, not patronizing her; and it's a business that pays. That reminds me that I must go back to it," said Bradley, rising and knocking the ashes from his pipe.

"Not *after* dinner, surely!" said Mainwaring, in surprise. "Come now, that's too much like the bolting Yankee of the travellers' books."

"There's a heavy run to get through to-night. We're working against time," returned Bradley. Even while speaking he had vanished within the house, returned quickly—having replaced his dark suit by jean trousers tucked in heavy boots, and a red flannel shirt over his starched white one—and, nodding gaily to Mainwaring, stepped from the lower end of the veranda. "The beggar actually looks pleased to go," said Mainwaring to himself in wonderment.

"Oh! Jim," said Mrs. Bradley, appearing at the door.

"Yes," said Bradley, faintly, from the bushes.

"Minty's ready. You might take her home."

"All right. I'll wait."

"I hope I haven't frightened Miss Sharpe away," said Mainwaring. "She isn't going, surely?"

"Only to get some better clothes, on account of company. I'm afraid you are giving her a good deal of trouble,

F

Mr. Mainwaring," said Mrs. Bradley, laughing.

"She wished me to say good-bye to you for her, as she couldn't come on the veranda in her old shawl and sun-bonnet," added Louise, who had joined them. "What do you really think of her, Mr. Mainwaring? I call her quite pretty, at times. Don't you?"

Mainwaring knew not what to say. He could not understand why they could have any special interest in the girl, or care to know what he, a perfect stranger, thought of her. He avoided a direct reply, however, by playfully wondering how Mrs. Bradley could subject her husband to Miss Minty's undivided fascinations.

"Oh, Jim always takes her home—if it's in the evening. He gets along with these people better than we do," returned Mrs. Bradley drily. "But," she added, with a return of her piquant Quaker-like coquettishness, "Jim says we are to devote our-

selves to you to-night—in retaliation, I
suppose. We are to amuse you, and not
let you get excited; and you are to be
sent to bed early."

It is to be feared that these latter wise
precautions—invaluable for all defenceless
and enfeebled humanity—were not carried
out; and it was late when Mainwaring
eventually retired, with brightened eyes
and a somewhat accelerated pulse. For
the ladies, who had quite regained that
kindly equanimity which Minty had rudely
interrupted, had also added a delicate and
confidential sympathy in their relations
with Mainwaring—as of people who had
suffered in common—and he experienced
these tender attentions at their hands
which any two women are emboldened by
each other's saving presence to show any
single member of our sex. Indeed, he
hardly knew if his satisfaction was the more
complete when Mrs. Bradley, withdrawing
for a few moments, left him alone on the

veranda with Louise and the vast, omni-
potent Night.

For awhile they sat silent, in the midst
of the profound and measureless calm.
Looking down upon the dim moonlit abyss
at their feet, they themselves seemed a part
of this night that arched above it; the
half-risen moon appeared to linger long
enough at their side to enwrap and suffuse
them with its glory; a few bright stars
quietly ringed themselves around them,
and looked wonderingly into the level of
their own shining eyes. For some vague
yearning to humanity seemed to draw this
dark and passionless void towards them.
The vast protecting maternity of Nature
leant hushed and breathless over this
solitude. Warm currents of air rose occa-
sionally from the valley, which one might
have believed were sighs from its full and
overflowing breast, or a grateful coolness
swept their cheeks and air when the
tranquil heights around them were moved

to slowly respond. Odours from invisible
bay and laurel sometimes filled the air ; the
incense of some rare and remoter cultivated
meadow beyond their ken, or the strong
germinating breath of leagues of wild oats,
that had yellowed the upland by day. In
the silence and shadow, their voices took
upon themselves, almost without their voli-
tion, a far-off confidential murmur, with
intervals of meaning silence—rather as if
their thoughts had spoken for themselves,
and they had stopped wonderingly to
listen. They talked at first vaguely to this
discreet audience of space and darkness,
and then, growing bolder, spoke to each
other and of themselves. Invested by the
infinite gravity of Nature, they had no fear
of human ridicule to restrain their youthful conceit or the extravagance of their un-
important confessions. They talked of
their tastes, of their habits, of their friends
and acquaintances. They settled some
points of doctrine, duty, and etiquette, with

the sweet seriousness of youth and its all-
powerful convictions. The listening vines
would have recognized no flirtation or love-
making in their animated but important
confidences ; yet when Mrs. Bradley re-
appeared to warn the invalid that it was
time to seek his couch, they both coughed
slightly in the nervous consciousness of
some unaccustomed quality in their voices,
and a sense of interruption far beyond their
own or the innocent intruder's ken.

"Well?" said Mrs. Bradley, in the sitting-room as Mainwaring's steps retreated
down the passage to his room.

"Well," said Louise with a slight yawn,
leaning her pretty shoulders languidly
against the door-post, as she shaded her
moonlight-accustomed eyes from the vulgar
brilliancy of Mrs. Bradley's bedroom candle.
" Well—oh, he talked a great deal about
' his people ' as he called them, and I talked
about us. He's very nice. You know, in
some things he's really like a boy."

" He looks much better."

" Yes ; but he is far from strong, yet."

Meantime, Mainwaring had no other confidant of his impressions than his own thoughts. Mingled with his exaltation, which was the more seductive that it had no well-defined foundation for existing, and implied no future responsibility, was a recurrence of his uneasiness at the impending visit of Richardson the next day. Strangely enough, it had increased under the stimulus of the evening. Just as he was really getting on with the family, he felt sure that this visitor would import some foreign element into their familiarity, as Minty had done. It was very possible they would not like him; now he remembered there was really something ostentatiously British and insular about this Richardson—something they would likely resent. Why couldn't this fellow have come later—or even before ? Before what ? But here he fell asleep, and almost instantly slipped from this veranda

in the Sierras, six thousand miles away, to
an ancient terrace, overgrown with moss
and tradition, that overlooked the sedate
glory of an English park.   Here he found
himself, restricted painfully by his inconsistent night-clothes, endeavouring to impress his mother and sisters with the
singular virtues and excellences of his
American host and hostesses—virtues and
excellences that he himself was beginning
to feel conscious had become more or less
apocryphal in that atmosphere.   He heard
his mother's voice saying severely, " When
you learn, Francis, to respect the opinions
and prejudices of your family enough to
prevent your appearing before them in this
uncivilized aboriginal costume, we will
listen to what you have to say of the friends
whose habits you seem to have adopted ; "
and he was frantically indignant that his
efforts to convince them that his negligence
was a personal oversight, and not a Californian custom, were utterly futile.   But

even then this vision was brushed away by the bewildering sweep of Louise's pretty skirt across the dreamy picture, and her delicate features and softly fringed eyes remained the last to slip from his fading consciousness.

The moon rose higher and higher above the sleeping house and softly breathing canyon. There was nothing to mar the idyllic repose of the landscape; only the growing light of the last two hours had brought out in the far eastern horizon a dim white peak, that gleamed faintly among the stars, like a bridal couch spread between the hills ringed with fading nuptial torches. No one would have believed that behind that impenetrable shadow to the west, in the heart of the forest, the throbbing saw-mill of James Bradley was even at that moment eating its destructive way through the conserved growth of Nature and centuries, and that the refined proprietor of house and greenwood, with the glow of his furnace fires on his red shirt, and his alert, intelligent eyes, was the geni of that devastation, and the toiling leader of the shadowy toiling figures around him.

CHAPTER III.

AMID the beauty of the most uncultivated
and untrodden wilderness there are certain
localities where the meaner and more
common processes of Nature take upon
themselves a degrading likeness to the
slovenly, wasteful, and improvident processes of man. The unrecorded landslip
disintegrating a whole hill-side will not
only lay bare the delicate framework of
strata and deposit to the vulgar eye, but
hurl into the valley a débris so monstrous
and unlovely as to shame even the hideous
ruins left by dynamite, hydraulic, or pick
and shovel; an overflown and forgotten
woodland torrent will leave in some remote
hollow a disturbed and ungraceful chaos of
inextricable logs, branches, rock, and soil

that will rival the unsavoury details of
some wrecked or abandoned settlement.
Of lesser magnitude and importance, there
are certain natural dust-heaps, sinks, and
cesspools, where the elements have collected the cast-off, broken, and frayed dis-
jecta of wood and field—the sweepings of
the sylvan household. It was remarkable
that Nature, so kindly considerate of mere
human ruins, made no attempt to cover up
or disguise these monuments of her own
mortality : no grass grew over the unsightly
landslides, no moss or ivy clothed the
stripped and bleached skeletons of over·
thrown branch and tree ; the dead leaves
and withered husks rotted in their open
grave uncrossed by vine or creeper. Even
the animals, except the lower organizations,
shunned those haunts of decay and ruin.

It was scarcely a hundred yards from
one of those dreary receptacles that Mr.
Bradley had taken leave of Miss Minty
Sharpe. The cabin occupied by her father,

herself, and a younger brother, stood, in
fact, on the very edge of the little hollow,
which was partly filled with decayed wood,
leaves, and displacements of the crumbling
bank, with the coal dust and ashes which
Mr. Sharpe had added from his forge, that
stood a few paces distant at the corner of
a cross-road. The occupants of the cabin
had also contributed to the hollow the
refuse of their household in broken boxes,
earthenware, tin cans, and cast-off clothing ;
and it is not improbable that the site of the
cabin was chosen with reference to this
convenient disposal of useless and en-
cumbering impedimenta. It was true that
the locality offered little choice in the way
of beauty. An outcrop of brown granite—
a portent of higher altitudes—extended a
quarter of a mile from the nearest fringe of
dwarf laurel and " brush " in one direction ;
in the other an advanced file of Bradley's
woods had suffered from some long-forgotten
fire, and still raised its blackened masts

and broken stumps over the scorched and
arid soil, swept of older underbrush and
verdure.   On the other side of the road a
dark ravine, tangled with briars and
haunted at night by owls and wild cats,
struggled wearily on, until blundering at
last upon the edge of the Great Canyon, it
slipped and lost itself for ever in a single
furrow of those mighty flanks.   When
Bradley had once asked Sharpe why he had
not built his house in the ravine, the blacksmith had replied : " That until the Lord
had appointed his time, he reckoned to
keep his head above ground and the
foundations thereof."   Howbeit the ravine,
or the " run " as it was locally known, was
Minty's only Saturday-afternoon resort for
recreation or berries.   " It was," she had
explained, " pow'ful soothin', and solitary."

She entered the house—a rude, square
building of unpainted boards—containing
a sitting-room, a kitchen, and two bed-
rooms.   A glance at these rooms, which

were plainly furnished, and whose canvas-
coloured walls were adorned with gorgeous
agricultural implement circulars, patent
medicine calendars, with poly-tinted
chromos and cheaply illuminated Scrip-
tural texts, showed her that a certain
neatness and order had been preserved
during her absence; and, finding the
house empty, she crossed the barren and
blackened intervening space between the
back door and her father's forge, and
entered the open shed. The light was
fading from the sky; but the glow of the
forge lit up the dusty road before it, and
accented the blackness of the rocky ledge
beyond. A small curly-headed boy, bearing a singular likeness to a smudged and
blackened crayon drawing of Minty, was
mechanically blowing the bellows, and
obviously intent upon something else;
while her father—a powerfully built man,
with a quaintly dissatisfied expression of
countenance—was with equal want of in-

terest mechanically hammering at a horse-
shoe. Without noticing Minty's advent,
he lazily broke into a querulous drawling
chaunt of some vague religious character :

> " O tur-ren, sinner ; tur-ren.
>   For the Lord bids you turn—ah !
>   O tur-ren, sinner ; tur-ren.
>   Why will you die ? "

The musical accent adapted itself to the
monotonous fall of the sledge-hammer ; and
at every repetition of the word " turn," he
suited the action to the word by turning
the horse-shoe with the iron in his left
hand. A slight grunt at the end of
every stroke, and the simultaneous repetition of " turn," seemed to offer him
amusement and relief. Minty, without
speaking, crossed the shop, and adminis-
tered a sound box on her brother's ear.
" Take that, and let me ketch you agen
layin' low when my back's turned, to put
on your store pants."

" The others had fetched away in the

laig," said the boy, opposing a knee and elbow at acute angle to further attack.

"You jest get and change 'em," said Minty.

The sudden collapse of the bellows broke in upon the soothing refrain of Mr. Sharpe, and caused him to turn also.

"It's Minty," he said, replacing the horse-shoe on the coals, and setting his powerful arms and the sledge on the anvil with an exaggerated expression of weariness.

"Yes; it's me," said Minty, "and Creation knows it's time I *did* come, to keep that boy from ruinin' us with his airs and conceits."

"Did ye bring over any o' that fever mixter?"

"No. Bradley sez you're loading yerself up with so much o' that bitter bark— kuinine they call it over there—that you'll lift the ruff off your head next. He allows ye aint got no ague; it's jest wind and

G

dyspepsy. He sez yer's strong ez a hoss."

"Bradley," said Sharpe, laying aside his sledge with an aggrieved manner, which was, however, as complacent as his fatigue and discontent, "ez one of them nat'ral born finikin skunks ez I despise. I reckon he began to give p'ints to his parents when he was about knee-high to Richelieu there. He's on them confidential terms with his-self and the Almighty that he reckons he ken run a saw-mill and a man's insides at the same time with one hand tied behind him. And his fininkin is up to his con-ceit: he wanted to tell me that that yer handy brush dump outside our shanty was unhealthy. Give a man with frills like that his own way and he'd be a sprinkling odor Cologne and peppermint all over the country."

"He set your shoulder as well as any doctor," said Minty.

"That's bone-settin', and a nat'ral gift,"

returned Sharpe, as triumphantly as his
habitual depression would admit; "it
aint conceit and finikin got out o' books!
Well," he added, after a pause, "wot's
happened ?"

Minty's face slightly changed. "Nothin';
I kem back to get some things," she said
shortly, moving away.

"And ye saw *him*?"

"Ye-e-s," drawled Minty carelessly, still
retreating.

"Bixby was along here about noon. He
says the stranger was suthin' high and
mighty in his own country, and them
'Frisco millionaires are quite sweet on
him. Where are ye goin'?"

"In the house."

"Well, look yer, Minty. Now that you're
here, ye might get up a batch o' hot biscuit
for supper. Dinner was that promiscous
and experimental to-day, along o' Richelieu's
nat'ral foolin', that I think I could git outside of a little suthin' now, if only to prop

up a kind of innard sinkin' that takes me.
Ye ken tell me the news at supper."

Later, however, when Mr. Sharpe had
quitted his forge for the night and, seated
at his domestic board, was, with a dismal
presentiment of future indigestion, vora-
ciously absorbing his favourite meal of hot
saleratus biscuits swimming in butter, he
had apparently forgotten his curiosity concerning Mainwaring and settled himself to a
complaining chronicle of the day's mishaps.
"Nat'rally, havin' an extra lot o' work on
hand and no time for foolin', what does
that ornery Richelieu get up and do this
mornin'? Ye know them ridiklus specimens
that he's been chippin' outer that ledge
that the yearth slipped from down the run,
and litterin' up the whole shanty with 'em.
Well, darn my skin! if he didn't run a
heap of 'em, mixed up with coal, unbe-
knownd to me, in the forge, to make what
he called a ' fire essay ' of 'em. Nat'rally I
couldn't get a blessed iron hot, and didn't

know what had gone of the fire, or the
coal either, for two hours, till I stopped
work and raked out the coal. That comes
from his hangin' round that saw-mill in the
woods, and listenin' to Bradley's high-
falutin' talk about rocks and strata and
sich."

"But Bradley don't go a cent on minin',
Pop," said Minty. "He sez the woods is
good enough for him; and there's millions
to be made when the railroad comes along,
and timber's wanted."

"But until then he's got to keep hisself,
to pay wages, and keep the mill runnin'.
Onless it's, ez Bixby says, that he hopes
to get that Englishman to rope in some o'
them 'Frisco friends of his to take a hand.
Ye didn't have any o' that kind o' talk, did
ye?"

"No; not *that* kind o' talk," said Minty.

"Not *that* kind o' talk!" repeated her
father with aggrieved curiosity. "Wot
kind, then?"

" Well," said Minty, lifting her black
eyes to her father's ; " I aint no account,
and you aint no account either ; you aint
got no college education, aint got no friends
in 'Frisco, and aint got no high-toned style ;
I can't play the pianner, jabber French, nor
get French dresses ; we aint got no fancy
' Shallet,' as they call it, with a first-class
view of nothing ; we've only a shanty on dry
rock !   But, afore *I'd* take advantage of a
lazy, gawky boy—for it aint anything else,
though he's good meanin' enough—-that
happened to fall sick in *my* house, and coax
and cosset him, and wrap him in white
cotton, and mother him, and sister him, and
Aunt Sukey him, and almost dry-nuss him
gin'rally, jist to get him sweet on me and
on mine, and take the inside track of others
—*I'd* be an Injin ! And if you'd allow it,
Pop, you'd be wuss nor a nigger ! "

" Sho ! " said her father, kindling with
that intense gratification with which the
male receives any intimation of alien femi-

nine weakness. "It aint that, Minty, I wanter know!"

"It's jist that, Pop; and I ez good ez let 'em know I seed it. I aint a fool, if some folk do drop their eyes and pertend to wipe the laugh out of their noses with a hand-kerchief when I let out to speak. I mayn't be good enough kempany——"

"Look yer, Minty," interrupted the blacksmith sternly, half rising from his seat with every trace of his former weakness vanished from his hard-set face; "do you mean to say that they put on airs to ye—to *my* darter?"

"No," said Minty quickly; "the men didn't, and don't you, a man, mix yourself up with women's meannesses. I ken manage 'em, Pop, with one hand."

Mr. Sharpe looked at his daughter's flashing black eyes. Perhaps an uneasy recollection of the late Mrs. Sharpe's remarkable capacity in that respect checked his further rage.

"No. Wot I was sayin'," resumed Minty, "ez that I mayn't be thought by others good enough to keep kempany with baronetts ez is to be—though baronetts mightn't object—but I aint mean enough to try to steal away some ole woman's darling boy in England, or snatch some likely young English girl's big brother outer the family without sayin' by your leave. How'd you like it if Richelieu was growed up, and went to sea—and it would be like his peartness—and he fell sick in some foreign land, and some princess or other skyugled *him* underhand away from us?"

Probably owing to the affair of the specimens, the elder Sharpe did not seem to regard the possible mesalliance of Richelieu with extraordinary disfavour. "That boy is conceited enough with hair ile and fine clothes for anything," he said plaintively. "But didn't that Louie Macy hev a feller already—that Captain Greyson? Wot's gone o' him?"

"That's it," said Minty; "he kin go out in the woods and whistle now. But all the same, she could hitch him in again at any time if the other stranger kicked over the traces. That's the style over there at The Lookout. There aint ez much heart in them two women put together ez would make a green gal flush up playin' forfeits. It's all in their breed, Pop. Love aint going to spile their appetites and complexions, give 'em nosebleed, nor put a drop o' water into their eyes in all their natural born days. That's wot makes me mad. Ef I thought that Loo cared a bit for that child I wouldn't mind; I'd just advise her to make him get up and get—pack his duds out o' camp, and go home and not come back until he had a written permit from his mother, or the other baronet in office."

"Looks sorter ef some one orter interfere," said the blacksmith reflectively.

" 'Taint exakly a case for a vigilance committee, tho' it's agin public morals this sorter kidnappin' o' strangers. Looks ez if it might bring the county into discredit in England."

" Well, don't *you* go and interfere and havin' folks say ez my nose was put out o' jint over there," said Minty curtly. "There's another Englishman comin' up from 'Frisco to see him to-morrow. Ef he aint scooped up by Jenny Bradley he'll guess there's a nigger in the fence somewhere. But there, Pop, let it drop. It's a bad aig, anyway," she concluded, rising from the table, and passing her hands down her frock and her shapely hips as if to wipe off further contamination of the subject. " Where's Richelieu agin ? "

"Said he didn't want supper, and like ez not he's gone over to see that fammerly at the Summit. There's a little girl thar he's sparkin', about his own age."

" His own age ! " said Minty indig-

nantly. "Why she's double that, if she's
a day. Well—if he aint the triflinest,
conceitednest little limb that ever grew!
I'd like to know where he got it from—
it wasn't mar's style."

Mr. Sharpe smiled darkly. Richelieu's
precocious gallantry evidently was not
considered as gratuitous as his experimental metallurgy. But as his eyes followed his daughter's wholesome, Phyllis-
like figure, a new idea took possession of
him ; needless to say, however, it was in
the line of another personal aggrievement,
albeit it took the form of religious reflec-
tion.

"It's curous, Minty, wot's fore-ordained,
and wot aint. Now, yer's one of them
high and mighty fellows, after the Lord,
ez comes meanderin' around here, and
drops off—ez fur ez I kin hear—in a kind
o' faint at the first house he kems to, and
is taken in and lodged and sumptuously
fed ; and nat'rally, they gets their reward

for it.   Now, wot's to hev kept that young
feller from coming *here* and droppin' down
in my forge, or in this very room, and *you*
a tendin' him, and jist layin' over them
folks at The Lookout ?"

"Wot's got hold o' ye, Pop ?   Don't I
tell ye he had a letter to Jim Bradley ?"
said Minty quickly, with an angry flash of
colour in her cheek.

"That aint it," said Sharpe confidently ;
"it's cos he *walked*.   Nat'rally you'd think
he'd *ride*, being high and mighty, and
that's where, ez the parson will tell ye,
wot's merely fi-nite and human wisdom
errs !   Ef that feller had ridden he'd have
had to come by this yer road, and by this
yer forge, and stop a spell like any other.
But it was fore-ordained that he should
walk, jest cos it wasn't generally kalkilated and reckoned on.   So *you* had no
show."

For a moment, Minty seemed struck
with her father's original theory.   But

with a vigorous shake of her shoulders she
threw it off. Her eyes darkened.

"I reckon you aint thinking, Pop"—
she began.

"I was only sayin' it was curous," he
rejoined quietly. Nevertheless, after a
pause, he rose, coughed, and going up to
the young girl, as she leaned over the
dresser, bent his powerful arm around her,
and drawing her and the plate she was
holding against his breast, laid his bearded
cheek for an instant softly upon her rebel-
lious head. "It's all right, Minty," he
said : "ain't it, pet ?" Minty's eyelids
closed gently under the familiar pressure.
"Wot's that in your hair, Minty ?" he
said tactfully, breaking an embarrassing
pause.

"Bar's grease. father," murmured Minty
in a child's voice—the grown-up woman,
under that magic touch, having lapsed
again into her father's motherless charge
of ten years before.

"It's pow'ful soothin', and pretty," said her father.

"I made it myself--do you want some?" asked Minty.

"Not now, girl!" For a moment they slightly rocked each other in that attitude —the man dextrously, the woman with infinite tenderness—and then they separated.

Late that night, after Richelieu had returned, and her father wrestled in his fitful sleep with the remorse of his guilty indulgence at supper, Minty remained alone in her room, hard at work, surrounded by the contents of one of her mother's trunks and the fragments of certain ripped-up and newly-turned dresses. For Minty had conceived the bold idea of altering one of her mother's gowns to the fashion of a certain fascinating frock worn by Louise Macy. It was late when her self-imposed task was completed. With a nervous trepidation that was novel to her,

Minty began to disrobe herself preparatory
to trying on her new creation. The light
of a tallow candle and a large swinging
lantern, borrowed from her father's forge,
fell shyly on her milky neck and shoulders,
and shone in her sparkling eyes, as she
stood before her largest mirror—the long
glazed door of a kitchen clock which she
had placed upon her chest of drawers.
Had poor Minty been content with the
full, free, and goddess-like outlines that it
reflected, she would have been spared her
impending disappointment. For, alas! the
dress of her model had been framed upon
a symmetrically attenuated French corset,
and the unfortunate Minty's fuller and
ampler curves had under her simple
country stays known no more restraining
cincture than knew the Venus of Milo.
The alteration was a hideous failure; it
was neither Minty's statuesque outline nor
Louise Macy's graceful contour. Minty
was no fool, and the revelation of this slow

education of the figure and training of outline—whether fair or false in art—struck
her quick intelligence with all its full
and hopeless significance. A bitter light
sprang to her eyes; she tore the wretched
sham from her shoulders, and then wrap-
ping a shawl around her, threw herself
heavily and sullenly on the bed. But inaction was not a characteristic of Minty's
emotion; she presently rose again, and,
taking an old work-box from her trunk,
began to rummage in its recesses. It was
an old shell-encrusted affair, and the apparent receptacle of such cheap odds and
ends of jewellery as she possessed: a
hideous cameo ring, the property of the
late Mrs. Sharpe, was missing. She again
rapidly explored the contents of the box,
and then an inspiration seized her, and she
darted into her brother's bedroom.

That precocious and gallant Lovelace of
ten, despite all sentiment, had basely
succumbed to the gross materialism of

youthful slumber. On a cot in the corner,
half hidden under the wreck of his own
careless and hurried disrobing, with one
arm hanging out of the coverlid, Richelieu
lay supremely unconscious. On the fore-
finger of his small but dirty hand the missing cameo was still glittering guiltily.
With a swift movement of indignation
Minty rushed with uplifted palm towards
the tempting expanse of youthful cheek
that lay invitingly exposed upon the pillow.
Then she stopped suddenly.

She had seen him lying thus a hundred
times before. On the pillow near him an
undistinguishable mass of golden fur—the
helpless bulk of a squirrel chained to the
leg of his cot; at his feet a wall-eyed cat,
who had followed his tyrannous caprices
with the long-suffering devotion of her sex;
on the shelf above him a loathsome collection of flies and tarantulas in dull green
bottles; a slab of ginger-bread for light
nocturnal refection, and her own pot of

bear's grease.   Perhaps it was the piteous
defencelessness of youthful sleep, perhaps
it was some lingering memory of her father's
caress ;   but as she gazed at him with
troubled eyes, the juvenile reprobate slipped
back into the baby-boy that she had carried
in her own childish arms such a short time
ago, when the maternal responsibility had
descended with the dead mother's ill-fitting
dresses upon her lank girlish figure and
scant virgin breast—and her hand fell
listlessly at her side.

The sleeper stirred slightly and awoke.
At the same moment, by some mysterious
sympathy, a pair of beady bright eyes
appeared in the bulk of fur near his curls,
the cat stretched herself, and even a vague
agitation was heard in the bottles on the
shelf.   Richelieu's blinking eyes wandered
from the candle to his sister, and then the
guilty hand was suddenly withdrawn under
the bedclothes.

"No matter, dear," said Minty ; "it's

mar's, and you kin wear it when you like,
if you'll only ask for it."

Richelieu wondered if he was dreaming !
This unexpected mildness—this inexplicable
tremor in his sister's voice : it must be some
occult influence of the night season on the
sisterly mind, possibly akin to a fear of
ghosts ! He made a mental note of it in
view of future favours, yet for the moment
he felt embarrassedly gratified. "Ye aint
wantin' anything, Minty," he said affectionately ; "a pail o' cold water from the far
spring—no, nothin' ?" He made an ostentatious movement as if to rise, yet suffi-
ciently protracted to prevent any hasty
acceptance of his prodigal offer.

"No, dear," she said, still gazing at him
with an absorbed look in her dark eyes.

Richelieu felt a slight creepy sensation
under that lovely far-off gaze. "Your eyes
look awful big at night, Minty," he said.
He would have added "and pretty," but
she was his sister, and he had the lofty

fraternal conviction of his duty in repress-
ing the inordinate vanity of the sex.
"Ye're sure ye aint wantin' nothin'?"

"Not now, dear." She paused a moment,
and then said deliberately: "But you
wouldn't mind turnin' out after sun-up and
runnin' an errand for me over to The Lookout?"

Richelieu's eyes sparkled so suddenly
that even in her absorption Minty noticed
the change. "But ye're not goin' to tarry
over there, ner gossip—you hear? Yer to
take this yer message. Yer to say, 'that
it will be onpossible for me to come back
there, on account—on account of'—— "

"Important business," suggested Richelieu; "that's the perlite style."

"Ef you like." She leaned over the bed
and put her lips to his forehead, still damp
with the dews of sleep, and then to his
long-lashed lids. "Mind Nip!"—the
squirrel—he practically suggested. For an
instant their blonde curls mingled on the
pillow. "Now go to sleep," she said curtly.

But Richelieu had taken her white neck in the short strangulatory hug of the small boy, and held her fast. " Ye'll let me put on my best pants ? "

" Yes."

" And wear that ring ? "

" Yes "—a little sadly.

" Then yer kin count me in, Minty; and see here "—his voice sank to a confidential whisper—" mebbee some day ye'll be beholden to *me* for a lot o' real jewellery."

She returned slowly to her room, and, opening the window, looked out upon the night. The same moon that had lent such supererogatory grace to the natural beauty of The Lookout, here seemed to have failed, as Minty had, in disguising the relentless limitations of Nature or the cruel bonds of custom. The black plain of granite, under its rays, appeared only to extend its poverty to some remoter barrier ; the blackened stumps of the burnt forest stood bleaker against the sky, like broken and twisted ledge where Richelieu had prospected was a hideous chasm of bluish blackness, over which a purple vapour seemed to hover; the " brush dump" beside the house showed a cavern of writhing and distorted objects stiffened into dark rigidity. She had often looked upon the prospect: it had never seemed so hard and changeless; yet she accepted it, as she had accepted it before.

She turned away, undressed herself mechanically, and went to bed. She had an idea that she had been very foolish; that her escape from being still more foolish was something miraculous, and in some measure connected with Providence, her father, her little brother, and her dead mother, whose dress she had recklessly spoiled. But that she had even so slightly touched the bitterness and glory of renunciation—as written of heroines and fine ladies by novelists and poets—never entered the foolish head of Minty Sharpe, the blacksmith's daughter.

CHAPTER IV.

IT was a little after daybreak next morning that Mainwaring awoke from the first unrefreshing night he had passed at The Lookout. He was so feverish and restless that he dressed himself at sunrise, and cautiously stepped out upon the still silent veranda. The chairs which he and Louise Macy had occupied were still, it seemed to him, conspicuously confidential with each other, and he separated them; but as he looked down into the Great Canyon at his feet he was conscious of some undefinable change in the prospect. A slight mist was rising from the valley, as if it were the last of last night's illusions; the first level sunbeams were obtrusively searching, and the keen morning air had a dryly practical insistance

which irritated him, until a light footstep
on the further end of the veranda caused
him to turn sharply.

It was the singular apparition of a small
boy, bearing a surprising resemblance to
Minty Sharpe, and dressed in a unique
fashion.   On a tumbled sea of blonde curls
a " chip " sailor hat, with a broad red ribbon,
rode jauntily.   But here the nautical
suggestion changed, as had the desire of
becoming a pirate which induced it.   A red
shirt, with a white collar, and a yellow
plaid ribbon tie, that also recalled Minty
Sharpe, lightly turned the suggestion of his
costume to mining.   Short black velvet
trousers, coming to his knee, and ostentatiously new short-legged boots, with
visible straps like curling ears, completed
the entirely original character of his lower
limbs.

Mainwaring, always easily gentle and
familiar with children and his inferiors,
looked at him with an encouraging smile.

Richelieu—for it was he—advanced gravely and held out his hand, with the cameo ring apparent. Mainwaring, with equal gravity, shook it warmly, and removed his hat. Richelieu, keenly observant, did the same.

"Is Jim Bradley out yet?" asked Richelieu carelessly.

"No; I think not. But I'm Frank Mainwaring. Will I do?"

Richelieu smiled. The dimples, the white teeth, the dark, laughing eyes, were surely Minty's?

"I'm Richelieu," he rejoined with equal candour.

"Richelieu?"

"Yes. That Frenchman—the Lord Cardinal—you know. Mar saw Forrest do him out in St. Louis."

"Do him?"

"Yes, in the theayter."

With a confused misconception of his meaning, Mainwaring tried to recall the historical dress of the great Cardinal and

fit it to the masquerader—if such he were
—before him.   But Richelieu relieved him
by adding—

"Richelieu Sharpe."

"Oh, that's your *name!*" said Mainwaring cheerfully.   "Then you're Miss
Minty's brother.   I know her.   How jolly
lucky!"

They both shook hands again.   Richelieu,
eager to get rid of the burden of his sister's
message, which he felt was in the way of
free-and-easy intercourse with this charming
stranger, looked uneasily towards the
house.

"I say," said Mainwaring, "if you're in
a hurry, you'd better go in there and knock.
I hear some one stirring in the kitchen."

Richelieu nodded, but first went back to
the steps of the veranda, picked up a small
blue knotted handkerchief, apparently containing some heavy objects, and repassed
Mainwaring.

"What! have you cut it, Richelieu, with

your valuables? What have you got there?"

"Specimens," said Richelieu shortly, and vanished.

He returned presently. " Well, Cardinal, did you see anybody?" asked Mainwaring.

"Mrs. Bradley; but Jim's over to the mill. I'm goin' there."

" Did you see Miss Macy?" continued Mainwaring carelessly.

" Loo?"

"Loo!—well; yes."

" No. She's philanderin' with Captain Greyson."

"Philandering with Greyson?" echoed Mainwaring, in wonder.

" Yes; on horseback on the ridge."

" You mean she's riding out with Mr.— with Captain Greyson?"

"Yes; ridin' *and* philanderin'," persisted Richelieu.

" And what do you call philandering?"

"Well; I reckon you and she oughter know," returned Richelieu, with a precocious air.

"Certainly," said Mainwaring with a faint smile. Richelieu really was like Minty.

There was a long silence. This young Englishman was becoming exceedingly un-interesting. Richelieu felt that he was gaining neither profit nor amusement, and losing time. "I'm going," he said.

"Good morning," said Mainwaring, without looking up.

Richelieu picked up his specimens, thoroughly convinced of the stranger's glittering deceitfulness, and vanished.

It was nearly eight o'clock when Mrs. Bradley came from the house. She apologized, with a slightly distrait smile, for the tardiness of the household. "Mr. Bradley stayed at the mill all night, and will not be here until breakfast, when he brings your friend Mr. Richardson with him"—

Mainwaring scarcely repressed a movement of impatience—"who arrives early. It's unfortunate that Miss Sharpe can't come to-day."

In his abstraction Mainwaring did not notice that Mrs. Bradley slightly accented Minty's formal appellation, and said carelessly—

"Oh, that's why her brother came over here so early!"

"Did *you* see him?" asked Mrs. Bradley, almost abruptly.

"Yes. He is an amusing little beggar; but I think he shares his sister's preference for Mr. Bradley. He deserted me here in the veranda for him at the mill."

"Louise will keep you company as soon as she has changed her dress," continued Mrs. Bradley. "She was out riding early this morning with a friend. She's very fond of early morning rides."

"*And* philandering," repeated Mainwaring to himself. It was quite natural for

Miss Macy to ride out in the morning, after
the fashion of the country, with an escort;
but why had the cub insisted on the "philandering"? He had said, "*and* philandering," distinctly. It was a nasty thing for
him to say. Any other fellow but he,
Mainwaring, might misunderstand the
whole thing. Perhaps he ought to warn
her—but no! he could not repeat the gossip
of a child, and that child the brother of one
of her inferiors. But was Minty an in-
ferior? Did she and Minty talk together
about this fellow Greyson? At all events,
it would only revive the awkwardness of
the preceding day, and he resolved to say
nothing.

He was rewarded by a half-inquiring,
half-confiding look in Louise's bright eyes,
when she presently greeted him on the
veranda. "She had quite forgotten," she
said, "to tell him last night of her morning's
engagement; indeed, she had half forgotten
it. It used to be a favourite practice of

hers, with Captain Greyson ; but she had
lately given it up. She believed she had
not ridden since—since——"

"Since when ? " asked Mainwaring.

"Well, since you were ill," she said
frankly.

A quick pleasure shone in Mainwaring's
cheek and eye ; but Louise's pretty lids did
not drop, nor her faint quiet bloom deepen.
Breakfast was already waiting when Mr.
Richardson arrived alone. He explained
that Mr. Bradley had some important and
unexpected business which had delayed
him, but which, he added, " Mr. Bradley
says may prove interesting enough to you
to excuse his absence this morning." Mainwaring was not displeased that his critical
and observant host was not present at their
meeting. Louise Macy was, however, as
demurely conscious of the different bearing
of the two compatriots. Richardson's
somewhat self-important patronage of the
two ladies, and that Californian familiarity

he had acquired, changed to a certain uneasy deference towards Mainwaring; while
the younger Englishman's slightly stiff and
deliberate cordiality was, nevertheless,
mingled with a mysterious understanding that appeared innate and unconscious.
Louise was quick to see that these two
men, more widely divergent in quality than
any two of her own countrymen, were yet
more subtly connected by some unknown
sympathy than the most equal of Americans.
Minty's prophetic belief of the effect of the
two women upon Richardson was certainly
true as regarded Mrs. Bradley. The banker
—a large material nature—was quickly
fascinated by the demure, puritanic graces
of that lady, and was inclined to exhibit a
somewhat broad and ostentatious gallantry
that annoyed Mainwaring. When they
were seated alone on the veranda, which
the ladies had discreetly left to them,
Richardson said—

"Odd I didn't hear of Bradley's wife

before. She seems a spicy, pretty, comfortable creature. Regularly thrown away with him up here."

Mainwaring replied coldly that she was "an admirable helpmeet of a very admirable man," not, however, without an uneasy recollection of her previous confidences respecting her husband. "They have been most thoroughly good and kind to me ; my own brother and sister could not have done more. And certainly not with better taste or delicacy," he added markedly.

"Certainly, certainly," said Richardson hurriedly. "I wrote to Lady Mainwaring that you were taken capital care of by some very honest people, and that——"

"Lady Mainwaring already knows what I think of them, and what she owes to their kindness," said Mainwaring drily.

"True, true," said Richardson apologetically. "Of course you must have seen a good deal of them. I only know Bradley

I

in a business way. He's been trying to
get the Bank to help him put up some
new mills here; but we didn't see it. I
daresay he is good company—rather
amusing, eh ?"

Mainwaring had the gift of his class
of snubbing by the polite and forgiving
oblivion of silence. Richardson shifted
uneasily in his chair, but continued with
assumed carelessness.

"No ; I only knew of this cousin, Miss
Macy. I heard of her when she was visiting some friends in Menlo Park last year.
Rather an attractive girl. They say
Colonel Johnson, of Sacramento, took
quite a fancy to her—it would have been
a good match, I daresay, for he is very
rich ; but the thing fell through in some
way. Then they say *she* wanted to marry
that Spaniard, young Pico, of the Amador
Ranche ; but his family wouldn't hear of
it. Somehow she's deuced unlucky. I suppose she'll make a mess of it with that

Captain Greyson she was out riding with this morning."

"Didn't the Bank think Bradley's mills a good investment?" asked Mainwaring quietly, when Richardson paused.

"Not with him in it; he is not a business man, you know."

"I thought he was. He seems to me an energetic man, who knows his work, and is not afraid to look after it himself."

"That's just it. He has got absurd ideas of co-operating with his workmen, you know, and doing everything slowly, and on a limited scale. The only thing to be done is to buy up all the land on this ridge, run off the settlers, freeze out all the other mills, and put it into a big San Francisco company on shares. That's the only way we would look at it."

"But you don't consider the investment bad, even from *his* point of view?"

" Perhaps not."

" And you only decline it because it isn't big enough for the Bank ? "

" Exactly."

" Richardson," said Mainwaring, slowly rising, putting his hands in his trouser pockets and suddenly looking down upon the banker from the easy level of habitual superiority, " I wish you'd attend to this thing for me. I desire to make some return to Mr. Bradley for his kindness. I wish to give him what help he wants— in his own way—you understand. I wish it, and I believe my father wishes it too. If you'd like him to write to you to that effect——"

" By no means ; it's not at all neces- sary," said Richardson, dropping with equal suddenness into his old-world obse- quiousness. " I shall certainly do as you wish. It is not a bad investment, Mr. Mainwaring, and, as you suggest, a very proper return for their kindness. And,

being here, it will come quite naturally for
me to take up the affair again."

" And—I say, Richardson."

"Yes, sir ? "

" As these ladies are rather short-
handed in their domestic service, you know,
perhaps you'd better *not* stay to luncheon
or dinner, but go on to the Summit
House—it's only a mile or two further—
and come back here this evening. I sha'n't
want you until then."

" Certainly ! " stammered Richardson.
" I'll just take leave of the ladies ! "

" It's not at all necessary," said Mainwaring quietly ; " you would only disturb
them in their household duties. I'll tell
them what I've done with you if they ask.
You'll find your stick and hat in the passage, and you can leave the veranda by
these steps. By the way, you had better
manage at the Summit to get some one
to bring my traps from here to be for-
warded to Sacramento to-morrow. I'll

want a conveyance, or a horse of some kind, myself, for I've given up walking for a while; but we can settle about that to-night. Come early. Good morning!"

He accompanied his thoroughly subjugated countryman — who, however, far from attempting to reassert himself, actually seemed easier and more cheerful in his submission—to the end of the veranda, and watched him depart. As he turned back he saw the pretty figure of Louise Macy leaning against the doorway. How graceful and refined she looked in that simple morning dress! What wonder that she was admired by Greyson, by Johnson, and by that Spaniard!—no, by Jove, it was *she* that wanted to marry him!

"What have you sent away Mr. Richardson for?" asked the young girl, with a half-reproachful, half-mischievous look in her bright eyes.

"I packed him off because I thought it

was a little too hard on you and Mrs. Bradley to entertain him without help."

"But as he was *our* guest, you might have left that to us," said Miss Macy.

"By Jove! I never thought of that," said Mainwaring, colouring in consternation. "Pray forgive me, Miss Macy—but, you see, I knew the man, and could say it, and you couldn't."

"Well, I forgive you, for you look really so cut up," said Louise, laughing. "But I don't know what Jenny will say of your disposing of her conquest so summarily." She stopped and regarded him more attentively. "Has he brought you any bad news? if so, it's a pity you didn't send him away before. He's quite spoiling our cure."

Mainwaring thought bitterly that he had. "But it's a cure for all that, Miss Macy," he said, with an attempt at cheerfulness; "and being a cure, you see, there's no longer an excuse for my staying here. I

have been making arrangements for leaving
here to-morrow."

"So soon?"

"Do you think it soon, Miss Macy?"
asked Mainwaring, turning pale in spite of
himself.

"I quite forgot—that you were here as
an invalid only, and that we owe our pleasure to the accident of your pain."

She spoke a little artificially, he thought,
yet her cheeks had not lost their pink
bloom, nor her eyes their tranquillity.   Had
he heard Minty's criticism he might have
believed that the organic omission noticed
by her was a fact.

"And now that your good work as Sister
of Charity is completed, you'll be able to
enter the world of gaiety again with a clear
conscience," said Mainwaring, with a smile
that he inwardly felt was a miserable failure.
"You'll be able to resume your morning
rides, you know, which the wretched invalid
interrupted."

Louise raised her clear eyes to his, without reproach, indignation, or even wonder. He felt as if he had attempted an insult and failed.

"Does my cousin know you are going so soon?" she asked finally.

"No, I did not know myself until to-day. You see," he added hastily, while his honest blood blazoned the lie in his cheek, "I've heard of some miserable business affairs that will bring me back to England sooner than I expected."

"I think you should consider your health more important than any mere business," said Louise. "I don't mean that you should remain *here*," she added with a hasty laugh, "but it would be a pity, now that you have reaped the benefit of rest and taking care of yourself, that you should not make it your only business to seek it elsewhere."

Mainwaring longed to say that within the last half-hour, living or dying had become of little moment to him; but he doubted the truth or efficacy of this time-worn heroic of passion. He felt, too, that anything he said was a mere subterfuge for the real reason of his sudden departure. And how was he to question her as to that reason? In escaping from these subterfuges, he was compelled to lie again. With an assumption of changing the subject, he said carelessly, "Richardson thought he had met you before—in Menlo Park, I think."

Amazed at the evident irrelevance of the remark, Louise said coldly that she did not remember having seen him before.

"I think it was at a Mr. Johnson's—or *with* a Mr. Johnson—or perhaps at one of those Spanish Ranches—I think he mentioned some name like Pico!"

Louise looked at him wonderingly for an instant and then gave way to a frank, irrepressible laugh, which lent her delicate but rather set little face all the colour he had missed. Partially relieved by her unconcern, and yet mortified that he had only provoked her sense of the ludicrous, he tried to laugh also.

"Then, to be quite plain," said Louise, wiping her now humid eyes, "you want me to understand that you really didn't pay sufficient attention to hear correctly! Thank you; that's a pretty English compliment, I suppose."

"I daresay you wouldn't call it 'philandering'?"

"I certainly shouldn't, for I don't know what 'philandering' means."

Mainwaring could not reply with Richelieu, "You ought to know"; nor did he dare explain what he thought it meant, and how he knew it. Louise, however, innocently solved the difficulty.

"There's a country song I've heard Minty sing," she said. "It runs—

'Come, Philander, let us be a-marchin',
    Every one for his true love a-sarchin';
    Choose your true love now or never. . . .'

Have you been listening to her also?"

" No," said Mainwaring, with a sudden incomprehensible, but utterly irrepressible, resolution ; "but *I'm* ' a-marchin'', you know, and perhaps I must ' choose my true love now or never.' Will you help me, Miss Macy ? "

He drew gently near her. He had become quite white, but also very manly, and it struck her, more deeply, thoroughly, and conscientiously sincere than any man who had before addressed her. She moved slightly away, as if to rest herself by laying both hands upon the back of the chair.

" Where do you expect to begin your ' sarchin' '? " she said, leaning on the chair and tilting it before her ; " or are you as vague as usual as to locality ? Is it at some ' Mr. Johnson ' or ' Mr. Pico,' or——— "

" Here," he interrupted boldly.

" I really think you ought to first tell my cousin that you are going away to-morrow," she said, with a faint smile : "it's

such short notice. She's just in there."
She nodded her pretty head, without raising
her eyes, towards the hall.

"But it may not be so soon," said Mainwaring.

"Oh, then the 'sarchin'' is not so important ?" said Louise, raising her head, and
looking towards the hall with some uneasy
but indefinable feminine instinct.

She was right; the sitting-room door
opened, and Mrs. Bradley made her smiling
appearance.

"Mr. Mainwaring was just looking for
you," said Louise, for the first time raising
her eyes to him. "He's not only sent off
Mr. Richardson, but he's going away himself to-morrow."

Mrs. Bradley looked from the one to the
other in mute wonder. Mainwaring cast
an imploring glance at Louise, which had
the desired effect. Much more seriously,
and in a quaint, businesslike way, the young
girl took it upon herself to explain to Mrs.

Bradley that Richardson had brought the invalid some important news that would, unfortunately, not only shorten his stay in America, but even compel him to leave The Lookout sooner than he expected—perhaps to-morrow. Mainwaring thanked her with his eyes, and then turned to Mrs. Bradley.

"Whether I go to-morrow or next day," he said with simple and earnest directness, "I intend, you know, to see you soon again, either here or in my own home in England. I do not know," he added with marked gravity, "that I have succeeded in convincing you that I have made your family already well known to my people, and that"—he fixed his eyes with a meaning look on Louise—"no matter when, or in what way, you come to them, your place is made ready for you. You may not like them, you know: the governor is getting to be an old man—perhaps too old for young Americans—but *they* will like *you*, and you must put up with that. My mother and sisters know Miss Macy as well as I do, and will make her one of the family."

The conscientious earnestness with which these apparent conventionalities were uttered, and some occult quality of quiet conviction in the young man's manner, brought a pleasant sparkle to the eyes of Mrs. Bradley and Louise.

"But," said Mrs. Bradley gaily, "our going to England is quite beyond our present wildest dreams; nothing but a windfall, an unexpected rise in timber, or even the tabooed hotel speculation could make it possible."

"But *I* shall take the liberty of trying to present it to Mr. Bradley to-night in some practical way that may convince even his critical judgment," said Mainwaring, still seriously. "It will be," he added more lightly, "the famous testimonial of my cure which I promised you."

"And you will find Mr. Bradley so sceptical that you will be obliged to defer

your going," said Mrs. Bradley triumphantly. "Come, Louise, we must not forget
that we have still Mr. Mainwaring's present
comfort to look after; that Minty has
basely deserted us, and that we ourselves
must see that the last days of our guest
beneath our roof are not remembered for
their privation."

She led Louise away with a half-mischievous suggestion of maternal propriety,
and left Mainwaring once more alone on
the veranda.

He had done it! Certainly she must
have understood his meaning, and there
was nothing left for him now but to
acquaint Bradley with his intentions to-
night, and press her for a final answer in
the morning. There would be no in-
delicacy then in asking her for an interview more free from interruption than this
public veranda. Without conceit he did
not doubt what the answer would be. His
indecision, his sudden resolution to leave

her, had been all based upon the uncertainty of *his* own feelings, the propriety of *his* declaration, the possibility of some previous experience of hers that might compromise *him*. Convinced by her unembarrassed manner of her innocence, or rather satisfied of her indifference to Richardson's gossip, he had been hurried by his feelings into an unexpected avowal. Brought up in the perfect security of his own social position and familiarly conscious—without vanity—of its importance and power in such a situation, he believed, without undervaluing Louise's charms or independence, that he had no one else than himself to consult. Even the slight uneasiness that still pursued him was more due to his habitual conscientiousness of his own intention than to any fear that she would not fully respond to it. Indeed, with his conservative ideas of proper feminine self-restraint, Louise's calm passivity and undemonstrative attitude were a proof of her

K

superiority; had she blushed over-much, cried, or thrown herself into his arms, he would have doubted the wisdom of so easy a selection. It was true he had known her scarcely three weeks; if he chose to be content with that his own accessible record of three centuries should be sufficient for her, and condone any irregularity.

Nevertheless, as an hour slipped away and Louise did not make her appearance —either on the veranda or in the little sitting-room off the hall—Mainwaring became more uneasy as to the incompleteness of their interview. Perhaps a faint suspicion of the inadequacy of her response began to trouble him; but he still fatuously regarded it rather as owing to his own hurried and unfinished declaration. It was true that he hadn't said half what he intended to say; it was true that she might have misunderstood it as the conventional gallantry of the situation, as —terrible thought!—the light banter of

the habitual love-making American, to
which she had been accustomed; perhaps
even now she relegated him to the level
of Greyson, and this accounted for her
singular impassiveness—an impassiveness
that certainly was singular now he reflected upon it—that might have been
even contempt! The last thought pricked
his deep conscientiousness; he walked
hurriedly up and down the veranda, and
then suddenly re-entering his room, took
up a sheet of note-paper and began to
write to her :—

"Can you grant me a few moments' interview alone? I cannot bear you should
think that what I was trying to tell you
when we were interrupted was prompted
by anything but the deepest sincerity and
conviction, or that I am willing it should
be passed over lightly by you or be forgotten. Pray give me a chance of proving
it by saying you will see me.

"F. M."

K 2

But how should he convey this to her? His delicacy revolted against handing it to her behind Mrs. Bradley's back, or the prestidigitation of slipping it into her lap or under her plate before them at luncheon; he thought for an instant of the Chinaman, but gentlemen—except in that "mirror of nature" the stage— usually hesitate to suborn other people's servants, or entrust a woman's secret to her inferiors. He remembered that Louise's room was at the further end of the house, and its low window gave upon the veranda, and was guarded at night by a film of white and blue curtains that were parted during the day to allow a triangular reve- lation of a pale blue and white draped interior. Mainwaring reflected that the low inside window-ledge was easily acces- sible from the veranda, would afford a capital lodgment for the note, and be quickly seen by the fair occupant of the room on entering. He sauntered slowly past the window; the room was empty, the moment propitious. A slight breeze was stirring the blue ribbons of the curtain; it would be necessary to secure the note with something; he returned along the veranda to the steps, where he had noticed a small irregular stone lying, which had evidently escaped from Richelieu's bag of treasure specimens, and had been overlooked by that ingenuous child. It was of a pretty peacock-blue colour, and, besides securing a paper, would be sure to attract her attention. He placed his note on the inside ledge and the blue stone atop, and went away with a sense of relief.

Another half-hour passed without incident. He could hear the voices of the two women in the kitchen and dining-room. After a while they appeared to cease, and he heard the sound of an opening door. It then occurred to him that the veranda was still too exposed for a confidential interview, and he resolved to

descend the steps, pass before the windows
of the kitchen where Louise might see him
and penetrate the shrubbery, where she
might be induced to follow him. They
would not be interrupted nor overheard
there.

But he had barely left the veranda
before the figure of Richelieu, who had
been patiently waiting for Mainwaring's
disappearance, emerged stealthily from the
shrubbery. He had discovered his loss on
handing his "fire assays" to the good-
humoured Bradley for later examination,
and he had retraced his way, step by step,
looking everywhere for his missing stone
with the unbounded hopefulness, lazy per-
sistency, and lofty disregard for time and
occupation known only to the genuine boy.
He remembered to have placed his knotted
bag upon the veranda, and, slipping off his
stiff boots, slowly and softly slid along
against the wall of the house, looking
carefully on the floor, and yet preserving a

studied negligence of demeanour, with one hand in his pocket and his small mouth contracted into a singularly soothing and almost voiceless whistle—Richelieu's own peculiar accomplishment. But no stone appeared. Like most of his genus he was superstitious, and repeated to himself the cabalistic formula : " Losin's seekin's, findin's keepin's"—presumed to be of great efficacy in such cases—with religious fervour. He had laboriously reached the end of the veranda when he noticed the open window of Louise's room, and stopped as a perfunctory duty to look in. And then Richelieu Sharpe stood for an instant utterly confounded and aghast at this crowning proof of the absolute infamy and sickening enormity of Man.

There was *his* stone—*his, Richelieu's, own specimen,* carefully gathered by himself and none other—and now stolen, abstracted, " skyugled," " smouged," " hooked " by this " rotten, skunkified, long-legged, splay-

footed, hoss-laughin', nigger-toothed, or'nary
despot!" And, worse than all, actually
made to do infamous duty as a love token!
—a "candy-gift"!—a "philanderin' box"!
to *his*, Richelieu's, girl—for Louise belonged
to that innocent and vague outside seraglio
of Richelieu's boyish dreams—and put atop
of a letter to her! and Providence permitted such an outrage! "Wot was he,
Richelieu, sent to school for, and organized
wickedness in the shape of gorilla Injins
like this allowed to ride high horses ram-
pant over Californcy!" He looked at the
heavens in mute appeal. And then—Providence not immediately interfering—he
thrust his own small arm into the window,
regained his priceless treasure, and fled
swiftly.

A fateful silence ensued. The wind
slightly moved the curtain outward, as if
in a playful attempt to follow him, and
then subsided. A moment later, apparently
reinforced by other winds, or sympathizing

with Richelieu, it lightly lifted the unlucky missive and cast it softly from the window. But here another wind, lying in wait, caught it cleverly, and tossed it, in a long curve, into the abyss. For an instant it seemed to float lazily, as on the mirrored surface of a lake, until, turning upon its side, it suddenly darted into utter oblivion.

When Mainwaring returned from the shrubbery, he went softly to the window. The disappearance of the letter and stone satisfied him of the success of his stratagem, and for the space of three hours relieved his anxiety. But at the end of that time, finding no response from Louise, his former uneasiness returned. Was she offended, or—the first doubt of her acceptance of him crossed his mind! A sudden and inexplicable sense of shame came upon him. At the same moment, he heard his name called from the steps, turned—and beheld Minty.

Her dark eyes were shining with a

pleasant light, and her lips parted on her white teeth with a frank, happy smile. She advanced and held out her hand. He took it with a mingling of disappointment and embarrassment.

"You're wondering why I kem on here, arter I sent word this morning that I kelkilated not to come. Well, 'twixt then and now suthin' 's happened. We've had fine doin's over at our house, you bet! Pop don't know which end he's standin' on; and I reckon that for about ten minutes I didn't know my own name. But ez soon ez I got fairly hold o' the hull thing, and had it put straight in my mind, I sez to myself, Minty Sharpe, sez I, the first thing for you to do now, is to put on yer bonnet and shawl, and trapse over to Jim Bradley's, and help them two womenfolks get dinner for themselves and that sick stranger. And," continued Minty, throwing herself into a chair and fanning her glowing face with her apron, " yer I am ! "

"But you have not told me *what* has happened," said Mainwaring, with a constrained smile, and an uneasy glance towards the house.

" That's so," said Minty, with a brilliant laugh. " I clean forgot the hull gist of the thing. Well, we're rich folks now—over thar on Barren Ledge! That onery brother of mine, Richelieu, hez taken some of his specimens over to Jim Bradley to be tested. And Bradley, just to please that child, takes 'em ; and not an hour ago Bradley comes running, likety switch, over to Pop to tell him to put up his notices, for the hull of that ledge where the forge stands is a mine o' silver and copper. Afore ye knew it, Lordy! half the folks outer the Summit and the mill was scattered down thar all over it. Richardson—that stranger ez knows you—kem thar too with Jim, and he allows, ef Bradley's essay is right, it's worth more than a hundred thousand dollars ez it stands ! "

" I suppose I must congratulate you, Miss Sharpe," said Mainwaring with an attempt at interest, but his attention still preoccupied with the open doorway.

" Oh, *they* know all about it!" said Minty, following the direction of his abstracted eyes with a slight darkening of her own, " I jest kem out o' the kitchen the other way, and Jim sent 'em a note ; but I allowed I'd tell *you* myself. Specially ez you was going away to-morrow."

"Who said I was going away to-morrow?" asked Mainwaring uneasily.

" Loo Macy ! "

" Ah—she did ? But I may change my mind, you know ! " he continued, with a faint smile.

Minty shook her curls decisively. " I reckon *she* knows," she said drily, " she's got law and Gospel for wot she says. But yer she comes. Ask her ! Look yer, Loo," she added, as the two women appeared at the doorway, with a certain exaggeration

of congratulatory manner that struck Mainwaring as being as artificial and disturbed
as his own; "didn't Sir Francis yer say he
was going to-morrow?"

"That's what I understood!" returned
Louise, with cold astonishment, letting her
clear indifferent eyes fall upon Mainwaring.
"I do not know that he has changed his
mind."

"Unless, as Miss Sharpe is a great
capitalist now, she is willing to use her
powers of persuasion," added Mrs. Bradley,
with a slight acidulous pointing of her usual
prim playfulness.

"I reckon Minty Sharpe's the same ez
she allus wos, unless more so," returned
Minty, with an honest egotism that carried
so much conviction to the hearer as to condone its vanity. "But I kem yer to do a
day's work, gals, and I allow to pitch in
and do it, and not sit yer swoppin' compli-
ments and keeping *him* from packin' his
duds. Onless," she stopped, and looked

around at the uneasy, unsympathetic circle
with a faint tremulousness of lip that belied
the brave black eyes above it, " onless I'm
in yer way."

The two women sprang forward with a
feminine bewildering excess of protesta-
tion ; and Mainwaring, suddenly pierced
through his outer selfish embarrassment
to his more honest depths, stammered
quickly—

" Look here, Miss Sharpe, if you think
of running away again, after having come
all the way here to make us share the
knowledge of your good fortune and your
better heart, by Jove ! I'll go back with
you."

But here the two women effusively
hurried her away from the dangerous prox-
imity of such sympathetic honesty, and a
moment later Mainwaring heard her laughing voice, as of old, ringing in the kitchen.
And then, as if unconsciously responding
to the significant common-sense that lay

in her last allusion to him, he went to his
room and grimly began his packing.

He did not again see Louise alone. At
their informal luncheon the conversation
turned upon the more absorbing topic of
the Sharpes' discovery, its extent, and its
probable effect upon the fortunes of the
locality. He noticed, abstractedly, that
both Mrs. Bradley and her cousin showed
a real or assumed scepticism of its value.
This did not disturb him greatly, except
for its intended check upon Minty's enthusiasm. He was more conscious, perhaps—
with a faint touch of mortified vanity—that
his own contemplated departure was of
lesser importance than this local excitement.
Yet, in his growing conviction that all was
over—if, indeed, it had ever begun—between
himself and Louise, he was grateful to this
natural diversion of incident which spared
them both an interval of embarrassing
commonplaces. And, with the suspicion of
some indefinable insincerity—either of his

own or Louise's—haunting him, Minty's
frank heartiness and outspoken loyalty gave
him a strange relief. It seemed to him as
if the clear cool breath of the forest had
entered with her homely garments, and the
steadfast truths of Nature were incarnate
in her shining eyes. How far this poetic
fancy would have been consistent or even
co-existent with any gleam of tenderness or
self-forgetfulness in Louise's equally pretty
orbs, I leave the satirical feminine reader
to determine.

It was late when Bradley at last returned,
bringing further and more complete cor-
roboration of the truth of Sharpe's good
fortune. Two experts had arrived, one
from Pine Flat and another from the
Summit, and upon this statement Richardson had offered to purchase an interest in
the discovery that would at once enable
the blacksmith to develop his mine.
"I shouldn't wonder, Mainwaring," he
added cheerfully, "if he'd put you

into it, too, and make your eternal fortune."

"With larks falling from the skies all round you, it's a pity *you* couldn't get put into something," said Mrs. Bradley, straightening her pretty brows.

"I'm not a gold-miner, my dear," said Bradley pleasantly.

"Nor a gold-finder," returned his wife, with a cruel little depression of her pink nostrils; "but you can work all night in that stupid mill and then," she added in a low voice, to escape Minty's attention, "spend the whole of the next day examining and following up a boy's discovery that his own relations had been too lazy and too ignorant to understand and profit by. I suppose that next you will be hunting up a site on the *other side* of the Canyon, where somebody else can put up an hotel and ruin your own prospects."

A sensitive shadow of pain quickly dimmed Bradley's glance—not the first or last time, evidently, for it was gradually bringing out a background of sadness in his intelligent eyes. But the next moment he turned kindly to Mainwaring, and began to deplore the necessity of his early departure, which Richardson had already made known to him with practical and satisfying reasons.

" I hope you won't forget, my dear fellow, that your most really urgent business is to look after your health; and if, hereafter, you'll only remember the old Lookout enough to impress that fact upon you, I shall feel that any poor service I have rendered you has been amply repaid."

Mainwaring, notwithstanding that he winced slightly at this fateful echo of Louise's advice, returned the grasp of his friend's hand with an honest pressure equal to his own. He longed now only for the coming of Richardson, to complete his scheme of grateful benefaction to his host.

The banker came, fortunately as the con-

versation began to flag ; and Mrs. Bradley's
half-coquettish ill-humour of a pretty
woman, and Louise's abstracted indifference, were becoming so noticeable as to
even impress Minty into a thoughtful
taciturnity. The graciousness of his reception by Mrs. Bradley somewhat restored
his former ostentatious gallantry, and his
self-satisfied, domineering manner had
enough masculine power in it to favourably
affect the three women, who, it must be
confessed, were a little bored by the finer
abstractions of Bradley and Mainwaring.
After a few moments, Mainwaring rose and,
with a significant glance at Richardson to
remind him of his proposed conference with
Bradley, turned to leave the room. He
was obliged to pass Louise, who was sitting
by the table. His attention was suddenly
arrested by something in her hand with
which she was listlessly playing. It was
the stone which he had put on his letter to
her.

As he had not been present when Bradley
arrived, he did not know that this fateful
object had been brought home by his host,
who, after receiving it from Richelieu, had
put it in his pocket to illustrate his story
of the discovery.   On the contrary, it
seemed that Louise's careless exposure of
his foolish stratagem was gratuitously and
purposely cruel.   Nevertheless, he stopped
and looked at her.

"That's a queer stone you have there,"
he said, in a tone which she recognized as
coldly and ostentatiously civil.

"Yes," she replied, without looking up;
"it's the outcrop of that mine."   She
handed it to him as if to obviate any further remark.   "I thought you had seen it
before."

"The outcrop," he repeated drily.   "That
is—it—it—it is the indication or sign of
something important that's below it—isn't
it?"

Louise shrugged her shoulders sceptically.

"It don't follow. It's just as likely to cover rubbish, after you've taken the trouble to look."

"Thanks," he said, with measured gentleness, and passed quietly out of the room.

The moon had already risen when Bradley, with his briar-wood pipe, preceded Richardson upon the veranda. The latter threw his large frame into Louise's rocking-chair near the edge of the abyss ; Bradley, with his own chair tilted against the side of the house after the national fashion, waited for him to speak. The absence of Mainwaring and the stimulus of Mrs. Bradley's graciousness had given the banker a certain condescending familiarity, which Bradley received with amused and ironical tolerance that his twinkling eyes made partly visible in the darkness.

"One of the things I wanted to talk to you about, Bradley, was that old affair of the advance you asked for from the Bank. We did not quite see our way to it then, and, speaking as a business man, it isn't really a matter of business now ; but it has lately been put to me in a light that would make the doing of it possible—you understand ?   The fact of the matter is this : Sir Robert Mainwaring, the father of the young fellow you've got in your house, is one of our directors and largest shareholders, and I can tell you—if you don't suspect it already—you've been lucky, Bradley— deucedly lucky—to have had him in your house, and to have rendered him a service. He's the heir to one of the largest landed estates in his county, one of the oldest county families, and will step into the title some day.   But, ahem !" he coughed patronizingly, " you knew all that !   No ?   Well, that charming wife of yours, at least, does ; for she's been talking about it.   Gad, Bradley, it takes those women to find out anything of that kind, eh ?"

The light in Bradley's eyes and his pipe went slowly out together.

"Then we'll say that affair of the advance is as good as settled. It's Sir Robert's wish, you understand—and this young fellow's wish—and if you'll come down to the Bank next week we'll arrange it for you; I think you'll admit they're doing the handsome thing to you and yours. And therefore," he lowered his voice confidentially, "you'll see, Bradley, that it will only be the honourable thing in you, you know, to look upon the affair as finished, and, in fact, to do all you can"—he drew his chair closer—"to—to—to drop this other foolishness."

"I don't think I quite understand you," said Bradley slowly.

"But your wife does, if you don't," returned Richardson bluntly; "I mean this foolish flirtation between Louise Macy and Mainwaring, which is utterly preposterous. Why, man, it can't possibly come to anything, and it couldn't be allowed for a moment. Look at his position and hers.

I should think, as a practical man, it would strike you—— ”

“ Only one thing strikes me, Richardson,” interrupted Bradley in a singularly distinct whisper, rising, and moving nearer the speaker : “ it is that you're sitting perilously near the edge of this veranda.   For, by the living God, if you don't take yourself out of that chair and out of this house, I won't be answerable for the consequences ! ”

“ Hold on there a minute, will you ? ” said Mainwaring's voice from the window.

Both men turned towards it.   A long leg was protruding from Mainwaring's window ; it was quickly followed by the other leg and body of the occupant, and the next moment Mainwaring came towards the two men, with his hands in his pockets.

“ Not so loud,” he said, looking towards the house.

“ Let that man go,” said Bradley, in a repressed voice.   “ You and I, Mainwaring, can speak together afterwards.”

"That man must stay until he hears what I have got to say," said Mainwaring, stepping between them. He was very white and grave in the moonlight, but very quiet; and he did not take his hands from his pockets. "I've listened to what he said because he came here on *my* business, which was simply to offer to do you a service. That was all, Bradley, that *I* told him to do. This rot about what he expects of you in return is his own impertinence. If you'd punched his head when he began it, it would have been all right. But since he has begun it, before he goes I think he ought to hear me tell you that I have already *offered* myself to Miss Macy, and she has *refused* me! If she had given me the least encouragement, I should have told you before. Further, I want to say that, in spite of that man's insinuations, I firmly believe that no one is aware of the circumstance except Miss Macy and myself."

"I had no idea of intimating that anything had happened that was not highly honourable and creditable to you and the young lady," began Richardson hurriedly.

" I don't know that it was necessary for you to have any ideas on the subject at all," said Mainwaring sternly; "nor that, having been shown how you have insulted this gentleman and myself, you need trouble us an instant longer with your company. You need not come back. I will manage my other affairs myself."

" Very well, Mr. Mainwaring—but—you may be sure that I shall certainly take the first opportunity to explain myself to Sir Robert," returned Richardson as, with an attempt at dignity, he strode away.

There was an interval of silence.

" Don't be too hard upon a fellow, Bradley," said Mainwaring, as Bradley remained dark and motionless in the shadow. " It is a poor return I'm making you for your kindness, but I swear I never thought of anything like—like—this."

" Nor did I," said Bradley bitterly.

" I know it, and that's what makes it so infernally bad for me. Forgive me, won't you ? Think of me, old fellow, as the wretchedest ass you ever met, but not such a cad as this would make me ! " As Mainwaring stepped out from the moonlight towards him with extended hand, Bradley finally grasped it.

" Thanks—there—thanks, old fellow ! And, Bradley—I say—don't say anything to your wife, for I don't think she knows it. And, Bradley—look here—I didn't like to be anything but plain before that fellow ; but I don't mind telling *you*, now that it's all over, that I really think Louise —Miss Macy—didn't altogether understand me either."

With another shake of the hand they separated for the night. For a long time after Mainwaring had gone, Bradley remained gazing thoughtfully into the Great Canyon. He thought of the time when

he had first come there, full of life and
enthusiasm, making an ideal world of his
pure and wholesome eyrie on the ledge.
What else he thought will, probably, never
be known until the misunderstanding of
honourable and chivalrous men by a charming and illogical sex shall be analysed and
explained by some more daring romancer.

When he returned to the house, he said
kindly to his wife, "I have been thinking
to-day about your hotel scheme, and I
shall write to Sacramento to-night to
accept that capitalist's offer."

Part II.

CHAPTER I.

THE sun was just rising. In two years of mutation and change it had seen the little cottage, clinging like a swallow's nest to the rocky eaves of a great Sierran canyon, give way to a straggling, many galleried hotel; and a dozen blackened chimneys rise above the barren tableland where once had stood the lonely forge. To that conservative orb of light and heat there must have been a peculiar satisfaction in looking down a few hours earlier upon the battlements and gables of Oldenhurst, whose base was deeply embedded in the matured foundations and settled traditions of an English county. For the rising sun had for the last ten centuries found Oldenhurst in its place,

from the heavy stone terrace that covered
the dead-and-forgotten wall where a Roman
sentinel had once paced, to the little
grating in the cloistered quadrangle, where
it had seen a Cistercian brother place the
morning dole. It had daily welcomed the
growth of this vast and picturesque excre-
scence of the times ; it had smiled every
morning upon this formidable yet quaint
incrustation of power and custom, ignoring, as Oldenhurst itself had ignored, the
generations who possessed it, the men who
built it, the men who carried it with fire
and sword, the men who had lied and
cringed for it, the king who had given it
to a favourite, the few brave hearts who
had died for it in exile, and the one or two
who had bought and paid for it. For
Oldenhurst had absorbed all these and
more until it had become a story of the
past, incarnate in stone, greenwood, and
flower ; it had even drained the life-blood
from adjacent hamlets, repaying them with

tumuli growths like its own, in the shape
of purposeless lodges, quaintly incompetent
hospitals and schools, and churches where
the inestimable blessing and knowledge of
its gospel were taught and fostered. Nor
had it dealt more kindly with the gentry
within its walls, sending some to the
scaffold, pillorying others in infamous office,
reducing a few to poverty, and halting its
later guests with gout and paralysis. It
had given them in exchange the dubious
immortality of a portrait gallery, from
which they stared with stony and equal
resignation ; it had preserved their useless
armour and accoutrements ; it had set up
their marble effigies in churches or laid
them in cross-legged attitudes to trip up
the unwary, until in death, as in life, they
got between the congregation and the
truth that was taught there. It had
allowed an Oldenhurst crusader, with a
broken nose like a pugilist, on the
strength of his having been twice to the

Holy Land, to hide the beautifully illuminated Word from the lowlier worshipper
on the humbler benches; it had sent an
iconoclastic Bishop of the Reformation to
a nearer minster to ostentatiously occupy
the place of the consecrated image he had
overthrown. Small wonder that crowding
the Oldenhurst retainers gradually into
smaller space, with occasional Sabbath
glimpses of the living rulers of Oldenhurst
already in railed-off exaltation, it had forced
them to accept Oldenhurst as a synonym of
eternity, and left the knowledge of a higher
Power to what time they should be turned
out to their longer sleep under the tender
grass of the beautiful outer churchyard.

And even thus, while every stone of the
pile of Oldenhurst and every tree in its
leafy park might have been eloquent with
the story of vanity, selfishness, and unequal
justice, it had been left to the infinite mercy
of Nature to seal their lips with a spell of
beaty that left mankind equally dumb;

earth, air, and moisture had entered into a gentle conspiracy to soften, mellow, and clothe its external blemishes of breach and accident, its irregular design, its additions, accretions, ruins, and lapses with a harmonious charm of outline and colour ; poets, romancers, and historians had equally conspired to illuminate the dark passages and uglier inconsistencies of its interior life with the glamour of their own fancy. The fragment of menacing keep, with its choked oubliettes, became a bower of tender ivy ; the grim story of its crimes, properly edited by a contemporary bard of the family, passed into a charming ballad. Even the superstitious darkness of its religious house had escaped through fallen roof and shattered wall, leaving only the foliated and sun-pierced screen of front, with its rose-window and pinnacle of cross behind. Pilgrims from all lands had come to see it ; fierce Republicans had crossed the seas to gaze at its mediæval outlines, and copy

M

them in wood and stucco on their younger soil. Politicians had equally pointed to it as a convincing evidence of their own principles and in refutation of each other; and it had survived both. For it was this belief in its own perpetuity that was its strength and weakness. And that belief was never stronger than on this bright August morning, when it was on the verge of dissolution. A telegram brought to Sir Robert Mainwaring had even then as completely shattered and disintegrated Oldenhurst, in all it was and all it meant, as if the brown-paper envelope had been itself charged with the electric fluid.

Sir Robert Mainwaring, whose family had for three centuries possessed Oldenhurst, had received the news of his financial ruin; and the vast pile which had survived the repeated invasion of superstition, force, intrigue, and even progress, had succumbed to a foe its founders and proprietors had loftily ignored and left to Jews and traders.

The acquisition of money, except by despoilment, gift, Royal favour, or inheritance, had been unknown at Oldenhurst. The present degenerate custodian of its fortunes, staggering under the weight of its sentimental mortmain already alluded to, had speculated in order to keep up its material strength, which was gradually shrinking through impoverished land and the ruined trade it had despised. He had invested largely in California mines, and was the chief shareholder in a San Francisco Bank. But the mines had proved worthless, the Bank had that morning suspended payment, owing to the failure of a large land and timber company on the Sierras, which it had imprudently " carried." The spark which had demolished Oldenhurst had been fired from the new telegraph-station in the hotel above the great Sierran canyon.

There was a large house-party at Oldenhurst that morning. But it had been a

part of the history of the Mainwarings to
accept defeat gallantly and as became their
blood. Sir Percival—the second gentleman
on the left as you entered the library—un-
horsed, dying on a distant moor, with a
handful of followers, abandoned by a charming Prince and a miserable cause, was
scarcely a greater hero than this ruined but
undaunted gentleman of eighty, entering
the breakfast-room a few hours later as
jauntily as his gout would permit, and conscientiously dispensing the hospitalities of
his crumbling house. When he had
arranged a few pleasure parties for the day,
and himself thoughtfully anticipated the
different tastes of his guests, he turned to
Lady Mainwaring.

"Don't forget that somebody ought to go
to the station to meet the Bradleys. Frank
writes from St. Moritz that they are due
here to-day."

Lady Mainwaring glanced quickly at her
husband, and said *sotto voce,* "Do you think

they'll care to come *now?* They probably have heard all about it."

"Not how it affects me," returned Sir Robert, in the same tone; "and as they might think that because Frank was with them on that California mountain we would believe it had something to do with Richardson involving the Bank in that wretched company, we must really *insist* upon their coming."

"Bradley!" echoed the Hon. Captain FitzHarry, overhearing the name during a late forage on the sideboard. "Bradley!— there was an awfully pretty American at Biarritz, travelling with a cousin, I think— a Miss Mason or Macy. Those sort of people, you know, who have a companion as pretty as themselves : bring you down with the other barrel if one misses—eh? Very clever, both of them, and hardly any accent."

"Mr. Bradley was a very dear friend of Frank's, and most kind to him," said Lady Mainwaring gravely.

"Didn't know there *was* a Mr. Bradley, really. He didn't come to the fore then," said the unabashed Captain. "Deuced hard to follow up those American husbands!"

"And their wives wouldn't thank you, if you did," said Lady Griselda Armiger, with a sweet smile.

"If it is the Mrs. Bradley I mean," said Lady Canterbridge from the lower end of the table, looking up from her letter, "who looks a little like Mrs. Summertree, and has a pretty cousin with her who wears very good frocks, I'm afraid you won't be able to get her down here. She's booked with engagements for the next six weeks. She and her cousin made all the running at Grigsby Royal, and she has quite deposed that other American beauty in Northforeland's good graces. She regularly *affiché'd* him, and it is piteous to see him follow her about. No, my dear; I don't believe they'll come to any one of less rank than a Marquis. If they did, I'm sure Canterbridge would have had them at Buckenthorpe already."

"I wonder if there was ever anything in Frank's admiration of this Miss Macy?" said Lady Mainwaring a few moments later, lingering beside her husband in his study.

"I really don't know," said Sir Robert abstractedly ; "his letters were filled with her praises, and Richardson thought—— "

"Pray don't mention that man's name again," said Lady Mainwaring, with the first indication of feeling she had shown. "I shouldn't trust him."

"But why do you ask ?" returned her husband.

Lady Mainwaring was silent for a moment. "She is very rich, I believe," she said slowly. "At least, Frank writes that some neighbours of theirs whom he met in the Engadine told him they had sold the site of that absurd cottage where he was ill for some extravagant sum."

"My dear Geraldine," said the old man affectionately, taking his wife's hand in his own, that now for the first time trembled, "if you have any hope based upon what you are thinking of now, let it be the last and least. You forget that Paget told us that with the best care he could scarcely ensure Frank's return to perfect health. Even if God in His mercy spared him long enough to take my place, what girl would be willing to tie herself to a man doomed to sickness and poverty? Hardly the one you speak of, my dear."

Lady Canterbridge proved a true prophet. Mrs. Bradley and Miss Macy did not come, regretfully alleging a previous engagement made on the Continent with the Duke of Northforeland and the Marquis of Dungeness; but the unexpected and apocryphal husband *did* arrive. "I have not seen my family," he said, "since I returned from visiting your son in Switzerland. I am glad they were able to amuse themselves without waiting for me at a London hotel, though I should prefer to have found them here." Sir Robert and Lady Mainwaring were courteous but slightly embarrassed. Lady Canterbridge, who had come to the station in bored curiosity, raised her clear blue eyes to his. He did not look like a fool, a complaisant or fashionably cynical husband—this well-dressed, well-mannered, but quietly and sympathetically observant man. Did he really care for his selfish wife? was it perfect trust or some absurd Transatlantic custom? She did not understand him. It wearied her and she turned her eyes indifferently away. Bradley, a little irritated, he knew not why, at the scrutiny of this tall, handsome, gentlemanly looking woman, who, however, in spite of her broad shoulders and narrow hips possessed a refined muliebrity superior to mere liberality of contour, turned slightly towards Sir Robert. "Lady Canterbridge,

Frank's cousin." explained Sir Robert
hesitatingly, as if conscious of some vague
awkwardness. Bradley and Lady Canterbridge both bowed—possibly the latter's
salutation was the most masculine—and
Bradley, eventually forgetting her presence,
plunged into an earnest, sympathetic, and
intelligent account of the condition in
which he had found the invalid at St.
Moritz. The old man at first listened
with an almost perfunctory courtesy and
a hesitating reserve: but as Bradley was
lapsing into equal reserve and they drove
up to the gates of the quadrangle, he
unexpectedly warmed with a word or two
of serious welcome. Looking up with a
half-unconscious smile, Bradley met Lady
Canterbridge's examining eyes.

The next morning, finding an opportunity to be alone with him, Bradley, with
a tactful mingling of sympathy and directness, informed his host that he was
cognisant of the disaster that had over-

taken the Bank, and delicately begged
him to accept of any service he could
render him. " Pardon me," he said, " if I
speak as plainly to you as I would to your
son; my friendship for him justifies an
equal frankness to any one he loves; but I
should not intrude upon your confidence
if I did not believe that my knowledge
and assistance might be of benefit to you.
Although *I* did not sell my lands to
Richardson or approve of his methods," he
continued. " I fear it was some suggestion
of mine that eventually induced him to
form the larger and more disastrous
scheme that ruined the Bank. So you
see," he added lightly, " I claim a right
to offer you my services." Touched by
Bradley's sincerity and discreet intelligence, Sir Robert was equally frank.
During the recital of his Californian in-
vestments—a chronicle of almost fatuous
speculation and imbecile enterprise—Bradley was profoundly moved at the naïve

ignorance of business and hopeless in-
genuousness of this old habitué of a
cynical world and an insincere society,
to whom no financial scheme had been
too wild for acceptance. As Bradley
listened with a half-saddened smile to the
grave visions of this aged enthusiast, he
remembered the son's unsophisticated simplicity; what he had considered as the
"boyishness" of immaturity was the taint
of the utterly unpractical Mainwaring
blood. It was upon this blood, and others
like it, that Oldenhurst had for centuries
waxed and fattened.

Bradley was true to his promise of
assistance, and with the aid of two or
three of his brother millionaires, whose
knowledge of the resources of the locality
was no less powerful and convincing than
the security of their actual wealth, managed to stay the immediate action of the
catastrophe until the affairs of the Sierran
Land and Timber Company could be

examined and some plan of reconstruction
arranged. During this interval of five
months, in which the credit of Sir Robert
Mainwaring was preserved with the secret
of his disaster, Bradley was a frequent
and welcome visitor to Oldenhurst. Apart
from his strange and chivalrous friendship
for the Mainwarings — which was as incomprehensible to Sir Robert as Sir
Robert's equally eccentric and Quixotic
speculations had been to Bradley—he
began to feel a singular and weird fasci-
nation for the place. A patient martyr in
the vast London house he had taken for
his wife and cousin's amusement, he loved
to escape the loneliness of its autumn
solitude or the occasional greater loneliness
of his wife's social triumphs. The handsome, thoughtful man who sometimes
appeared at the foot of his wife's table or
melted away like a well-bred ghost in the
hollow emptiness of her brilliant recep-
tions, piqued the languid curiosity of a few.

A distinguished personage, known for his tactful observance of *convenances* that others forgot, had made a point of challenging this gentlemanly apparition, and had followed it up with courteous civilities, which led to exchange of much respect but no increase of acquaintance. He had even spent a week at Buckenthorpe, with Canterbridge in the coverts and Lady Canterbridge in the music-room and library. He had returned more thoughtful, and for some time after was more frequent in his appearances at home, and more earnest in his renewed efforts to induce his wife to return to America with him.

"You'll never be happy anywhere but in California, among those common people," she replied; "and while I was willing to share your poverty *there*," she added drily, "I prefer to share your wealth among civilized ladies and gentlemen. Besides," she continued, "we must consider Louise.

She is as good as engaged to Lord Dunshunner, and I do not intend that you
shall make a mess of her affairs here as
you did in California."

It was the first time he had heard of
Lord Dunshunner's proposals ; it was the
first allusion she had ever made to Louise
and Mainwaring.

Meantime, the autumn leaves had fallen
silently over the broad terraces of Oldenhurst with little changes to the fortunes
of the great house itself. The Christmas
house-party included Lady Canterbridge,
whose husband was still detained at Homburg in company with Dunshunner ; and
Bradley, whose wife and cousin lingered
on the Continent. He was slightly embarrassed when Lady Canterbridge turned
to him one afternoon as they were returning from the lake and congratulated him
abruptly upon Louise's engagement.

" Perhaps you don't care to be congratulated," she said, as he did not immediately

respond, " and you had as little to do with
it as with that other ?   It is a woman's
function."

" What other ? " echoed Bradley.

Lady Canterbridge slightly turned her
handsome head towards him as she walked
unbendingly at his side.   " Tell me how
you manage to keep your absolute simplicity so fresh.   Do you suppose it wasn't
known at Oldenhurst that Frank had quite
compromised himself with Miss Macy over
there ? "

" It certainly was not known ' over
there,' " said Bradley curtly.

" Don't be angry with me."

Such an appeal from the tall, indifferent
woman at his side, so confidently superior
to criticism, and uttered in a lower tone,
made him smile, albeit uneasily.

" I only meant to congratulate you," she
continued carelessly.   " Dunshunner is not
a bad sort of fellow, and will come into a
good property some day.   And then, society

is so made up of caprice, just now, that it is well for your wife's cousin to make the most of her opportunities while they last. She is very popular now; but next season——" Seeing that Bradley remained silent, she did not finish her sentence, but said with her usual abruptness, "Do you know a Miss Araminta Eulalie Sharpe?"

Bradley started. Could any one recognize honest Minty in the hopeless vulgarity which this fine lady had managed to carelessly import into her name? His eye kindled.

"She is an old friend of mine, Lady Canterbridge."

"How fortunate! Then I can please you by giving you good news of her. She is the coming sensation. They say she is very rich, but quite one of the people, you know: in fact, she makes no scruples of telling you her father was a blacksmith, I think, and takes the dear old man with her everywhere. FitzHarry raves about her,

N

and says her *naïveté* is something too
delicious. She is regularly in with some of
the best people already. Lady Dungeness
has taken her up, and Northforeland is only
waiting for your cousin's engagement to
be able to go over decently. Shall I ask
her to Buckenthorpe ?—come, now, as an
apology for my rudeness to your cousin ? "
She was very womanly now in spite of her
high collar, her straight back, and her
tightly fitting jacket, as she stood there
smiling. Suddenly, her smile faded; she
drew her breath in quickly.

She had caught a glimpse of his usually
thoughtful face and eyes, now illuminated
with some pleasant memory.

"Thank you," he said smilingly, yet with
a certain hesitation, as he thought of The
Lookout and Araminta Eulalie Sharpe,
and tried to reconcile them with the
lady before him. " I should like it very
much."

" Then you have known Miss Sharpe a

long time?" continued Lady Canterbridge as they walked on.

"While we were at The Lookout she was our nearest neighbour."

"And I suppose your wife will consider it quite proper for you to see her again at my house?" said Lady Canterbridge, with a return of conventional levity.

"Oh! quite," said Bradley.

They had reached the low Norman-arched side-entrance to the quadrangle. As Bradley swung open the bolt-studded oaken door to let her pass, she said carelessly—

"Then you are not coming in now?"

"No; I shall walk a little longer."

"And I am quite forgiven?"

"I am thanking you very much," he said, smiling directly into her blue eyes. She lowered them, and vanished into the darkness of the passage.

The news of Minty's success was further corroborated by Sir Robert, who later that evening called Bradley into the study. "Frank has been writing from Nice that he has renewed his acquaintance with some old Californian friends of yours—a Mr. and Miss Sharpe. Lady Canterbridge says that they are well known in London to some of our friends, but I would like to ask you something about them. Lady Mainwaring was on the point of inviting them here when I received a letter from Mr. Sharpe asking for a *business* interview. Pray, who is this Sharpe?"

"You say he writes for a *business* interview?" asked Bradley.

"Yes."

Bradley hesitated for a moment and then said quietly, "Perhaps, then, I am justified in a breach of confidence to him, in order to answer your question. He is the man who has assumed all the liabilities of the Sierran Land and Timber Company to enable the Bank to resume payment. But he did it on the condition that you were never to

know it. For the rest, he was a blacksmith
who made a fortune, as Lady Canterbridge
will tell you."

" How very odd—how kind, I mean ! I
should like to have been civil to him on
Frank's account alone."

" I should see him on business and be
civil to him afterwards." Sir Robert received the American's levity with his usual
seriousness.

" No, they must come here for Christmas.
His daughter is—— "

"Araminta Eulalie Sharpe," said Bradley,
in defiant memory of Lady Canterbridge.

Sir Robert winced audibly. " I shall
rely on you, my dear boy, to help me make
it pleasant for them," he said.

Christmas came, but not Minty. It drew
a large contingent from Oldenhurst to the
quaint old church, who came to view the
green-wreathed monuments, and walls
spotted with crimson berries, as if with the
blood of former Oldenhurst warriors, and

to impress the wondering villagers with the
ineffable goodness and bounty of the Creator
towards the Lords of Oldenhurst and their
friends.   Sir Robert, a little gouty, kept the
house, and Bradley, somewhat uneasy at
the Sharpes' absence, but more distrait with
other thoughts, wandered listlessly in the
long library.   At the lower angle it was
embayed into the octagon space of a former
tower, which was furnished as a quaint
recess for writing or study, pierced through
its enormous walls with a lance-shaped
window, hidden by heavy curtains.   He
was gazing abstractedly at the melancholy
eyes of Sir Percival, looking down from the
dark panel opposite, when he heard the crisp
rustle of a skirt.   Lady Canterbridge,
tightly and stiffly buttoned in black from
her long narrow boots to her slim white-
collared neck, stood beside him with a
prayer-book in her ungloved hand.   Bradley
coloured quickly; the penetrating incense
of the Christmas boughs and branches that

decked the walls and ceilings, mingling with some indefinable intoxicating aura from the woman at his side, confused his senses. He seemed to be losing himself in some forgotten past coeval with the long, quaintly lighted room, the rich hangings, and the painted ancestor of this handsome woman. He recovered himself with an effort, and said, " You are going to church ? "

" I may meet them coming home ; it's all the same. You like *him ?* " she said abruptly, pointing to the portrait. " I thought you did not care for that sort of man over there."

" A man like that must have felt the impotence of his sacrifice before he died, and that condoned everything," said Bradley thoughtfully.

" Then you don't think him a fool ? Bob says it was a fair bargain for a title and an office, and that by dying he escaped trial and the confiscation of what he had."

Bradley did not reply.

"I am disturbing your illusions again. Yet I rather like them. I think you are quite capable of a sacrifice—perhaps you know what it is already."

He felt that she was looking at him ; he felt equally that he could not respond with a commonplace. He was silent.

"I have offended you again, Mr. Bradley," she said. " Please be Christian, and pardon me. You know this is a season of peace and goodwill." She raised her blue eyes at the same moment to the Christmas decorations on the ceiling. They were standing before the parted drapery of the lance window. Midway between the arched curtains hung a spray of mistletoe—the conceit of a mischievous housemaid. Their eyes met it simultaneously.

Bradley had Lady Canterbridge's slim, white hand in his own. The next moment voices were heard in the passage, and the door nearly opposite to them opened deliberately. The idea of their apparent

seclusion and half compromising attitude
flashed through the minds of both at the
same time. Lady Canterbridge stepped
quickly backward, drawing Bradley with
her, into the embrasure of the window ; the
folds of the curtain swung together and
concealed them from view.

The door had been opened by the footman, ushering in a broad-shouldered man,
who was carrying a travelling-bag and an
umbrella in his hand. Dropping into an
armchair before the curtain he waved
away the footman, who, even now, mechanically repeated a previously vain attempt
to relieve the stranger of his luggage.

"You leave that 'ere grip sack where it
is, young man, and tell Sir Robert Mainwaring that Mr. Demander Sharpe, of
Californy, wishes to see him—on business—on *business,* do ye hear ? You hang
onter that sentence—*on business!* it's about
ez much ez you kin carry, I reckon, and
leave that grip sack alone."

From behind the curtain Bradley made a sudden movement to go forward; but Lady Canterbridge—now quite pale but collected—restrained him with a warning movement of her hand. Sir Robert's stick and halting step were next heard along the passage, and he entered the room. His simple and courteous greeting of the stranger was instantly followed by a renewed attack upon the "grip sack," and a renewed defence of it by the stranger.

"No, Sir Robert," said the voice argumentatively, "this yer's a *business* interview, and until it's over—if *you* please —we'll remain ez we air. I'm Demander Sharpe, of Californy, and I and my darter, Minty, oncet had the pleasure of knowing your boy over thar, and of meeting him agin the other day at Nice."

"I think," said Sir Robert's voice gently, "that these are not the only claims you have upon me. I have only a day or two ago heard from Mr. Bradley that I owe to your generous hands and your disinterested liberality the saving of my California fortune."

There was the momentary sound of a pushed-back chair, a stamping of feet, and then Mr. Sharpe's voice rose high with the blacksmith's old querulous aggrieved utterance :

"So it's that finikin', conceited Bradley agin—that's giv' me away! Ef that man's all-fired belief in his being the Angel Gabriel and Dan'l Webster rolled inter one don't beat anythin'! I suppose that high-flyin' jay-bird kalkilated to put you and me and my gal and yer boy inter harness for his four-hoss chariot and he sittin' kam on the box drivin' us! Why don't he 'tend to his own business, and look arter his own concerns—instead o' leaving Jinny Bradley and Loo Macy dependent on Kings and Queens and titled folks gen'rally, and he, Jim Bradley, philanderin' with another

man's wife—while that thar man is hard
at work tryin' to make a honest livin' fer
his wife, buckin' agin' faro an' the tiger
gen'rally at Monaco! Eh? And that man
a-intermeddlin' with me! Ef," continued
the voice dropped to a tone of hopeless
moral conviction, "Ef there's a man I
mor'lly despise — it's that finikin' Jim
Bradley."

"You quite misunderstand me, my dear
sir," said Sir Robert's hurried voice; "he
told me you had pledged him to secrecy,
and he only revealed it to explain why you
wished to see me."

There was a grunt of half-placated wrath
from Sharpe, and then the voice resumed,
but more deliberately, "Well, to come back
to business: you've got a boy, Francis,
and I've got a darter, Araminty. They've
sorter taken a shine to each other and they
want to get married. Mind yer—wait a
moment!—it wasn't allus so. No, sir;
when my gal Araminty first seed your boy

in Californy she was poor, and she didn't
kalkilate to get into anybody's family un-
beknownst or on sufferance. Then she got
rich and you got poor; and then—hold on
a minit!—she allows, does my girl, that
there aint any nearer chance o' their
making a match than they were afore,
for she isn't goin' to hev it said that she
married your son fur the chance of some
day becomin' Lady Mainwaring."

"One moment, Mr. Sharpe," said the
voice of the Baronet gravely: "I am both
flattered and pained by what I believe to
be the kindly object of your visit. Indeed,
I may say I have gathered a suspicion of
what might be the sequel of this most unhappy acquaintance of my son and your
daughter; but I cannot believe that he
has kept you in ignorance of his unfortunate prospects and his still more unfortunate state of health."

"When I told ye to hold on a minit,"
continued the blacksmith's voice, with a

touch of querulousness in its accent, "that
was jist wot I was comin' to. I knowed
part of it from my own pocket, she knowed
the rest of it from his lips and the doctors
she interviewed. And then she says to
me—sez my girl Minty—'Pop,' she sez,
'he's got nothing to live for now but his
title, and that he never may live to get, so
that I think ye kin jist go, Pop, and fairly
and squarely, as a honest man, ask his
father to let me hev him.' Them's my
darter's own words, Sir Robert; and when
I tell yer that she's got a million o' dollars
to back them, ye'll know she means business every time."

"Did Francis know that you were
coming here?"

"Bless ye, no! He don't know that she
would have him. Ef it kem to that, he
aint even asked her! She wouldn't let
him until she was sure of *you.*"

"Then you mean to say there is no engagement?"

"In course not. I reckoned to do the square thing first with ye."

The halting step of the baronet crossing the room was heard distinctly. He had stopped beside Sharpe. "My dear Mr. Sharpe," he said, in a troubled voice, "I cannot permit this sacrifice. It is too— too great!"

"Then," said Sharpe's voice querulously, "I'm afraid we must do without your permission. I didn't reckon to find a sort o' British Jim Bradley in you. If *you* can't permit my darter to sacrifice herself by marryin' your son, I can't permit her to sacrifice her love and him by *not* marryin' him. So I reckon this yer interview is over."

"I am afraid we are both old fools, Mr. Sharpe; but—we will talk this over with Lady Mainwaring. Come." There was evidently a slight struggle near the chair over some inanimate object. But the next moment the Baronet's voice rose, persuasively, "Really, I must insist upon relieving you of your bag and umbrella."

"Well, if you'll let me telegraph 'yes' to Minty, I don't care if yer do."

When the room was quiet again, Lady Canterbridge and James Bradley silently slipped from the curtain, and, without a word, separated at the door.

There was a merry Christmas at Oldenhurst and at Nice. But whether Minty's loving sacrifice was accepted or not, or whether she ever reigned as Lady Mainwaring, or lived an untitled widow, I cannot say. But as Oldenhurst still exists in all its pride and power, it is presumed that the peril that threatened its fortunes was averted, and that if another heroine was not found worthy of a frame in its picture-gallery, at least it had been sustained as of old by devotion and renunciation.

A DRIFT FROM REDWOOD CAMP.

o

A DRIFT FROM REDWOOD CAMP.

THEY had all known him as a shiftless, worthless creature. From the time he first entered Redwood Camp, carrying his entire effects in a red handkerchief on the end of a long-handled shovel, until he lazily drifted out of it on a plank in the terrible inundation of 1856, they never expected anything better of him. In a community of strong men with sullen virtues and dangerously fascinating vices, he was tolerated as possessing neither—not even rising by any dominant human weakness or ludicrous quality to the importance of a butt. In the *dramatis personæ* of Redwood Camp he was a simple "super"—who had only passive, speechless rôles in those fierce dramas that were sometimes unrolled beneath its green-curtained pines. Nameless and penniless, he was overlooked by the census and ignored by the tax collector, while in a hotly contested election for sheriff, when even the head-boards of the scant cemetery were consulted to fill the poll-lists, it was discovered that neither candidate had thought fit to avail himself of his actual vote. He was debarred the rude heraldry of a nickname of achievement, and in a camp made up of "Euchre Bills," "Poker Dicks," "Profane Pete," and "Snapshot Harry," was known vaguely as "him," "Skeesicks," or "that coot." It was remembered long after, with a feeling of superstition, that he had never even met with the dignity of an accident, nor received the fleeting honour of a chance shot meant for somebody else in any of the liberal and broadly comprehensive encounters which distinguished the camp. And the inundation that finally carried him out of it was partly anticipated by his passive incompetency, for while the others escaped—or were drowned in escaping—he calmly floated off on his plank without an opposing effort.

For all that Elijah Martin—which was his real name—was far from being unamiable or repellent. That he was cowardly, untruthful, selfish, and lazy, was undoubtedly the fact; perhaps it was his peculiar misfortune that, just then, courage, frankness, generosity, and activity were the dominant factors in the life of Redwood Camp. His submissive gentleness, his unquestioned modesty, his half refinement, and his amiable exterior consequently availed him nothing against the fact that he was missed during a raid of the Digger Indians, and lied to account for it; or that he lost his right to a gold discovery by failing to make it good against a

bully, and selfishly kept this discovery
from the knowledge of the camp. Yet
this weakness awakened no animosity in
his companions, and it is probable that the
indifference of the camp to his fate in
this final catastrophe came purely from a
simple forgetfulness of one who at that
supreme moment was weakly incapable.

Such was the reputation and such the
antecedents of the man who, on the 15th
of March, 1856, found himself adrift in a
swollen tributary of the Minyo. A spring
freshet of unusual volume had flooded the
adjacent river until, bursting its bounds, it
escaped through the narrow, wedge-shaped
valley that held Redwood Camp. For a
day and a night the surcharged river
poured half its waters through the straggling camp. At the end of that time
every vestige of the little settlement was
swept away; all that was left was scattered far and wide in the country, caught
in the hanging branches of water-side

willows and alders, embayed in sluggish
pools, dragged over submerged meadows,
and one fragment—bearing up Elijah
Martin—pursuing the devious courses of
an unknown tributary fifty miles away.
Had he been a rash, impatient man, he
would have been speedily drowned in some
earlier desperate attempt to reach the
shore; had he been an ordinarily bold man,
he would have succeeded in transferring
himself to the branches of some obstruct-
ing tree; but he was neither, and he clung
to his broken raft-like berth with an en-
durance that was half the paralysis of
terror and half the patience of habitual
misfortune. Eventually he was caught in
a side current, swept to the bank, and cast
ashore on an unexplored wilderness.

His first consciousness was one of hunger,
that usurped any sentiment of gratitude
for his escape from drowning. As soon as
his cramped limbs permitted, he crawled
out of the bushes in search of food. He

did not know where he was; there was no sign of habitation—or even occupation—anywhere. He had been too terrified to notice the direction in which he had drifted —even if he had possessed the ordinary knowledge of a backwoodsman, which he did not. He was helpless. In his bewildered state, seeing a squirrel cracking a nut on the branch of a hollow tree near him, he made a half-frenzied dart at the frightened animal, which ran away. But the same association of ideas in his torpid and confused brain impelled him to search for the squirrel's hoard in the hollow of the tree. He ate the few hazel-nuts he found there ravenously. The purely animal instinct satisfied, he seemed to have borrowed from it a certain animal strength and intuition. He limped through the thicket not unlike some awkward, shy quadrumane, stopping here and there to peer out through the openings over the marshes that lay beyond. His sight, hearing, and even the sense of smell had become preternaturally acute. It was the latter which suddenly arrested his steps with the odour of dried fish. It had a significance beyond the mere instincts of hunger—it indicated the contiguity of some Indian encampment. And as such—it meant danger, torture, and death.

He stopped, trembled violently, and tried to collect his scattered senses. Redwood Camp had embroiled itself needlessly and brutally with the surrounding Indians, and only held its own against them by reckless courage and unerring marksmanship. The frequent use of a casual wandering Indian as a target for the practising rifles of its members had kept up an undying hatred in the heart of the aborigines and stimulated them to terrible and isolated reprisals. The scalped and skinned dead body of Jack Trainer, tied on his horse and held hideously upright by a cross of wood behind his saddle, had passed, one night, a slow and ghastly

apparition, into camp; the corpse of Dick
Ryner had been found anchored on the river-
bed, disembowelled and filled with stone
and gravel. The solitary and unprotected
member of Redwood Camp who fell into the
enemy's hands was doomed.

Elijah Martin remembered this, but his
fears gradually began to subside in a certain
apathy of the imagination, which, perhaps,
dulled his apprehensions and allowed the
instinct of hunger to become again upper-
most. He knew that the low bark tents,
or wigwams, of the Indians were hung with
strips of dried salmon, and his whole being
was now centred upon an attempt to
stealthily procure a delicious morsel. As
yet he had distinguished no other sign of
life or habitation; a few moments later,
however, and grown bolder with an animal-
like trustfulness in his momentary security,
he crept out of the thicket and found himself near a long, low mound or burrow-like
structure of mud and bark on the river-

bank. A single narrow opening, not unlike the entrance of an Esquimaux hut, gave upon the river. Martin had no difficulty in recognizing the character of the building. It was a "sweat-house," an institution common to nearly all the aboriginal tribes of California. Half a religious temple, it was also half a sanitary asylum, was used as a Russian bath or superheated vault, from which the braves, sweltering and stifling all night, by smothered fires, at early dawn plunged, perspiring, into the ice-cold river. The heat and smoke were further utilized to dry and cure the long strips of fish hanging from the roof, and it was through the narrow aperture that served as a chimney that the odour escaped which Martin had detected. He knew that, as the bathers only occupied the house from midnight to early morn, it was now probably empty. He advanced confidently toward it.

He was a little surprised to find that the small open space between it and the river was occupied by a rude scaffolding, like that on which certain tribes exposed their dead, but in this instance it only contained the feathered leggings, fringed blanket, and eagle-plumed head-dress of some brave. He did not, however, linger in this plainly visible area, but quickly dropped on all-fours and crept into the interior of the house. Here he completed his feast with the fish, and warmed his chilled limbs on the embers of the still smouldering fires. It was while drying his tattered clothes and shoeless feet that he thought of the dead brave's useless leggings and moccasins, and it occurred to him that he would be less likely to attract the Indians' attention from a distance and provoke a ready arrow, if he were disguised as one of them. Crawling out again, he quickly secured, not only the leggings, but the blanket and head-dress, and putting them on, cast his own clothes into the stream. A bolder, more energetic, or more provident man would have followed the act by quickly making his way back to the thicket to reconnoitre, taking with him a supply of fish for future needs. But Elijah Martin succumbed again to the recklessness of inertia; he yielded once more to the animal instinct of momentary security. He returned to the interior of the hut, curled himself again on the ashes, and weakly resolving to sleep until moonrise, and as weakly hesitating, ended by falling into uneasy but helpless stupor.

When he awoke, the rising sun, almost level with the low entrance to the sweat-house, was darting its direct rays into the interior, as if searching it with fiery spears. He had slept ten hours. He rose trembblingly to his knees. Everything was quiet without; he might yet escape. He crawled to the opening. The open space before it was empty, but the scaffolding was gone. The clear, keen air revived him. As he sprang out, erect, a shout that nearly stunned him seemed to rise from the earth

on all sides.   He glanced around him in a
helpless agony of fear.   A dozen concentric
circles of squatting Indians, whose heads
were visible above the reeds, encompassed
the banks around the sunken base of the
sweat-house with successive dusky rings.
Every avenue of escape seemed closed.
Perhaps for that reason the attitude of his
surrounding captors was passive rather than
aggressive, and the shrewd, half-Hebraic
profiles nearest him expressed only stoical
waiting.   There was a strange similarity of
expression in his own immovable apathy of
despair.   His only sense of averting his fate
was a confused idea of explaining his intrusion.   His desperate memory yielded a few
common Indian words.   He pointed auto-
matically to himself and the stream.   His
white lips moved.

"I come—from—the river!"

A guttural cry, as if the whole assembly
were clearing their throats, went round the
different circles.   The nearest rocked them-

selves to and fro and bent their feathered
heads toward him. A hollow-cheeked,
decrepit old man arose and said, simply :

"It is he! The great chief has come!"

* * * *

He was saved. More than that, he was
re-created. For, by signs and intimations
he was quickly made aware that since the
death of their late chief, their medicine-men
had prophesied that his perfect successor
should appear miraculously before them,
borne noiselessly on the river *from the sea*,
in the plumes and insignia of his prede-
cessor. This mere coincidence of appearance and costume might not have been convincing to the braves had not Elijah Martin's
actual deficiencies contributed to their unquestioned faith in him. Not only his inert
possession of the sweat-house and his
apathetic attitude in their presence, but his
utter and complete unlikeness to the white
frontiersmen of their knowledge and tradition—creatures of fire and sword and

malevolent activity—as well as his manifest
dissimilarity to themselves, settled their
conviction of his supernatural origin.   His
gentle, submissive voice, his yielding will,
his lazy helplessness, the absence of strange
weapons and fierce explosives in his possession, his unwonted sobriety—all proved him
an exception to his apparent race that was
in itself miraculous.   For it must be confessed that, in spite of the cherished theories
of most romances and all statesmen and
commanders, that *fear* is the great civilizer
of the savage barbarian, and that he is
supposed to regard the prowess of the white
man and his mysterious death-dealing
weapons as evidence of his supernatural
origin and superior creation, the facts have
generally pointed to the reverse.   Elijah
Martin was not long in discovering that
when the Minyo hunter, with his obsolete
bow, dropped dead by a bullet from a view-
less and apparently noiseless space, it was
not considered the lightnings of an avenging

Deity, but was traced directly to the ambushed rifle of Kansas Joe, swayed by a viciousness quite as human as their own; the spectacle of Blizzard Dick, verging on *delirium tremens,* and riding "amuck" into an Indian village with a revolver in each hand, did *not* impress them as a supernatural act, nor excite their respectful awe as much as the less harmful frenzy of one of their own medicine-men; they were *not* influenced by implacable white gods, who relaxed only to drive hard bargains and exchange mildewed flour and shoddy blankets for their fish and furs. I am afraid they regarded these raids of Christian civilization as they looked upon grasshopper plagues, famines, inundations, and epidemics; while an utterly impassive God washed his hands of the means he had employed, and even encouraged the faithful to resist and overcome his emissaries—the white devils! Had Elijah Martin been a student of theology, he would have been struck with the singular resem-

P

blance of these theories—although the application thereof was reversed—to the Christian faith. But Elijah Martin had neither the imagination of a theologian nor the insight of a politician. He only saw that he, hitherto ignored and despised in a community of half-barbaric men, now translated to a community of men wholly savage, was respected and worshipped !

It might have turned a stronger head than Elijah's. He was at first frightened, fearful lest his reception concealed some hidden irony, or that, like the flower-crowned victim of ancient sacrifice, he was exalted and sustained to give importance and majesty to some impending martyrdom. Then he began to dread that his innocent deceit—if deceit it was—should be discovered ; at last, partly from meekness and partly from the animal contentment of present security, he accepted the situation. Fortunately for him it was purely passive. The Great Chief of the

Minyo tribe was simply an expressionless
idol of flesh and blood. The previous in-
cumbent of that office had been an old
man, impotent and senseless of late years
through age and disease. The chieftains
and braves had consulted in council before
him, and perfunctorily submitted their
decisions, like offerings, to his unresponsive
shrine. In the same way, all material
events—expeditions, trophies, industries—
were supposed to pass before the dull, impassive eyes of the great chief, for direct
acceptance. On the second day of Elijah's
accession, two of the braves brought a
bleeding human scalp before him. Elijah
turned pale, trembled, and averted his
head, and then, remembering the danger
of giving way to his weakness, grew still
more ghastly. The warriors watched him
with impassioned faces. A grunt—but
whether of astonishment, dissent, or ap-
proval, he could not tell—went round the
circle. But the scalp was taken away

and never again appeared in his presence.

An incident still more alarming quickly followed. Two captives, white men, securely bound, were one day brought before him on their way to the stake, followed by a crowd of old and young squaws and children. The unhappy Elijah recognized in the prisoners two packers from a distant settlement who sometimes passed through Redwood Camp. An agony of terror, shame, and remorse shook the pseudo-chief to his crest of high feathers, and blanched his face beneath its paint and yellow ochre. To interfere to save them from the torture they were evidently to receive at the hands of those squaws and children, according to custom, would be exposure and death to him as well as themselves; while to assist by his passive presence at the horrible sacrifice of his countrymen was too much for even his weak selfishness. Scarcely knowing what he did as the lugubrious procession passed before him, he hurriedly hid his face in his blanket and turned his back upon the scene. There was a dead silence. The warriors were evidently unprepared for this extraordinary conduct of their chief. What might have been their action it was impossible to conjecture, for at that moment a little squaw, perhaps impatient for the sport and partly emboldened by the fact that she had been selected, only a few days before, as the betrothed of the new chief, approached him slyly from the other side. The horrified eyes of Elijah, momentarily raised from his blanket, saw and recognized her. The feebleness of a weak nature, that dared not measure itself directly with the real cause, vented its rage on a secondary object. He darted a quick glance of indignation and hatred at the young girl. She ran back in startled terror to her companions, a hurried consultation followed, and in another moment the whole bevy of girls, old women, and children were on the wing, shrieking and crying, to their wigwams.

"You see," said one of the prisoners coolly to the other in English, "I was right. They never intended to do anything to us. It was only a bluff. These Minyos are a different sort from the other tribes. They never kill anybody if they can help it."

"You're wrong," said the other excitedly. "It was that big chief there, with his head in a blanket, that sent those dogs to the rightabout. Hell! did you see them run at just a look from him? He's a high and mighty feller, you bet. Look at his dignity!"

"That's so—he ain't no slouch," said the other, gazing at Elijah's muffled head critically. "D——d if he ain't a born king."

The sudden conflict and utter revulsion of emotion that those simple words caused in Elijah's breast was almost incredible.

He had been at first astounded by the
revelation of the peaceful reputation of the
unknown tribe he had been called upon to
govern; but even this comforting assur-
ance was as nothing compared to the
greater revelations implied in the speaker's
praise of himself. He, Elijah Martin!
the despised, the rejected, the worthless
outcast of Redwood Camp, recognized as
a "born king," a leader; his power felt by
the very men who had scorned him! And
he had done nothing—stop! had he
actually done *nothing?* Was it not possible that he was *really* what they thought
him? His brain reeled under the strong,
unaccustomed wine of praise; acting upon
his weak selfishness, it exalted him for a
moment to their measure of his strength,
even as their former belief in his in-
efficiency had kept him down. Courage
is too often only the memory of past success. This was his first effort; he forgot
he had not earned it, even as he now

ignored the danger of earning it. The few words of unconscious praise had fallen like the blade of knighthood on his cowering shoulders; he had risen ennobled from the contact. Though his face was still muffled in his blanket, he stood erect and seemed to have gained in stature.

The braves had remained standing irresolute, and yet watchful, a few paces from their captives. Suddenly Elijah, still keeping his back to the prisoners, turned upon the braves with blazing eyes, violently throwing out his hands with the gesture of breaking bonds. Like all sudden demonstrations of undemonstrative men, it was extravagant, weird, and theatrical. But it was more potent than speech—the speech that, even if effective, would still have betrayed him to his countrymen. The braves hurriedly cut the thongs of the prisoners; another impulsive gesture from Elijah, and they, too, fled. When he lifted his eyes cautiously from his blanket, captors

and captives had dispersed in opposite directions, and he was alone—and triumphant !

From that moment Elijah Martin was
another man. He went to bed that night
in an intoxicating dream of power; he
arose a man of will, of strength. He read
it in the eyes of the braves, albeit at times
averted in wonder. He understood now,
that although peace had been their habit
and custom, they had nevertheless sought
to test his theories of administration with
the offering of the scalps and the captives,
and in this detection of their common
weakness he forgot his own. Most heroes
require the contrast of the unheroic to set
them off; and Elijah actually found himself devising means for strengthening the
defensive and offensive character of the
tribe, and was himself strengthened by it.
Meanwhile the escaped packers did not fail
to heighten the importance of their adventure by elevating the character and achieve-
ments of their deliverer; and it was pre-

sently announced throughout the frontier
settlements that the hitherto insignificant
and peaceful tribe of Minyos, who inhabited
a large territory bordering on the Pacific
Ocean, had developed into a powerful
nation, only kept from the war-path by a
more powerful but mysterious chief. The
Government sent an Indian agent to treat
with them, in its usual half-paternal, half-
aggressive, and wholly inconsistent policy.
Elijah, who still retained the imitative
sense and adaptability to surroundings
which belong to most lazy, impressible
natures, and in striped yellow and vermilion
features looked the chief he personated,
met the agent with silent and becoming
gravity. The council was carried on by
signs. Never before had an Indian treaty
been entered into with such perfect knowledge of the intentions and designs of the
whites by the Indians, and such profound
ignorance of the qualities of the Indians
by the whites. It need scarcely be said that

the treaty was an unquestionable Indian
success. They did not give up their arable
lands; what they did sell to the agent
they refused to exchange for extravagant-
priced shoddy blankets, worthless guns,
damp powder, and mouldy meal. They
took pay in dollars, and were thus enabled
to open more profitable commerce with the
traders at the settlements for better goods
and better bargains; they simply declined
beads, whisky, and Bibles at any price.
The result was that the traders found it profitable to protect them from their countrymen, and the chances of wantonly shooting
down a possible valuable customer stopped
the old indiscriminate rifle-practice. The
Indians were allowed to cultivate their
fields in peace. Elijah purchased for them
a few agricultural implements. The catch-
ing, curing, and smoking of salmon became
an important branch of trade. They
waxed prosperous and rich; they lost their
nomadic habits—a centralized settlement

bearing the external signs of an Indian
village took the place of their old tempo-
rary encampments, but the huts were inter-
nally an improvement on the old wigwams.
The dried fish were banished from the
tent-poles to long sheds especially con-
structed for that purpose. The sweat-
house was no longer utilized for worldly
purposes. The wise and mighty Elijah did
not attempt to reform their religion, but
to preserve it in its integrity.

That these improvements and changes
were due to the influence of one man was
undoubtedly true, but that he was necessarily a superior man did not follow. Elijah's
success was due partly to the fact that he
had been enabled to impress certain negative
virtues, which were part of his own nature,
upon a community equally constituted to
receive them. Each was strengthened by
the recognition in each other of the unexpected value of those qualities; each
acquired a confidence begotten of their

success. "*He-hides-his-face*," as Elijah
Martin was known to the tribe after the
episode of the released captives, was really
not so much of an autocrat as many constitutional rulers.

* * * *

Two years of tranquil prosperity passed.
Elijah Martin, foundling, outcast, without
civilized ties or relationship of any kind,
forgotten by his countrymen, and lifted into
alien power, wealth, security, and respect,
became—home-sick!

It was near the close of a summer afternoon. He was sitting at the door of his
lodge, which overlooked, on one side, the
far-shining levels of the Pacific, and, on the
other, the slow descent to the cultivated
meadows and banks of the Minyo River,
that debouched through a waste of salt-
marsh, beach-grass, sand-dunes, and foamy
estuary into the ocean. The headland, or
promontory—the only eminence of the
Minyo territory—had been reserved by him

for his lodge, partly on account of its isolation from the village at its base, and partly
for the view it commanded of his territory.
Yet his wearying and discontented eyes
were more often found on the ocean, as a
possible highway of escape from his irksome
position, than on the plain and the distant
range of mountains, so closely connected
with the nearer past and his former de-
tractors. In his vague longing he had no
desire to return to them, even in triumph ;
in his present security there still lingered a
doubt of his ability to cope with the old
conditions. It was more like his easy,
indolent nature—which revived in his prosperity—to trust to this least practical and
remote solution of his trouble. His home-
sickness was as vague as his plan for escape
from it ; he did not know exactly what he
regretted, but it was probably some life he
had not enjoyed, some pleasure that had
escaped his former incompetency and
poverty.

He had sat thus a hundred times, as aimlessly blinking at the vast possibilities of the shining sea beyond, turning his back upon the nearer and more practicable mountains, lulled by the far-off beating of monotonous rollers, the lonely cry of the curlew and plover, the drowsy changes of alternate breaths of cool, fragrant reeds and warm, spicy sands that blew across his eyelids, and succumbed to sleep, as he had done a hundred times before. The narrow strips of coloured cloth, insignia of his dignity, flapped lazily from his tent-poles, and at last seemed to slumber with him; the shadows of the leaf-tracery thrown by the bay-tree on the ground at his feet scarcely changed its pattern. Nothing moved but the round, restless, berry-like eyes of Wachita, his child-wife, the former heroine of the incident with the captive packers, who sat near her lord, armed with a willow wand, watchful of intruding wasps, sand-flies, and even the more ostentatious advances of a rotund and clerical-looking humble-bee, with his monotonous homily. Content, dumb, submissive, vacant, at such times, Wachita, debarred her husband's confidences through the native customs and his own indifferent taciturnity, satisfied herself by gazing at him with the wondering but ineffectual sympathy of a faithful dog. Unfortunately for Elijah her purely mechanical ministration could not prevent a more dangerous intrusion upon his security.

He awoke with a light start, and eyes that gradually fixed upon the woman a look of returning consciousness. Wachita pointed timidly to the village below.

"The Messenger of the Great White Father has come to-day, with his waggons and horses ; he would see the chief of the Minyos, but I would not disturb my lord."

Elijah's brow contracted. Relieved of its characteristic metaphor, he knew that this meant that the new Indian agent had made his usual official visit, and had exhibited the usual anxiety to see the famous chieftain.

"Good!" he said. "White Rabbit (his lieutenant) will see the messenger and exchange gifts. It is enough."

"The white messenger has brought his wangee (white) woman with him. They would look upon the face of him who hides it," continued Wachita dubiously. "They would that Wachita should bring them nearer to where my lord is, that they might see him when he knew it not."

Elijah glanced moodily at his wife, with the half suspicion with which he still regarded her alien character. "Then let Wachita go back to the squaws and old women, and let her hide herself with them until the wangee strangers are gone," he said curtly. "I have spoken. Go!"

Accustomed to these abrupt dismissals, which did not necessarily indicate displeasure, Wachita disappeared without a word. Elijah, who had risen, remained for

Q

a few moments leaning against the tent-poles, gazing abstractedly toward the sea. The bees droned uninterruptedly in his ears, the far-off roll of the breakers came to him distinctly ; but suddenly, with greater distinctness, came the murmur of a woman's voice.

"He don't look savage a bit! Why, he's real handsome."

"Hush! you——" said a second voice, in a frightened whisper.

"But if he *did* hear he couldn't understand," returned the first voice. A suppressed giggle followed.

Luckily, Elijah's natural and acquired habits of repression suited the emergency. He did not move, although he felt the quick blood fly to his face, and the voice of the first speaker had suffused him with a strange and delicious anticipation. He restrained himself, though the words she had naïvely dropped were filling him with new and tremulous suggestion. He was motionless,

even while he felt that the vague longing
and yearning which had possessed him
hitherto was now mysteriously taking some
unknown form and action.

The murmuring ceased. The humble-
bee's drone again became ascendant—a
sudden fear seized him. She was *going;*
he should never see her! While he had
stood there a dolt and sluggard, she had
satisfied her curiosity and stolen away.
With a sudden yielding to impulse, he
darted quickly in the direction where he
had heard her voice. The thicket moved,
parted, crackled, and rustled, and then un-
dulated thirty feet before him in a long
wave, as if from the passage of some lithe,
invisible figure. But at the same moment
a little cry, half of alarm, half of laughter,
broke from his very feet, and a bent man-
zanito-bush, relaxed by frightened fingers,
flew back against his breast. Thrusting it
hurriedly aside, his stooping, eager face
came almost in contact with the pink,

flushed cheeks and tangled curls of a woman's head. He was so near, her moist and laughing eyes almost drowned his eager glance ; her parted lips and white teeth were so close to his that her quick breath took away his own.

She had dropped on one knee, as her companion fled, expecting he would overlook her as he passed, but his direct onset had extracted the feminine outcry. Yet even then she did not seem greatly frightened.

" It's only a joke, sir," she said, ignoring her late belief that he knew no English, but coolly lifting herself to her feet, by grasping his arm. " I'm Mrs. Dall, the Indian agent's wife. They said you wouldn't let anybody see you—and *I* determined I would. That's all ! " She stopped, threw back her tangled curls behind her ears, shook the briars and thorns from her skirt, and added : " Well, I reckon you aren't afraid of a woman, are you ? So no harm's done. Good-by ! "

She drew slightly back as if to retreat, but the elasticity of the manzanito against which she was leaning threw her forward once more. He again inhaled the perfume of her hair; he saw even the tiny freckles that darkened her upper lip and brought out the moist, red curve below. A sudden recollection of a playmate of his vagabond childhood flashed across his mind; a wild inspiration of lawlessness, begotten of his past experience, his solitude, his dictatorial power, and the beauty of the woman before him, mounted to his brain. He threw his arms passionately around her, pressed his lips to hers, and with a half-hysterical laugh drew back and disappeared in the thicket.

Mrs. Dall remained for an instant dazed and stupefied. Then she lifted her arm mechanically, and with her sleeve wiped her bruised mouth and the ochre stain that his paint had left, like blood, upon her cheek. Her laughing face had become instantly grave, but not from fear; her dark eyes had clouded, but not entirely with indignation. She suddenly brought down her hand sharply against her side with a gesture of discovery. "That's no Injun!" she said, with prompt decision. The next minute she plunged back into the trail again, and the dense foliage once more closed around her. But as she did so the broad, vacant face and the mutely wondering eyes of Wachita rose, like a placid moon, between the branches of a tree where she had been hidden, and shone serenely and impassively after her.

*   *   *   *

A month elapsed. But it was a month filled with more experience to Elijah than his past two years of exaltation. In the first few days following his meeting with Mrs. Dall, he was possessed by terror, mingled with flashes of desperation, at the remembrance of his rash imprudence. His recollection of extravagant frontier chivalry

to womankind, and the swift retribution
of the insulted husband or guardian, alter-
nately filled him with abject fear or extravagant recklessness. At times prepared
for flight, even to the desperate abandonment of himself in a canoe to the waters of
the Pacific ; at times he was on the point
of inciting his braves to attack the Indian
agency and precipitate the war that he felt
would be inevitable. As the days passed,
and there seemed to be no interruption to
his friendly relations with the agency, with
that relief a new, subtle joy crept into
Elijah's heart. The image of the agent's
wife framed in the leafy screen behind his
lodge, the perfume of her hair and breath
mingled with the spicing of the bay, the
brief thrill and tantalization of the stolen
kiss still haunted him. Through his long,
shy abstention from society, and his two
years of solitary exile, the fresh beauty of
this young Western wife, in whom the frank
artlessness of girlhood still lingered,

appeared to him like a superior creation.
He forgot his vague longings in the incep-
tion of a more tangible but equally unpractical passion.   He remembered her unconscious and spontaneous admiration of him ;
he dared to connect it with her forgiving
silence.   If she had withheld her confidences
from her husband, he could hope—he knew
not exactly what !

One afternoon Wachita put into his
hand a folded note.   With an instinctive
presentiment of its contents, Elijah turned
red and embarrassed in receiving it from
the woman who was recognized as his wife.
But the impassive, submissive manner of
this household drudge, instead of touching
his conscience, seemed to him a vulgar and
brutal acceptance of the situation that
dulled whatever compunction he might
have had.   He opened the note and read
hurriedly as follows :—

" You took a great freedom with me

the other day, and I am justified in taking
one with you now. I believe you understand English as well as I do. If you
want to explain that, and your conduct to
me, I will be at the same place this afternoon. My friend will accompany me, but
she need not hear what you have to
say."

Elijah read the letter, which might have
been written by an ordinary school-girl, as
if it had conveyed the veiled rendezvous of
a princess. The reserve, caution, and shy-
ness which had been the safeguard of his
weak nature were swamped in a flow of
immature passion. He flew to the interview with the eagerness and inexperience
of first love. He was completely at her
mercy. So utterly was he subjugated by
her presence that she did not even run the
risk of his passion. Whatever sentiment
might have mingled with her curiosity, she
was never conscious of a necessity to guard

herself against it.   At this second meeting she was in full possession of his secret.
He had told her everything; she had
promised nothing in return—she had
not even accepted anything.   Even her
actual after-relations to the *dénouement*
of his passion are still shrouded in
mystery.

Nevertheless, Elijah lived two weeks on
the unsubstantial memory of this meeting.
What might have followed could not be
known, for at the end of that time an outrage—so atrocious that even the peaceful
Minyos were thrilled with savage indignation—was committed on the outskirts of
the village.   An old chief, who had been
specially selected to deal with the Indian
agent, and who kept a small trading out-
post, had been killed and his goods de-
spoiled by a reckless Redwood packer.
The murderer had coolly said that he was
only "serving out" the tool of a fraudu-
lent imposture on the Government, and

that he dared the arch-impostor himself, the so-called Minyo chief, to help himself. A wave of ungovernable fury surged up to the very tent-poles of Elijah's lodge and demanded vengeance. Elijah trembled and hesitated. In the thraldom of his selfish passion for Mrs. Dall he dared not contemplate a collision with her country-men. He would have again sought refuge in his passive, non-committal attitude, but he knew the impersonal character of Indian retribution and compensation—a sacrifice of equal value, without reference to the culpability of the victim—and he dreaded some spontaneous outbreak. To prevent the enforced expiation of the crime by some innocent brother packer, he was obliged to give orders for the pursuit and arrest of the criminal, secretly hoping for his escape or the interposition of some circumstance to avert his punishment. A day of sullen expectancy to the old men and squaws in camp, of gloomy anxiety to

Elijah alone in his lodge, followed the departure of the braves on the war-path. It was midnight when they returned. Elijah, who from his habitual reserve and the accepted etiquette of his exalted station had remained impassive in his tent, only knew from the guttural rejoicings of the squaws that the expedition had been successful and the captive was in their hands. At any other time he might have thought it an evidence of some growing scepticism of his infallibility of judgment and a diminution of respect that they did not confront him with their prisoner. But he was too glad to escape from the danger of exposure and possible arraignment of his past life by the desperate captive, even though it might not have been understood by the spectators. He reflected that the omission might have arisen from their recollection of his previous aversion to a retaliation on other prisoners. Enough that they would wait his signal for the torture and execution at sunrise the next day.

The night passed slowly. It is more than probable that the selfish and ignoble torments of the sleepless and vacillating judge were greater than those of the prisoner who dozed at the stake between his curses. Yet it was part of Elijah's fatal weakness that his kinder and more human instincts were dominated even at that moment by his lawless passion for the Indian agent's wife, and his indecision as to the fate of his captive was equally due to his preoccupation and a selfish consideration of her possible relations to the result. He hated the prisoner for his infelicitous and untimely crime, yet he could not make up his mind to his death. He paced the ground before his lodge in dishonourable incertitude. The small eyes of the submissive Wachita watched him with vague solicitude.

Towards morning he was struck by a

shameful inspiration. He would creep un-
perceived to the victim's side, unloose his
bonds, and bid him fly to the Indian
agency! There he was to inform Mrs.
Dall that her husband's safety depended
upon his absenting himself for a few days,
but that she was to remain and com-
municate with Elijah. She would understand everything, perhaps; at least she
would know that the prisoner's release was
to please her, and even if she did not, no
harm would be done, a white man's life
would be saved, and his real motive would
not be suspected. He turned with feverish
eagerness to the lodge. Wachita had disappeared—probably to join the other
women. It was well; she would not suspect him.

The tree to which the doomed man was
bound was, by custom, selected nearest the
chief's lodge, within its sacred enclosure,
with no other protection than that offered
by its reserved seclusion and the outer

semicircle of warriors' tents before it. To escape, the captive would therefore have to pass beside the chief's lodge to the rear and descend the hill towards the shore. Elijah would show him the way, and make it appear as if he had escaped unaided. As he glided into the shadow of a group of pines, he could dimly discern the outline of the destined victim, secured against one of the larger trees in a sitting posture, with his head fallen forward on his breast as if in sleep. But at the same moment another figure glided out from the shadow and approached the fatal tree. It was Wachita!

He stopped in amazement. But in another instant a flash of intelligence made it clear to him. He remembered her vague uneasiness and solicitude at his agitation and her sudden disappearance; she had fathomed his perplexity, as she had once before! Of her own accord she was going to release the prisoner! The knife to cut his cords glittered in her hand. Brave and faithful animal!

He held his breath as he drew nearer. But, to his horror, the knife suddenly flashed in the air and darted down, again and again, upon the body of the helpless man. There was a convulsive struggle, but no outcry, and the next moment the body hung limp and inert in its cords. Elijah would himself have fallen, half fainting, against a tree, but by a revulsion of feeling, came the quick revelation that the desperate girl had rightly solved the problem! She had done what *he* ought to have done—and his loyalty and manhood were preserved. That conviction and the courage to act upon it—to have called the sleeping braves to witness his sacrifice—would have saved him, but—it was ordered otherwise!

As the girl rapidly passed him he threw out his hand and seized her wrist. "What did you do this for?" he demanded.

"For you," she said stupidly.

"And why?"

"Because you no kill him—you love his squaw."

"*His* squaw!" He staggered back. A terrible suspicion flashed upon him. He dashed Wachita aside and ran to the tree. It was the body of the Indian agent!

Aboriginal justice had been satisfied. The warriors had not caught the *murderer*, but, true to their idea of vicarious retribution, they had determined upon the expiatory sacrifice of a life as valuable and innocent as the one they had lost, and had carried off the unfortunate representative of the Government.

"So the Gov'rment hev at last woke up and wiped out them cussed Digger Minyos," said Snap-shot Harry, three months later, as he laid down the newspaper, in the brand-new saloon of the brand-new town of Redwood. "I see they've stampeded both banks of the Minyo River, and sent off a lot to the reservation. I reckon the soldiers at Fort Cass got sick o' sentiment after those hounds killed the Ingun agent, and are beginning to agree with us that the only 'good Injun' is a dead one."

"And it turns out that that wonderful chief, that them two packers used to rave about, woz about as big a devil ez any, and tried to run off with the agent's wife, only the warriors killed her. I'd like to know what become of him. Some says he was killed, others allow that he got away. I've heerd tell that he was originally some kind of Methodist preacher!—a kind o' saint that got a sort o' spiritooal holt on the old squaws and children."

"Why don't you ask old Skeesicks? I see he's back here ag'in—and grubbin' along at a dollar a day on tailin's. He's been somewhere up north, they say."

"What, Skeesicks? That shiftless,

o'n'ry cuss! You bet he wusn't anywhere where there was danger or fighting.
Why, you might as well hev suspected *him*
of being the big chief himself! There he
comes—ask him."

And the laughter was so general that
Elijah Martin—*alias* Skeesicks—lounging
shyly into the bar-room, joined in it
weakly.

PRINTED BY BALLANTYNE, HANSON AND CO.
LONDON AND EDINBURGH

BY DUTTON COOK.
Leo. | Paul Foster's Daughter.

BY C. EGBERT CRADDOCK.
The Prophet of the Great Smoky Mountains.

BY WILLIAM CYPLES.
Hearts of Gold.

BY ALPHONSE DAUDET.
The Evangelist; or, Port Salvation.

BY JAMES DE MILLE.
A Castle in Spain.

BY J. LEITH DERWENT.
Our Lady of Tears. | Circe's Lovers.

BY CHARLES DICKENS.
Sketches by Boz.
The Pickwick Papers.
Oliver Twist. | Nicholas Nickleby.

BY MRS. ANNIE EDWARDES.
A Point of Honour. | Archie Lovell.

BY M. BETHAM-EDWARDS.
Felicia. | Kitty.

BY EDWARD EGGLESTON.
Roxy.

BY PERCY FITZGERALD.
Bella Donna. | Second Mrs. Tillotson.
Seventy-five Brooke Street. | Polly.
Never Forgotten. | Fatal Zero.
The Lady of Brantome.

BY ALBANY DE FONBLANQUE.
Filthy Lucre.

BY R. E. FRANCILLON.
Olympia. | Queen Cophetua.
One by One. | A Real Queen.

PREF. BY SIR BARTLE FRERE.
Pandurang Hari.

BY HAIN FRISWELL.
One of Two.

BY EDWARD GARRETT.
The Capel Girls.

BY CHARLES GIBBON.
Robin Gray. | For Lack of Gold.
What will the World Say?
In Honour Bound. | For the King.
In Love and War. | In Pastures Green.
Queen of the Meadow.
The Flower of the Forest.
A Heart's Problem. | Heart's Delight.
The Braes of Yarrow.
The Golden Shaft. | Fancy Free.
Of High Degree. | Loving a Dream.
By Mead and Stream. | A Hard Knot.

BY WILLIAM GILBERT.
James Duke. | Dr. Austin's Guests.
The Wizard of the Mountain.

BY JAMES GREENWOOD.
Dick Temple.

BY JOHN HABBERTON.
Brueton's Bayou. | Country Luck.

BY ANDREW HALLIDAY.
Every-Day Papers.

BY LADY DUFFUS HARDY.
Paul Wynter's Sacrifice.

BY THOMAS HARDY.
Under the Greenwood Tree.

BY J. BERWICK HARWOOD.
The Tenth Earl.

BY JULIAN HAWTHORNE.
Garth. | Ellice Quentin.
Sebastian Strome.
Prince Saroni's Wife. | Dust.
Fortune's Fool. | Beatrix Randolph.
Miss Cadogna. | Love—or a Name.

BY SIR ARTHUR HELPS.
Ivan de Biron.

BY MRS. CASHEL HOEY.
The Lover's Creed.

BY TOM HOOD.
A Golden Heart.

BY MRS. GEORGE HOOPER.
The House of Raby.

BY TIGHE HOPKINS.
'Twixt Love and Duty.

BY MRS. ALFRED HUNT.
Thornicroft's Model.
The Leaden Casket. | Self-Condemned.
That other Person.

BY JEAN INGELOW.
Fated to be Free.

BY HARRIETT JAY.
The Dark Colleen.
The Queen of Connaught.

BY MARK KERSHAW.
Colonial Facts and Fictions.

BY R. ASHE KING.
A Drawn Game.
'The Wearing of the Green.'

BY HENRY KINGSLEY.
Oakshott Castle.

BY E. LYNN LINTON.
Patricia Kemball. | Leam Dundas.
The World Well Lost.
Under Which Lord? | 'My Love!'
With a Silken Thread. | Ione.
The Rebel of the Family.

BY HENRY W. LUCY.
Gideon Fleyce.

London : CHATTO & WINDUS, Piccadilly, W.

BY JUSTIN McCARTHY.

Dear Lady Disdain.
The Waterdale Neighbours.
My Enemy's Daughter.
A Fair Saxon. | Linley Rochford.
Miss Misanthrope. | Donna Quixote.
The Comet of a Season.
Maid of Athens. | Camiola.

BY MRS. MACDONELL.

Quaker Cousins.

BY KATHARINE S. MACQUOID.

The Evil Eye. | Lost Rose.

BY W. H. MALLOCK.

The New Republic.

BY FLORENCE MARRYAT.

Open! Sesame! | A Little Stepson.
Fighting the Air. | Written in Fire.
A Harvest of Wild Oats.

BY J. MASTERMAN.

Half-a-Dozen Daughters.

BY BRANDER MATTHEWS.

A Secret of the Sea.

BY JEAN MIDDLEMASS.

Touch and Go. | Mr. Dorillion.

BY MRS. MOLESWORTH.

Hathercourt Rectory.

BY D. CHRISTIE MURRAY.

A Life's Atonement. | A Model Father.
Joseph's Coat. | Coals of Fire.
Val Strange. | Hearts.
By the Gate of the Sea.
The Way of the World.
A Bit of Human Nature.
First Person Singular.
Cynic Fortune.

BY ALICE O'HANLON.

The Unforeseen.

BY MRS. OLIPHANT.

Whiteladies. | The Primrose Path.
The Greatest Heiress in England.

BY MRS. ROBERT O'REILLY.

Phœbe's Fortunes.

BY OUIDA.

Held in Bondage. | Pascarel.
Strathmore. | Signa.
Chandos. | In a Winter City.
Under Two Flags. | Ariadne.
Idalia. | Moths.
Cecil Castlemaine. | Friendship.
Tricotrin. | Pipistrello.
Puck. | Bimbi.
Folle Farine. | In Maremma.
A Dog of Flanders. | Wanda.

BY OUIDA—continued.

Frescoes. | Princess Napraxine.
Two Little Wooden Shoes.
A Village Commune. | Othmar.

BY MARGARET AGNES PAUL.

Gentle and Simple.

BY JAMES PAYN.

Lost Sir Massingberd.
A Perfect Treasure.
Bentinck's Tutor.
Murphy's Master.
A County Family. | At Her Mercy.
A Woman's Vengeance.
Cecil's Tryst. | Clyffards of Clyffe.
Family Scapegrace.
Foster Brothers. | Found Dead.
Best of Husbands. | Walter's Word.
Halves. | Fallen Fortunes.
What He Cost Her.
Humorous Stories.
Gwendoline's Harvest.
Like Father, Like Son.
A Marine Residence.
Married Beneath Him.
Mirk Abbey.
Not Wooed, but Won. | £200 Reward.
Less Black than We're Painted.
By Proxy. | Under One Roof.
High Spirits. | Carlyon's Year.
A Confidential Agent.
Some Private Views. | From Exile.
A Grape from a Thorn. | Kit.
For Cash Only. | The Canon's Ward.
The Talk of the Town. | Holiday Tasks.

BY C. L. PIRKIS.

Lady Lovelace.

BY EDGAR A. POE.

The Mystery of Marie Roget.

BY E. C. PRICE.

Valentina. | Mrs. Lancaster's Rival.
Gerald. | The Foreigners.

BY CHARLES READE.

Never Too Late to Mend.
Hard Cash. | Peg Woffington.
Christie Johnstone. | Griffith Gaunt.
Put Yourself in His Place.
The Double Marriage.
Love Little, Love Long. | Foul Play.
The Cloister and the Hearth.
The Course of True Love.

London : CHATTO & WINDUS, Piccadilly, W.

BY CHARLES READE—*continued.*
The Autobiography of a Thief, &c.
A Terrible Temptation. | The Jilt.
The Wandering Heir. | A Simpleton.
A Woman-Hater. | Readiana.
Singleheart and Doubleface.
Good Stories of Men & other Animals.

BY MRS. J. H. RIDDELL.
Her Mother's Darling.
The Uninhabited House.
Weird Stories. | Fairy Water.
The Prince of Wales's Garden Party.
The Mystery in Palace Gardens.

BY F. W. ROBINSON.
Women are Strange.
The Hands of Justice.

BY JAMES RUNCIMAN.
Skippers and Shellbacks.
Grace Balmaign's Sweetheart.
Schools and Scholars.

BY W. CLARK RUSSELL.
Round the Galley Fire.
On the Fo'k'sle Head.
In the Middle Watch.
A Voyage to the Cape.

BY BAYLE ST. JOHN.
A Levantine Family.

BY G. A. SALA.
Gaslight and Daylight.

BY JOHN SAUNDERS.
Bound to the Wheel.
One Against the World.
The Lion in the Path.
The Two Dreamers. | Guy Waterman.

BY KATHARINE SAUNDERS.
Joan Merryweather. | The High Mills.
Margaret and Elizabeth.
Sebastian. | Heart Salvage.

BY GEORGE R. SIMS.
Rogues and Vagabonds.
The Ring o' Bells.
Mary Jane's Memoirs.

BY ARTHUR SKETCHLEY.
A Match in the Dark.

BY T. W. SPEIGHT.
The Mysteries of Heron Dyke.

BY R. A. STERNDALE.
The Afghan Knife.

BY R. LOUIS STEVENSON.
New Arabian Nights. | Prince Otto.

BY BERTHA THOMAS.
Proud Maisie. | The Violin-Player.
Cressida.

BY W. MOY THOMAS.
A Fight for Life.

BY WALTER THORNBURY.
Tales for the Marines.

BY T. ADOLPHUS TROLLOPE.
Diamond Cut Diamond.

BY ANTHONY TROLLOPE.
The Way We Live Now.
Mr. Scarborough's Family.
The Golden Lion of Granpere.
American Senator. | Kept in the Dark.
Frau Frohmann. | Land-Leaguers.
Marion Fay. | John Caldigate.

BY F. ELEANOR TROLLOPE.
Anne Furness. | Mabel's Progress.
Like Ships upon the Sea.

BY J. T. TROWBRIDGE.
Farnell's Folly.

BY IVAN TURGENIEFF, &c.
Stories from Foreign Novelists.

BY MARK TWAIN.
Tom Sawyer. | A Tramp Abroad.
The Stolen White Elephant.
A Pleasure Trip on the Continent.
Huckleberry Finn.
Life on the Mississippi.
The Prince and the Pauper.

BY C. C. FRASER TYTLER.
Mistress Judith.

BY SARAH TYTLER.
What She Came Through.
Beauty and the Beast.
The Bride's Pass. | St. Mungo's City.
Noblesse Oblige. | Lady Bell.
Citoyenne Jacqueline.
Disappeared.

BY J. S. WINTER.
Cavalry Life. | Regimental Legends.

BY LADY WOOD.
Sabina.

BY EDMUND YATES.
Castaway. | The Forlorn Hope.
Land at Last.

London : CHATTO & WINDUS, Piccadilly, W.

A LIST OF BOOKS

PUBLISHED BY

CHATTO & WINDUS,

214, PICCADILLY, LONDON, W.

Sold by all Booksellers, or sent post-free for the published price by the Publishers:

About.—The Fellah: An Egyptian Novel. By EDMOND ABOUT. Translated by Sir RANDAL ROBERTS. Post 8vo, illustrated boards, **2s.** ; cloth limp, **2s. 6d.**

Adams (W. Davenport), Works by:
A Dictionary of the Drama. Being a comprehensive Guide to the Plays, Playwrights, Players, and Playhouses of the United Kingdom and America, from the Earliest to the Present Times. Crown 8vo, half-bound, **12s. 6d.** [*Preparing.*
Quips and Quiddities. Selected by W. DAVENPORT ADAMS. Post 8vo, cloth limp, **2s. 6d.**

Advertising, A History of, from the Earliest Times. Illustrated by Anecdotes, Curious Specimens, and Notices of Successful Advertisers. By HENRY SAMPSON. Crown 8vo, with Coloured Frontispiece and Illustrations, cloth gilt, **7s. 6d.**

Agony Column (The) of "The Times," from 1800 to 1870. Edited, with an Introduction, by ALICE CLAY. Post 8vo, cloth limp, **2s. 6d.**

Aïdé (Hamilton), Works by:
Post 8vo, illustrated boards, **2s.** each.
Carr of Carrlyon. | Confidences.

Alexander (Mrs.), Novels by:
Post 8vo, illustrated boards, **2s.** each.
Maid, Wife, or Widow?
Valerie's Fate.

Allen (Grant), Works by:
Crown 8vo, cloth extra, **6s.** each.
The Evolutionist at Large. Second Edition, revised.
Vignettes from Nature.
Colin Clout's Calendar

ALLEN (GRANT)—*continued.*
Strange Stories. With Frontispiece by GEORGE DU MAURIER. Cr. 8vo, cl. ex., **6s.** ; post 8vo, illust. bds., **2s.**
Philistia: A Novel. Crown 8vo, cloth extra, **3s. 6d.**; post 8vo, illust. bds., **2s.**
Babylon: A Novel. Post 8vo, illust. boards, **2s.**
For Malmie's Sake: A Tale of Love and Dynamite. Cr. 8vo, cl. ex., **6s.**
In all Shades: A Novel. New and Cheaper Edition. Crown 8vo, cloth extra, **3s. 6d.**
The Beckoning Hand, &c. With a Frontispiece by TOWNLEY GREEN. Crown 8vo, cloth extra, **6s.**

Architectural Styles, A Handbook of. Translated from the German of A. ROSENGARTEN, by W. COLLETT-SANDARS. Crown 8vo, cloth extra, with 639 Illustrations, **7s. 6d.**

Artemus Ward :
Artemus Ward's Works: The Works of CHARLES FARRER BROWNE, better known as ARTEMUS WARD. With Portrait and Facsimile. Crown 8vo, cloth extra, **7s. 6d.**
The Genial Showman: Life and Adventures of Artemus Ward. By EDWARD P. HINGSTON. With a Frontispiece. Cr. 8vo, cl. extra, **3s. 6d.**

Arnold.—Bird Life in England. By EDWIN LESTER ARNOLD. Crown 8vo, cloth extra, **6s.**

Art (The) of Amusing : A Collection of Graceful Arts, Games, Tricks, Puzzles, and Charades. By FRANK BELLEW. With 300 Illustrations. Cr. 8vo cloth extra, **4s. 6d.**

Ashton (John), Works by:

Crown 8vo, cloth extra, 7s. 6d. each.

A History of the Chap-Books of the Eighteenth Century. With nearly 400 Illustrations, engraved in facsimile of the originals.

Social Life in the Reign of Queen Anne. From Original Sources. With nearly 100 Illustrations.

Humour, Wit, and Satire of the Seventeenth Century. With nearly 100 Illustrations.

English Caricature and Satire on Napoleon the First. With 120 Illustrations from Originals. Two Vols., demy 8vo, cloth extra, 28s.

Bacteria.—A Synopsis of the

Bacteria and Yeast Fungi and Allied Species. By W. B. GROVE, B.A. With 87 Illusts. Crown 8vo, cl. extra, 3s. 6d.

Bankers, A Handbook of Lon-

don; together with Lists of Bankers from 1677. By F. G. HILTON PRICE. Crown 8vo, cloth extra, 7s. 6d.

Bardsley (Rev. C.W.), Works by:

Crown 8vo, cloth extra, 7s. 6d. each.

English Surnames: Their Sources and Significations. Third Ed., revised.

Curiosities of Puritan Nomenclature.

Bartholomew Fair, Memoirs

of. By HENRY MORLEY. With 100 Illusts. Crown 8vo, cloth extra, 7s. 6d.

Beaconsfield, Lord: A Biogra-

phy. By T. P. O'CONNOR, M.P. Sixth Edition, with a New Preface. Crown 8vo, cloth extra, 7s. 6d.

Beauchamp. — Grantley

Grange: A Novel. By SHELSLEY BEAUCHAMP. Post 8vo, illust. bds., 2s.

Beautiful Pictures by British

Artists: A Gathering of Favourites from our Picture Galleries. All engraved on Steel in the highest style of Art. Edited, with Notices of the Artists, by SYDNEY ARMYTAGE, M.A. Imperial 4to, cloth extra, gilt and gilt edges, 21s.

Bechstein. — As Pretty as

Seven, and other German Stories. Collected by LUDWIG BECHSTEIN. With Additional Tales by the Brothers GRIMM, and 100 Illusts. by RICHTER. Small 4to, green and gold, 6s. 6d. gilt edges, 7s. 6d.

Beerbohm. — Wanderings in

Patagonia; or, Life among the Ostrich Hunters. By JULIUS BEERBOHM. With Illusts. Crown 8vo, cloth extra, 3s. 6d.

Belgravia. One Shilling Monthly.

A New Serial Story by W. CLARK RUSSELL, entitled The Frozen Pirate, began in the JULY Number. Two New Serial Stories will begin in the Number for JANUARY, 1888, and will be continued through the year: Undercurrents, by the Author of " Phyllis ;" and The Blackhall Ghosts, by SARAH TYTLER.

. *Now ready, the Volume for* JULY *to* OCTOBER, 1887, *cloth extra, gilt edges,* 7s. 6d.; *Cases for binding Vols.,* 2s. *each.*

Belgravia Holiday Number,

1887. Demy 8vo, with Illustrations, 1s.

Belgravia Annual, 1887: A

Collection of Powerful Short Stories, each complete in itself. With Illustrations. Demy 8vo, 1s.   [*Nov.* 10.

Bennett (W.C., LL.D.), Works by:

Post 8vo, cloth limp, 2s. each.

A Ballad History of England.

Songs for Sailors.

Besant (Walter) and James

Rice, Novels by. Crown 8vo, cloth extra, 3s. 6d. each; post 8vo, illust. boards, 2s. each; cloth limp, 2s. 6d. each.

Ready-Money Mortiboy.

With Harp and Crown.

This Son of Vulcan.

My Little Girl.

The Case of Mr. Lucraft.

The Golden Butterfly.

By Celia's Arbour.

The Monks of Thelema.

'Twas in Trafalgar's Bay.

The Seamy Side.

The Ten Years' Tenant.

The Chaplain of the Fleet.

Besant (Walter), Novels by:

Crown 8vo, cloth extra, 3s. 6d. each post 8vo, illust. boards, 2s. each; cloth limp, 2s. 6d. each.

All Sorts and Conditions of Men: An Impossible Story. With Illustrations by FRED. BARNARD.

The Captains' Room, &c. With Frontispiece by E. J. WHEELER.

All in a Garden Fair. With 6 Illusts. by H. FURNISS.

Dorothy Forster. With Frontispiece by CHARLES GREEN.

Uncle Jack and other Stories.

Besant, Walter, *continued—*
Children of Gibeon: A Novel. New and Cheaper Edition. Crown 8vo, cloth extra, 3s. 6d.
The World Went Very Well Then. With Etching of Portrait by John Pettie, R.A., and Illustrations by A. Forestier. Three Vols., cr. 8vo.

The Art of Fiction. Demy 8vo, 1s.

Library Edition of the Novels of
Besant and Rice.
Messrs. Chatto & Windus *are now issuing a choicely-printed Library Edition of the Novels of Messrs.* Besant *and* Rice. *The Volumes (each one containing a Complete Novel) are printed from a specially-cast fount of type on a large crown 8vo page by Messrs.* Ballantyne & Hanson, *and handsomely bound in cloth by Messrs.* Burn & Co. *Price Six Shillings each. The First Volume is*
Ready-Money Mortiboy,
with Portrait of James Rice, *etched by* Daniel A. Wehrschmidt, *and a New Preface by* Walter Besant, *telling the story of his literary partnership with* James Rice. *To be followed by the following :—*
My Little Girl. [*Ready.*
With Harp and Crown. [*Ready.*
This Son of Vulcan. [*Oct.*
The Golden Butterfly. With Etched Portrait of Walter Besant. [*Nov.*
The Monks of Thelema.
By Celia's Arbour.
The Chaplain of the Fleet.
The Seamy Side. &c. &c.

Betham-Edwards (M.), Novels
by :
Felicia. Cr. 8vo, cloth extra, 3s. 6d. ; post 8vo, illust. bds., 2s.
Kitty. Post 8vo, illust. bds., 2s.

Bewick (Thos.) and his Pupils.
By Austin Dobson. With 95 Illustrations. Square 8vo, cloth extra, 10s. 6d.

Birthday Books :—
The Starry Heavens: A Poetical Birthday Book. Square 8vo, handsomely bound in cloth, 2s. 6d.
Birthday Flowers: Their Language and Legends. By W. J. Gordon. Beautifully Illustrated in Colours by Viola Boughton. In illuminated cover, crown 4to, 6s.
The Lowell Birthday Book. With Illusts. Small 8vo, cloth extra, 4s. 6d.

Blackburn's (Henry) Art Handbooks. Demy 8vo, Illustrated, uniform in size for binding.
Academy Notes, separate years, from 1875 to 1886, each 1s.

Blackburn, Henry, *continued—*
Academy Notes, 1887. With numerous Illustrations. 1s.
Academy Notes, 1875-79. Complete in One Vol.,with nearly 600 Illusts. in Facsimile. Demy 8vo, cloth limp, 6s.
Academy Notes, 1880-84. Complete in One Volume, with about 700 Facsimile Illustrations. Cloth limp, 6s.
Grosvenor Notes, 1877. 6d.
Grosvenor Notes, separate years, from 1878 to 1886, each 1s.
Grosvenor Notes, 1887. With numerous Illusts. 1s.
Grosvenor Notes, 1877-82. With upwards of 300 Illustrations. Demy 8vo, cloth limp, 6s.
Grosvenor Notes, 1883-87. With upwards of 300 Illustrations. Demy 8vo, cloth limp, 6s.
Pictures at South Kensington. With 70 Illusts. 1s. [*New Edit. preparing.*
The English Pictures at the National Gallery. 114 Illustrations. 1s.
The Old Masters at the National Gallery. 128 Illustrations. 1s. 6d.
A Complete Illustrated Catalogue to the National Gallery. With Notes by H. Blackburn, and 242 Illusts. Demy 8vo, cloth limp, 3s.

Illustrated Catalogue of the Luxembourg Gallery. Containing about 250 Reproductions after the Original Drawings of the Artists. Edited by F. G. Dumas. Demy 8vo, 3s. 6d.
The Paris Salon, 1887. With about 300 Facsimile Sketches. Demy 8vo, 3s.

Blake (William) : Etchings from
his Works. By W. B. Scott. With descriptive Text. Folio, half-bound boards, India Proofs, 21s.

Boccaccio's Decameron ; or,
Ten Days' Entertainment. Translated into English, with an Introduction by Thomas Wright, F.S.A. With Portrait and Stothard's beautiful Copperplates. Cr. 8vo, cloth extra, gilt, 7s. 6d.

Bowers'(G.) Hunting Sketches:
Oblong 4to, half-bound boards, 21s. each.
Canters in Crampshire.
Leaves from a Hunting Journal. Coloured in facsimile of the originals.

Boyle (Frederick), Works by :
Crown 8vo, cloth extra, 3s. 6d. each; post 8vo, illustrated boards, 2s. each.
Camp Notes: Stories of Sport and Adventure in Asia, Africa, and America. [*Trotter.*
Savage Life: Adventures of a Globe-
Chronicles of No-Man's Land Post 8vo, illust. boards, 2s.

Brand's Observations on Popular Antiquities, chiefly Illustrating the Origin of our Vulgar Customs, Ceremonies, and Superstitions. With the Additions of Sir HENRY ELLIS. Crown 8vo, cloth extra, gilt, with numerous Illustrations, 7s. 6d.

Bret Harte, Works by :

Bret Harte's Collected Works. Arranged and Revised by the Author. Complete in Five Vols., crown 8vo, cloth extra, 6s. each.
Vol. I. COMPLETE POETICAL AND DRAMATIC WORKS. With Steel Portrait, and Introduction by Author.
Vol. II. EARLIER PAPERS—LUCK OF ROARING CAMP, and other Sketches —BOHEMIAN PAPERS — SPANISH AND AMERICAN LEGENDS.
Vol. III. TALES OF THE ARGONAUTS —EASTERN SKETCHES.
Vol. IV. GABRIEL CONROY.
Vol. V. STORIES — CONDENSED NOVELS, &c.

The Select Works of Bret Harte, in Prose and Poetry. With Introductory Essay by J. M. BELLEW, Portrait of the Author, and 50 Illustrations. Crown 8vo cloth extra, 7s. 6d.

Bret Harte's Complete Poetical Works. Author's Copyright Edition. Beautifully printed on hand-made paper and bound in buckram. Cr. 8vo, 4s. 6d.

Gabriel Conroy : A Novel. Post 8vo, illustrated boards, 2s.

An Heiress of Red Dog, and other Stories. Post 8vo, illust. boards, 2s.

The Twins of Table Mountain. Fcap. 8vo, picture cover, 1s.

Luck of Roaring Camp, and other Sketches. Post 8vo, illust. bds., 2s.

Jeff Briggs's Love Story. Fcap. 8vo, picture cover, 1s. [2s. 6d.

Flip. Post 8vo, illust. bds., 2s.; cl. limp,

Californian Stories (including THE TWINS OF TABLE MOUNTAIN, JEFF BRIGGS'S LOVE STORY, &c.) Post 8vo, illustrated boards, 2s.

Maruja: A Novel. Post 8vo, illust. boards, 2s.; cloth limp, 2s. 6d.

The Queen of the Pirate Isle. With 28 original Drawings by KATE GREENAWAY, Reproduced in Colours by EDMUND EVANS. Sm. 4to, bds., 5s.

Brewer (Rev. Dr.), Works by :

The Reader's Handbook of Allusions, References, Plots, and Stories. Fifth Edition, revised throughout, with a New Appendix, containing a COMPLETE ENGLISH BIBLIOGRAPHY. Cr. 8vo, 1,400 pp., cloth extra, 7s. 6d.

Authors and their Works, with the Dates: Being the Appendices to "The Reader's Handbook," separately printed. Cr. 8vo, cloth limp, 2s.

BREWER (REV. DR.), *continued—*

A Dictionary of Miracles: Imitative, Realistic, and Dogmatic. Crown 8vo, cloth extra, 7s. 6d.; half-bound, 9s.

Brewster (Sir David), Works by:

More Worlds than One: The Creed of the Philosopher and the Hope of the Christian. With Plates. Post 8vo, cloth extra, 4s. 6d.

The Martyrs of Science: Lives of GALILEO, TYCHO BRAHE, and KEPLER. With Portraits. Post 8vo, cloth extra, 4s. 6d.

Letters on Natural Magic. A New Edition, with numerous Illustrations, and Chapters on the Being and Faculties of Man, and Additional Phenomena of Natural Magic, by J. A. SMITH. Post 8vo, cl. ex., 4s. 6d.

Briggs, Memoir of Gen. John.
By Major EVANS BELL. With a Portrait. Royal 8vo, cloth extra, 7s. 6d.

Brillat-Savarin.—Gastronomy
as a Fine Art. By BRILLAT-SAVARIN. Translated by R. E. ANDERSON, M.A. Post 8vo, cloth limp, 2s. 6d.

Buchanan's (Robert) Works :
Crown 8vo, cloth extra, 6s. each.
Ballads of Life, Love, and Humour. Frontispiece by ARTHUR HUGHES.
Undertones. | **London Poems.**
The Book of Orm.
White Rose and Red: A Love Story.
Idylls and Legends of Inverburn.
Selected Poems of Robert Buchanan With a Frontispiece by T. DALZIEL.
The Hebrid Isles: Wanderings in the Land of Lorne and the Outer Hebrides. With Frontispiece by WILLIAM SMALL.
A Poet's Sketch-Book: Selections from the Prose Writings of ROBERT BUCHANAN.
The Earthquake; or, Six Days and a Sabbath.

Robert Buchanan's Complete Poetical Works. With Steel-plate Portrait. Crown 8vo, cloth extra, 7s. 6d.

Crown 8vo, cloth extra, 3s. 6d. each; post 8vo, illust. boards, 2s. each.
The Shadow of the Sword.
A Child of Nature. With a Frontispiece.
God and the Man. With Illustrations by FRED. BARNARD.
The Martyrdom of Madeline. With Frontispiece by A. W. COOPER.
Love Me for Ever. With a Frontispiece by P. MACNAB.
Annan Water. | **The New Abelard.**
Foxglove Manor.
Matt: A Story of a Caravan.
The Master of the Mine.

Bunyan's Pilgrim's Progress.

Edited by Rev. T. SCOTT. With 17 Steel Plates by STOTHARD engraved by GOODALL, and numerous Woodcuts. Crown 8vo, cloth extra, gilt, 7s. 6d.

Burnett (Mrs.), Novels by:

Surly Tim, and other Stories. Post 8vo, illustrated boards, 2s.

Fcap. 8vo, picture cover, 1s. each.
Kathleen Mavourneen.
Lindsay's Luck.
Pretty Polly Pemberton.

Burton (Captain), Works by:

To the Gold Coast for Gold: A Personal Narrative. By RICHARD F. BURTON and VERNEY LOVETT CAMERON. With Maps and Frontispiece. Two Vols., crown 8vo, cloth extra, 21s.

The Book of the Sword: Being a History of the Sword and its Use in all Countries, from the Earliest Times. By RICHARD F. BURTON. With over 400 Illustrations. Square 8vo, cloth extra, 32s.

Burton (Robert):

The Anatomy of Melancholy. A New Edition, complete, corrected and enriched by Translations of the Classical Extracts. Demy 8vo, cloth extra, 7s. 6d.

Melancholy Anatomised: Being an Abridgment, for popular use, of BURTON'S ANATOMY OF MELANCHOLY. Post 8vo, cloth limp, 2s. 6d.

Byron (Lord):

Byron's Childe Harold. An entirely New Edition of this famous Poem, with over One Hundred new Illusts. by leading Artists. (Uniform with the Illustrated Editions of "The Lady of the Lake" and "Marmion.") Elegantly and appropriately bound, small 4to, 16s.

Byron's Letters and Journals. With Notices of his Life. By THOMAS MOORE. A Reprint of the Original Edition. Cr. 8vo, cloth extra, 7s. 6d.

Byron's Don Juan. Complete in One Vol., post 8vo, cloth limp, 2s.

Caine (T. Hall), Novels by:

The Shadow of a Crime. Cr. 8vo, cloth extra, 3s. 6d.; post 8vo, illustrated boards, 2s.

A Son of Hagar. New and Cheaper Edition. Crown 8vo, cloth extra, 3s. 6d.

Cameron (Comdr.), Works by:

To the Gold Coast for Gold: A Personal Narrative. By RICHARD F. BURTON and VERNEY LOVETT CAMERON. With Frontispiece and Maps. Two Vols., crown 8vo, cloth extra, 21s.

The Cruise of the "Black Prince" Privateer, Commanded by ROBERT HAWKINS, Master Mariner. By Commander V. LOVETT CAMERON, R.N., C.B., D.C.L. With Frontispiece and Vignette by P. MACNAB. Crown 8vo, cl. ex., 5s.

Cameron (Mrs. H. Lovett), Novels by:

Crown 8vo, cloth extra, 3s. 6d. each post 8vo, illustrated boards, 2s. each.
Juliet's Guardian. | Deceivers Ever.

Carlyle (Thomas):

On the Choice of Books. By THOMAS CARLYLE. With a Life of the Author by R. H. SHEPHERD. New and Revised Edition, post 8vo, cloth extra, Illustrated, 1s. 6d.

The Correspondence of Thomas Carlyle and Ralph Waldo Emerson, 1834 to 1872. Edited by CHARLES ELIOT NORTON. With Portraits. Two Vols., crown 8vo, cloth extra, 24s.

Chapman's (George) Works:

Vol. I. contains the Plays complete, including the doubtful ones. Vol. II., the Poems and Minor Translations, with an Introductory Essay by ALGERNON CHARLES SWINBURNE. Vol. III., the Translations of the Iliad and Odyssey. Three Vols., crown 8vo, cloth extra, 18s.; or separately, 6s. each.

Chatto & Jackson.—A Treatise

on Wood Engraving, Historical and Practical. By WM. ANDREW CHATTO and JOHN JACKSON. With an Additional Chapter by HENRY G. BOHN; and 450 fine Illustrations. A Reprint of the last Revised Edition. Large 4to, half-bound, 28s.

Chaucer:

Chaucer for Children: A Golden Key. By Mrs. H.R. HAWEIS. With Eight Coloured Pictures and numerous Woodcuts by the Author. New Ed., small 4to, cloth extra, 6s.

Chaucer for Schools. By Mrs. H. R. HAWEIS. Demy 8vo, cloth limp, 2s. 6d.

Chronicle (The) of the Coach:

Charing Cross to Ilfracombe. By J. D CHAMPLIN. With 75 Illustrations by EDWARD L. CHICHESTER. Square 8vo, cloth extra, 7s. 6d.

City (The) of Dream: A Poem.

Fcap. 8vo, cloth extra, 6s. [In the press.

Clodd. — Myths and Dreams.
By EDWARD CLODD, F.R.A.S., Author of " The Childhood of Religions," &c. Crown 8vo, cloth extra, 5s.

Cobban.—The Cure of Souls:
A Story. By J. MACLAREN COBBAN. Post 8vo, illustrated boards, 2s.

Coleman.—Curly: An Actor's
Story. By JOHN COLEMAN. Illustrated by J. C. DOLLMAN. Crown 8vo, 1s.; cloth, 1s. 6d.

Collins (Wilkie), Novels by:
Crown 8vo, cloth extra, Illustrated, 3s.6d. each ; post 8vo, illustrated bds., 2s. each; cloth limp, 2s. 6d. each.
Antonina. Illust. by Sir JOHN GILBERT.
Basil. Illustrated by Sir JOHN GILBERT and J. MAHONEY.
Hide and Seek. Illustrated by Sir JOHN GILBERT and J. MAHONEY.
The Dead Secret. Illustrated by Sir JOHN GILBERT.
Queen of Hearts. Illustrated by Sir JOHN GILBERT.
My Miscellanies. With a Steel-plate Portrait of WILKIE COLLINS.
The Woman in White. With Illustrations by Sir JOHN GILBERT and F. A. FRASER.
The Moonstone. With Illustrations by G. Du MAURIER and F. A. FRASER.
Man and Wife. Illust. by W. SMALL.
Poor Miss Finch. Illustrated by G. Du MAURIER and EDWARD HUGHES.
Miss or Mrs.? With Illustrations by S. L. FILDES and HENRY WOODS.
The New Magdalen. Illustrated by G.Du MAURIER and C.S.REINHARDT.
The Frozen Deep. Illustrated by G. Du MAURIER and J. MAHONEY.
The Law and the Lady. Illustrated by S. L. FILDES and SYDNEY HALL.
The Two Destinies.
The Haunted Hotel. Illustrated by ARTHUR HOPKINS.
The Fallen Leaves.
Jezebel's Daughter.
The Black Robe.
Heart and Science: A Story of the Present Time.
"I Say No."
The Evil Genius.

Little Novels. Three Vols., cr. 8vo.

Collins (Mortimer), Novels by:
Crown 8vo, cloth extra, 3s. 6d. each ; post 8vo, illustrated boards, 2s. each.
Sweet Anne Page. | Transmigration.
From Midnight to Midnight.

A Fight with Fortune. Post 8vo, illustrated boards, 2s.

Collins (Mortimer & Frances),
Novels by :
Crown 8vo, cloth extra, 3s. 6d. each ; post 8vo, illustrated boards, 2s. each.
Blacksmith and Scholar.
The Village Comedy.
You Play Me False.

Post 8vo, illustrated boards, 2s. each.
Sweet and Twenty. | Frances.

Collins (C. Allston).—The Bar
Sinister: A Story. By C. ALLSTON COLLINS. Post 8vo, illustrated bds.,2s.

Colman's Humorous Works:
" Broad Grins," " My Nightgown and Slippers," and other Humorous Works, Prose and Poetical, of GEORGE COLMAN. With Life by G. B. BUCKSTONE, and Frontispiece by HOGARTH. Crown 8vo cloth extra, gilt, 7s. 6d.

Convalescent Cookery: A
Family Handbook. By CATHERINE RYAN. Crown 8vo, 1s.; cloth, 1s. 6d.

Conway (Moncure D.), Works
by :
Demonology and Devil-Lore. Two Vols., royal 8vo, with 65 Illusts., 28s.
A Necklace of Stories. Illustrated by W. J. HENNESSY. Square 8vo, cloth extra, 6s.

Cook (Dutton), Works by:
Crown 8vo, cloth extra, 6s. each.
Hours with the Players. With a Steel Plate Frontispiece.
Nights at the Play: A View of the English Stage.

Leo: A Novel. Post 8vo, illustrated boards, 2s.
Paul Foster's Daughter. crown 8vo, cloth extra, 3s. 6d.; post 8vo, illustrated boards, 2s.

Copyright. — A Handbook of
English and Foreign Copyright in Literary and Dramatic Works. By SIDNEY JERROLD, of the Middle Temple, Esq., Barrister-at-Law. Post 8vo, cloth limp, 2s. 6d.

Cornwall.—Popular Romances
of the West of England; or, The Drolls, Traditions, and Superstitions of Old Cornwall. Collected and Edited by ROBERT HUNT, F.R.S. New and Revised Edition, with Additions, and Two Steel-plate Illustrations by GEORGE CRUIKSHANK. Crown 8vo, cloth extra, 7s. 6d.

Craddock. — The Prophet of
the Great Smoky Mountains. By CHARLES EGBERT CRADDOCK. Post 8vo, illust. bds., 2s.; cloth limp, 2s. 6d.

Creasy.—Memoirs of Eminent Etonians : with Notices of the Early History of Eton College. By Sir EDWARD CREASY, Author of " The Fifteen Decisive Battles of the World." Crown 8vo, cloth extra, gilt, with 13 Portraits, 7s. 6d.

Cruikshank (George):

The Comic Almanack. Complete in TWO SERIES : The FIRST from 1835 to 1843; the SECOND from 1844 to 1853. A Gathering of the BEST HUMOUR of THACKERAY, HOOD, MAYHEW, ALBERT SMITH, A'BECKETT, ROBERT BROUGH, &c. With 2,000 Woodcuts and Steel Engravings by CRUIKSHANK, HINE, LANDELLS, &c. Crown 8vo, cloth gilt, two very thick volumes, 7s. 6d. each.

The Life of George Cruikshank. By BLANCHARD JERROLD, Author of " The Life of Napoleon III.," &c. With 84 Illustrations. New and Cheaper Edition, enlarged, with Additional Plates, and a very carefully compiled Bibliography. Crown 8vo, cloth extra, 7s. 6d.

Robinson Crusoe. A beautiful reproduction of Major's Edition, with 37 Woodcuts and Two Steel Plates by GEORGE CRUIKSHANK, choicely printed. Crown 8vo, cloth extra, 7s. 6d.

Cumming (C. F. Gordon), Works by:
Demy 8vo, cloth extra, 8s. 6d. each.

In the Hebrides. With Autotype Facsimile and numerous full-page Illustrations.

In the Himalayas and on the Indian Plains. With numerous Illustrations.

Via Cornwall to Egypt. With a Photogravure Frontispiece. Demy 8vo, cloth extra, 7s. 6d.

Cussans.—Handbook of Heraldry; with Instructions for Tracing Pedigrees and Deciphering Ancient MSS., &c. By JOHN E. CUSSANS. Entirely New and Revised Edition, illustrated with over 400 Woodcuts and Coloured Plates. Crown 8vo, cloth extra, 7s. 6d.

Cyples.—Hearts of Gold: A Novel. By WILLIAM CYPLES. Crown 8vo, cloth extra, 3s. 6d.; post 8vo, illustrated boards, 2s.

Daniel. — Merrie England in the Olden Time. By GEORGE DANIEL. With Illustrations by ROBT. CRUIKSHANK. Crown 8vo, cloth extra, 3s. 6d.

Daudet.—The Evangelist; or, Port Salvation. By ALPHONSE DAUDET. Translated by C. HARRY MELTZER. With Portrait of the Author. Crown 8vo, cloth extra, 3s. 6d.; post 8vo, illust. boards, 2s.

Davies (Dr. N. E.), Works by:
Crown 8vo, 1s. each; cloth limp, 1s. 6d. each.

One Thousand Medical Maxims.
Nursery Hints: A Mother's Guide.
Aids to Long Life. Crown 8vo, 2s.; cloth limp, 2s. 6d.

Davies' (Sir John) Complete Poetical Works, including Psalms I. to L. in Verse, and other hitherto Unpublished MSS., for the first time Collected and Edited, with Memorial-Introduction and Notes, by the Rev. A. B. GROSART, D.D. Two Vols. crown 8vo, cloth boards, 12s.

De Maistre.—A Journey Round My Room. By XAVIER DE MAISTRE. Translated by HENRY ATTWELL. Post 8vo, cloth limp, 2s. 6d.

De Mille.—A Castle in Spain: A Novel. By JAMES DE MILLE. With a Frontispiece. Crown 8vo, cloth extra, 3s. 6d.; post 8vo, illust. bds., 2s.

Derwent (Leith), Novels by:
Crown 8vo, cloth extra, 3s. 6d. each; post 8vo, illustrated boards, 2s. each.
Our Lady of Tears. | Circe's Lovers.

Dickens (Charles), Novels by:
Post 8vo, illustrated boards, 2s. each.
Sketches by Boz. | Nicholas Nickleby.
Pickwick Papers. | Oliver Twist.

The Speeches of Charles Dickens, 1841-1870. With a New Bibliography, revised and enlarged. Edited and Prefaced by RICHARD HERNE SHEPHERD. Cr. 8vo, cloth extra, 6s.—Also a SMALLER EDITION, in the *Mayfair Library*. Post 8vo, cloth limp, 2s. 6d.

About England with Dickens. By ALFRED RIMMER. With 57 Illustrations by C. A. VANDERHOOF, ALFRED RIMMER, and others. Sq. 8vo, cloth extra, 10s. 6d.

Dictionaries:
A Dictionary of Miracles: Imitative, Realistic, and Dogmatic. By the Rev. E. C. BREWER, LL.D. Crown 8vo, cloth extra, 7s. 6d.; hf.-bound, 9s.

The Reader's Handbook of Allusions, References, Plots, and Stories. By the Rev. E. C. BREWER, LL.D. Fifth Edition, revised throughout, with a New Appendix, containing a Complete English Bibliography. Crown 8vo, 1,400 pages, cloth extra, 7s. 6d.

DICTIONARIES—*continued.*

Authors and their Works, with the Dates. Being the Appendices to "The Reader's Handbook," separately printed. By the Rev. Dr. BREWER. Crown 8vo, cloth limp, 2s.

Familiar Allusions: A Handbook of Miscellaneous Information; including the Names of Celebrated Statues, Paintings, Palaces, Country Seats, Ruins, Churches, Ships, Streets, Clubs, Natural Curiosities, and the like. By WM. A: WHEELER and CHARLES G. WHEELER. Demy 8vo, cloth extra, 7s. 6d.

Familiar Short Sayings of Great Men. With Historical and Explanatory Notes. By SAMUEL A. BENT, M.A. Fifth Edition, revised and enlarged. Cr. 8vo, cloth extra, 7s. 6d.

A Dictionary of the Drama: Being a comprehensive Guide to the Plays, Playwrights, Players, and Playhouses of the United Kingdom and America, from the Earliest to the Present Times. By W. DAVENPORT ADAMS. A thick volume, crown 8vo, half-bound, 12s. 6d. [*In preparation.*

The Slang Dictionary: Etymological, Historical, and Anecdotal. Crown 8vo, cloth extra, 6s. 6d.

Women of the Day: A Biographical Dictionary. By FRANCES HAYS. Cr. 8vo, cloth extra, 5s.

Words, Facts, and Phrases: A Dictionary of Curious, Quaint, and Out-of-the-Way Matters. By ELIEZER EDWARDS. New and Cheaper Issue. Cr. 8vo, cl. ex., 7s. 6d.; hf.-bd., 9s.

Diderot.—The Paradox of Acting. Translated, with Annotations, from Diderot's "Le Paradoxe sur le Comédien," by WALTER HERRIES POLLOCK. With a Preface by HENRY IRVING. Cr. 8vo, in parchment, 4s. 6d.

Dobson (W. T.), Works by:
Post 8vo, cloth limp, 2s. 6d. each.
Literary Frivolities, Fancies, Follies, and Frolics. [cities.
Poetical Ingenuities and Eccentri-

Doran. — Memories of our Great Towns; with Anecdotic Gleanings concerning their Worthies and their Oddities. By Dr. JOHN DORAN, F.S.A. With 38 Illustrations. New and Cheaper Edition. Crown 8vo, cloth extra, 7s. 6d.

Drama, A Dictionary of the. Being a comprehensive Guide to the Plays, Playwrights, Players, and Playhouses of the United Kingdom and America, from the Earliest to the Present Times. By W. DAVENPORT ADAMS. (Uniform with BREWER'S "Reader's Handbook.") Crown 8vo, half-bound, 12s. 6d. [*In preparation.*

Dramatists, The Old. Cr. 8vo, cl. ex., Vignette Portraits, 6s. per Vol.

Ben Jonson's Works. With Notes Critical and Explanatory, and a Biographical Memoir by WM. GIFFORD. Edit. by Col. CUNNINGHAM. 3 Vols.

Chapman's Works. Complete in Three Vols. Vol. I. contains the Plays complete, including doubtful ones; Vol. II., Poems and Minor Translations, with Introductory Essay by A. C. SWINBURNE; Vol. III., Translations of the Iliad and Odyssey.

Marlowe's Works. Including his Translations. Edited, with Notes and Introduction, by Col. CUNNINGHAM. One Vol.

Massinger's Plays. From the Text of WILLIAM GIFFORD. Edited by Col. CUNNINGHAM. One Vol.

Dyer. — The Folk - Lore of Plants. By Rev. T. F. THISELTON DYER, M.A. Crown 8vo, cloth extra, 7s. 6d. [*In preparation.*

Early English Poets. Edited, with Introductions and Annotations, by Rev. A. B. GROSART, D.D. Crown 8vo, cloth boards, 6s. per Volume.

Fletcher's (Giles, B.D.) Complete Poems. One Vol.

Davies' (Sir John) Complete Poetical Works. Two Vols.

Herrick's (Robert) Complete Collected Poems. Three Vols.

Sidney's (Sir Philip) Complete Poetical Works. Three Vols.

Herbert (Lord) of Cherbury's Poems. Edited, with Introduction, by J. CHURTON COLLINS. Crown 8vo, parchment, 8s.

Edgcumbe. — Zephyrus: A Holiday in Brazil and on the River Plate. By E. R. PEARCE EDGCUMBE. With 41 Illustrations. Crown 8vo, cloth extra, 5s. [*Preparing.*

Edwardes (Mrs. A.), Novels by:
A Point of Honour. Post 8vo, illustrated boards, 2s.
Archie Lovell. Crown 8vo, cloth extra, 3s. 6d.; post 8vo, illust. bds., 2s.

Eggleston.—Roxy: A Novel. By EDWARD EGGLESTON. Post 8vo, illust. boards, 2s.

Emanuel.—On Diamonds and Precious Stones: their History, Value, and Properties; with Simple Tests for ascertaining their Reality. By HARRY EMANUEL, F.R.G.S. With numerous Illustrations, tinted and plain. Crown 8vo, cloth extra, gilt, 6s.

Ewald (Alex. Charles, F.S.A.), Works by.

The Life and Times of Prince Charles Stuart, Count of Albany, commonly called the Young Pretender. From the State Papers and other Sources. New and Cheaper Edition, with a Portrait, crown 8vo, cloth extra, 7s. 6d.

Stories from the State Papers. With an Autotype Facsimile. Crown 8vo, cloth extra, 6s.

Studies Re-studied: Historical Sketches from Original Sources. Demy 8vo, cloth extra, 12s.

Eyes, Our: How to Preserve Them from Infancy to Old Age. By JOHN BROWNING, F.R.A.S., &c. Sixth Edition. With 55 Illustrations. Crown 8vo, cloth, 1s.

Fairholt.—Tobacco: Its History and Associations; with an Account of the Plant and its Manufacture, and its Modes of Use in all Ages and Countries. By F. W. FAIRHOLT, F.S.A. With upwards of 100 Illustrations by the Author. Crown 8vo, cloth extra, 6s.

Familiar Allusions: A Hand-book of Miscellaneous Information; including the Names of Celebrated Statues, Paintings, Palaces, Country Seats, Ruins, Churches, Ships, Streets, Clubs, Natural Curiosities, and the like. By WILLIAM A. WHEELER, Author of "Noted Names of Fiction;" and CHARLES G. WHEELER. Demy 8vo, cloth extra, 7s. 6d.

Familiar Short Sayings of Great Men. By SAMUEL ARTHUR BENT, A.M. Fifth Edition, Revised and Enlarged. Crown 8vo, cloth extra, 7s. 6d.

Farrer (James Anson), Works by:
Military Manners and Customs. Crown 8vo, cloth extra, 6s.
War: Three Essays, Reprinted from "Military Manners." Crown 8vo, 1s.; cloth, 1s. 6d.

Faraday (Michael), Works by:
Post 8vo, cloth extra, 4s. 6d. each.
The Chemical History of a Candle: Lectures delivered before a Juvenile Audience at the Royal Institution. Edited by WILLIAM CROOKES, F.C.S. With numerous Illustrations.
On the Various Forces of Nature, and their Relations to each other: Lectures delivered before a Juvenile Audience at the Royal Institution. Edited by WILLIAM CROOKES, F.C.S. With numerous Illustrations.

Fin-Bec.—The Cupboard Papers: Observations on the Art of Living and Dining. By FIN-BEC. Post 8vo, cloth limp, 2s. 6d.

Fireworks, The Complete Art of Making; or, The Pyrotechnist's Treasury. By THOMAS KENTISH. With 267 Illustrations. A New Edition, Revised throughout and greatly Enlarged. Crown 8vo, cloth extra, 5s.

Fitzgerald (Percy), Works by:
The Recreations of a Literary Man; or, Does Writing Pay? With Recollections of some Literary Men, and a View of a Literary Man's Working Life. Cr. 8vo, cloth extra, 6s.
The World Behind the Scenes. Crown 8vo, cloth extra, 3s. 6d.
Little Essays: Passages from the Letters of CHARLES LAMB. Post 8vo, cloth limp, 2s. 6d.
Fatal Zero: A Homburg Diary. Cr. 8vo, cloth extra, 3s. 6d.
A Day's Tour: A Journey through France and Belgium. With Sketches in facsimile of the Original Drawings. Crown 4to, picture cover, 1s.

Post 8vo, illustrated boards, 2s. each.
Bella Donna. | Never Forgotten
The Second Mrs. Tillotson.
Polly.
Seventy-five Brooke Street.
The Lady of Brantome.

Fletcher's (Giles, B.D.) Com-plete Poems: Christ's Victorie in Heaven, Christ's Victorie on Earth, Christ's Triumph over Death, and Minor Poems. With Memorial-Introduction and Notes by the Rev. A. B. GROSART, D.D. Cr. 8vo, cloth bds., 6s.

Fonblanque.—Filthy Lucre: A Novel. By ALBANY DE FONBLANQUE. Post 8vo, illustrated boards, 2s.

Fox-Bourne (H. R.), Works by:
English Merchants: Memoirs in Illustration of the Progress of British Commerce. With numerous Illustrations. Cr. 8vo, cloth extra, 7s. 6d.
English Newspapers: Contributions to the History of Journalism. Two vols., demy 8vo, cloth extra, 25s.
[Preparing.

Francillon (R. E.), Novels by:
Crown 8vo, cloth extra, 3s. 6d. each; post 8vo, illust. boards, 2s. each.
One by One. | A Real Queen.
Queen Cophetua. |

Olympia. Post 8vo, illust. boards, 2s.
Esther's Glove. Fcap. 8vo, 1s.

French Literature, History of.
By HENRY VAN LAUN. Complete in 3 Vols., demy 8vo, cl. bds., 7s. 6d. each.

Frere.—Pandurang Hari; or, Memoirs of a Hindoo. With a Preface by Sir H. BARTLE FRERE, G.C.S.I., &c. Crown 8vo, cloth extra, 3s. 6d.; post 8vo, illustrated boards, 2s.

Friswell.—One of Two: A Novel.
By HAIN FRISWELL. Post 8vo, illustrated boards, 2s.

Frost (Thomas), Works by:
Crown 8vo, cloth extra, 3s. 6d. each.
Circus Life and Circus Celebrities.
The Lives of the Conjurers.
The Old Showmen and the Old London Fairs.

Fry's (Herbert) Royal Guide
to the London Charities, 1887-8. Showing their Name, Date of Foundation, Objects, Income, Officials, &c. Published Annually. Cr. 8vo, cloth, 1s. 6d.

Gardening Books:
Post 8vo, 1s. each; cl. limp, 1s. 6d. each.
A Year's Work in Garden and Greenhouse: Practical Advice to Amateur Gardeners as to the Management of the Flower, Fruit, and Frame Garden. By GEORGE GLENNY.
Our Kitchen Garden: The Plants we Grow, and How we Cook Them. By TOM JERROLD.
Household Horticulture: A Gossip about Flowers. By TOM and JANE JERROLD. Illustrated.
The Garden that Paid the Rent. By TOM JERROLD.

My Garden Wild, and What I Grew there. By F. G. HEATH. Crown 8vo, cloth extra, 5s.; gilt edges, 6s.

Garrett.—The Capel Girls: A Novel. By EDWARD GARRETT. Cr. 8vo, cl. ex., 3s. 6d.; post 8vo, illust. bds., 2s.

Gentleman's Magazine (The).
One Shilling Monthly. In addition to the Articles upon subjects in Literature, Science, and Art, for which this Magazine has so high a reputation, "Science Notes," by W. MATTIEU WILLIAMS, F.R.A.S., and "Table Talk," by SYLVANUS URBAN, appear monthly.
⁎ *Now ready, the Volume for* JANUARY *to* JUNE, 1887, *cloth extra, price* 8s. 6d.; *Cases for binding,* 2s. *each.*

Gentleman's Annual (The) for
1887. Consisting of one entire Novel, entitled The Golden Hoop: An After-Marriage Interlude. By T. W. SPEIGHT Author of "The Mysteries of Heron Dyke." Demy 8vo, picture cover, 1s.
[*Nov.* 10.

German Popular Stories. Collected by the Brothers GRIMM, and Translated by EDGAR TAYLOR. Edited, with an Introduction, by JOHN RUSKIN. With 22 Illustrations on Steel by GEORGE CRUIKSHANK. Square 8vo, cloth extra, 6s. 6d.; gilt edges, 7s. 6d.

Gibbon (Charles), Novels by:
Crown 8vo, cloth extra, 3s. 6d. each
post 8vo, illustrated boards, 2s. each.

Robin Gray.	Braes of Yarrow.
What will the World Say?	A Heart's Problem.
In Honour Bound.	The Golden Shaft.
Queen of the Meadow.	Of High Degree.
	Fancy Free.
The Flower of the Forest.	Loving a Dream.
	A Hard Knot.

Post 8vo, illustrated boards, 2s. each.
For Lack of Gold.
For the King. | In Pastures Green.
In Love and War.
By Mead and Stream.
Heart's Delight.   [*Preparing.*

Gilbert (William), Novels by:
Post 8vo, illustrated boards, 2s. each.
Dr. Austin's Guests.
The Wizard of the Mountain.
James Duke, Costermonger.

Gilbert (W. S.), Original Plays
by: In Two Series, each complete in itself, price 2s. 6d. each.
The FIRST SERIES contains—The Wicked World—Pygmalion and Galatea—Charity—The Princess—The Palace of Truth—Trial by Jury.
The SECOND SERIES contains—Broken Hearts—Engaged—Sweethearts—Gretchen—Dan'l Druce—Tom Cobb—H.M.S. Pinafore—The Sorcerer—The Pirates of Penzance.

Eight Original Comic Operas. Written by W. S. GILBERT. Containing: The Sorcerer—H.M.S. "Pinafore" —The Pirates of Penzance—Iolanthe — Patience — Princess Ida — The Mikado—Trial by Jury. Demy 8vo, cloth limp, 2s. 6d.

Glenny.—A Year's Work in Garden and Greenhouse: Practical Advice to Amateur Gardeners as to the Management of the Flower, Fruit, and Frame Garden. By GEORGE GLENNY. Post 8vo, 1s.; cloth, 1s. 6d.

Godwin.—Lives of the Necro- mancers. By WILLIAM GODWIN. Post 8vo, limp, 2s.

Golden Library, The:

Square 16mo (Tauchnitz size), cloth limp, 2s. per volume.

Bayard Taylor's Diversions of the Echo Club.

Bennett's (Dr. W. C.) Ballad History of England.

Bennett's (Dr.) Songs for Sailors.

Byron's Don Juan.

Godwin's (William) Lives of the Necromancers.

Holmes's Autocrat of the Breakfast Table. Introduction by SALA.

Holmes's Professor at the Breakfast Table.

Hood's Whims and Oddities. Complete. All the original Illustrations.

Irving's (Washington) Tales of a Traveller.

Jesse's (Edward) Scenes and Occupations of a Country Life.

Lamb's Essays of Ella. Both Series Complete in One Vol.

Leigh Hunt's Essays: A Tale for a Chimney Corner, and other Pieces. With Portrait, and Introduction by EDMUND OLLIER.

Mallory's (Sir Thomas) Mort d'Arthur: The Stories of King Arthur and of the Knights of the Round Table. Edited by B. MONTGOMERIE RANKING.

Pascal's Provincial Letters. A New Translation, with Historical Introduction and Notes, by T. M'CRIE, D.D.

Pope's Poetical Works. Complete.

Rochefoucauld's Maxims and Moral Reflections. With Notes, and Introductory Essay by SAINTE-BEUVE.

St. Pierre's Paul and Virginia, and The Indian Cottage. Edited, with Life, by the Rev. E. CLARKE.

Golden Treasury of Thought,

The: AN ENCYCLOPÆDIA OF QUOTATIONS from Writers of all Times and Countries. Selected and Edited by THEODORE TAYLOR. Crown 8vo, cloth gilt and gilt edges, 7s. 6d.

Graham. — The Professor's

Wife: A Story. By LEONARD GRAHAM. Fcap. 8vo, picture cover, 1s.

Greeks and Romans, The Life

of the, Described from Antique Monuments. By ERNST GUHL and W. KONER. Translated from the Third German Edition, and Edited by Dr. F. HUEFFER. 545 Illusts. New and Cheaper Edit., demy 8vo, cl. ex., 7s. 6d.

Greenaway (Kate) and Bret

Harte.—The Queen of the Pirate Isle. By BRET HARTE. With 25 original Drawings by KATE GREENAWAY, Reproduced in Colours by E. EVANS. Sm. 4to, bds., 5s.

Greenwood (James), Works by:

Crown 8vo, cloth extra, 3s. 6d. each.

The Wilds of London.

Low-Life Deeps: An Account of the Strange Fish to be Found There.

Dick Temple: A Novel. Post 8vo, illustrated boards, 2s.

Guyot.—The Earth and Man;

or, Physical Geography in its relation to the History of Mankind. By ARNOLD GUYOT. With Additions by Professors AGASSIZ, PIERCE, and GRAY; 12 Maps and Engravings on Steel, some Coloured, and copious Index. Crown 8vo, cloth extra, gilt, 4s. 6d.

Habberton (John), Author of

"Helen's Babies," Novels by:

Post 8vo, illustrated boards, 2s. each; cloth limp, 2s. 6d. each.

Brueton's Bayou.

Country Luck. [*Preparing.*

Hair (The): Its Treatment in

Health, Weakness, and Disease. Translated from the German of Dr. J. PINCUS. Crown 8vo, 1s.; cloth, 1s. 6d.

Hake (Dr. Thomas Gordon),

Poems by:

Crown 8vo, cloth extra, 6s. each.

New Symbols.

Legends of the Morrow.

The Serpent Play.

Maiden Ecstasy. Small 4to, cloth extra, 8s.

Hall.—Sketches of Irish Cha-

racter. By Mrs. S. C. HALL. With numerous Illustrations on Steel and Wood by MACLISE, GILBERT, HARVEY, and G. CRUIKSHANK. Medium 8vo, cloth extra, gilt, 7s. 6d.

Halliday.—Every-day Papers.

By ANDREW HALLIDAY. Post 8vo, illustrated boards, 2s.

Handwriting, The Philosophy

of. With over 100 Facsimiles and Explanatory Text. By DON FELIX DE SALAMANCA. Post 8vo, cl. limp, 2s. 6d.

Hanky-Panky: A Collection of

Very Easy Tricks, Very Difficult Tricks, White Magic, Sleight of Hand, &c. Edited by W. H. CREMER. With 200 Illusts. Crown 8vo, cloth extra, 4s. 6d.

Hardy (Lady Duffus). — Paul
Wynter's Sacrifice: A Story. By
Lady DUFFUS HARDY. Post 8vo, illust.
boards, 2s.

Hardy (Thomas).—Under the
Greenwood Tree. By THOMAS HARDY,
Author of "Far from the Madding
Crowd." With numerous Illustrations.
Crown 8vo, cloth extra, 3s. 6d. ; post
8vo, illustrated boards, 2s.

Harwood.—The Tenth Earl.
By J. BERWICK HARWOOD. Post 8vo,
illustrated boards, 2s.

Haweis (Mrs. H. R.), Works by :
The Art of Dress. With numerous
Illustrations. Small 8vo, illustrated
cover, 1s. ; cloth limp, 1s. 6d.
The Art of Beauty. New and Cheaper
Edition. Crown 8vo, cloth extra,
Coloured Frontispiece and Illusts.6s.
The Art of Decoration. Square 8vo,
handsomely bound and profusely
Illustrated, 10s. 6d.
Chaucer for Children: A Golden
Key. With Eight Coloured Pictures
and numerous Woodcuts. New
Edition, small 4to, cloth extra, 6s.
Chaucer for Schools. Demy 8vo,
cloth limp, 2s. 6d.

Haweis (Rev. H. R.).—American
Humorists. Including WASHINGTON
IRVING, OLIVER WENDELL HOLMES,
JAMES RUSSELL LOWELL, ARTEMUS
WARD, MARK TWAIN, and BRET HARTE.
By the Rev. H. R. HAWEIS, M.A.
Crown 8vo, cloth extra, 6s.

Hawthorne (Julian), Novels by.
Crown 8vo, cloth extra, 3s. 6d. each ;
post 8vo, illustrated boards, 2s. each.

Garth. | Sebastian Strome.
Ellice Quentin. | Dust.
Prince Saroni's Wife.
Fortune's Fool. | Beatrix Randolph.

Crown 8vo, cloth extra, 3s. 6d. each.
Miss Cadogna.
Love—or a Name.

Mrs. Gainsborough's Diamonds.
Fcap. 8vo, illustrated cover, 1s.

Hays.—Women of the Day: A
Biographical Dictionary of Notable
Contemporaries. By FRANCES HAYS.
Crown 8vo, cloth extra, 5s.

Heath (F. G.). — My Garden
Wild, and What I Grew There. By
FRANCIS GEORGE HEATH, Author of
"The Fern World," &c. Crown 8vo,
cloth extra, 5s. ; cl. gil gilt edges, 6s.

Helps (Sir Arthur), Works by .
Post 8vo, cloth limp, 2s. 6d. each.
Animals and their Masters.
Social Pressure.

Ivan de Biron: A Novel. Crown 8vo,
cloth extra, 3s. 6d. ; post 8vo, illustrated boards, 2s.

Herman.—One Traveller Re-
turns: A Romance. By HENRY HER-
MAN and D. CHRISTIE MURRAY. Crown
8vo, cloth extra, 6s. [Preparing

Herrick's (Robert) Hesperides,
Noble Numbers, and Complete Collected Poems. With Memorial-Introduction and Notes by the Rev. A. B.
GROSART, D.D., Steel Portrait, Index
of First Lines, and Glossarial Index,
&c. Three Vols., crown 8vo, cloth, 18s.

Hesse-Wartegg (Chevalier
Ernst von), Works by :
Tunis: The Land and the People.
With 22 Illustrations. Crown 8vo,
cloth extra, 3s. 6d.
The New South-West: Travelling
Sketches from Kansas, New Mexico,
Arizona, and Northern Mexico.
With 100 fine Illustrations and Three
Maps. Demy 8vo, cloth extra,
14s. [In preparation.

Herbert.—The Poems of Lord
Herbert of Cherbury. Edited, with
Introduction, by J. CHURTON COLLINS.
Crown 8vo, bound in parchment, 8s.

Hindley (Charles), Works by :
Crown 8vo, cloth extra, 3s. 6d. each.
Tavern Anecdotes and Sayings: In-
cluding the Origin of Signs, and
Reminiscences connected with
Taverns, Coffee Houses, Clubs, &c.
With Illustrations.
The Life and Adventures of a Cheap
Jack. By One of the Fraternity.
Edited by CHARLES HINDLEY.

Hoey.—The Lover's Creed.
By Mrs. CASHEL HOEY. With Frontispiece by P. MACNAB. Post 8vo, illustrated boards, 2s.

Holmes (O. Wendell), Works by :
The Autocrat of the Breakfast-
Table. Illustrated by J. GORDON
THOMSON. Post 8vo, cloth limp,
2s. 6d.—Another Edition in smaller
type, with an Introduction by G. A.
SALA. Post 8vo, cloth limp, 2s.
The Professor at the Breakfast-
Table ; with the Story of Iris. Post
8vo, cloth limp, 2s.

Holmes. — The Science of
Voice Production and Voice Preservation: A Popular Manual for the Use of Speakers and Singers. By GORDON HOLMES, M.D. With Illustrations. Crown 8vo, 1s.; cloth, 1s. 6d.

Hood (Thomas):
Hood's Choice Works, in Prose and Verse. Including the Cream of the COMIC ANNUALS. With Life of the Author, Portrait, and 200 Illustrations. Crown 8vo, cloth extra, 7s. 6d.

Hood's Whims and Oddities. Complete. With all the original Illustrations. Post 8vo, cloth limp, 2s.

Hood (Tom), Works by:
From Nowhere to the North Pole: A Noah's Arkæological Narrative. With 25 Illustrations by W. BRUNTON and E. C. BARNES. Square crown 8vo, cloth extra, gilt edges, 6s.

A Golden Heart: A Novel. Post 8vo, illustrated boards, 2s.

Hook's (Theodore) Choice Humorous Works, including his Ludicrous Adventures, Bons Mots, Puns and Hoaxes. With a New Life of the Author, Portraits, Facsimiles, and Illusts. Cr. 8vo, cl. extra, gilt, 7s. 6d.

Hooper. — The House of Raby:
A Novel. By Mrs. GEORGE HOOPER. Post 8vo, illustrated boards, 2s.

Hopkins — "'Twixt Love and
Duty:" A Novel. By TIGHE HOPKINS. Crown 8vo, cloth extra, 6s.; post 8vo, illustrated boards, 2s.

Horne. — Orion : An Epic Poem,
in Three Books. By RICHARD HENGIST HORNE. With Photographic Portrait from a Medallion by SUMMERS. Tenth Edition, crown 8vo, cloth extra, 7s.

Howell. — Conflicts of Capital
and Labour, Historically and Economically considered: Being a History and Review of the Trade Unions of Great Britain. By GEO. HOWELL M.P. Crown 8vo, cloth extra, 7s. 6d.

Hunt (Mrs. Alfred), Novels by:
Crown 8vo, cloth extra, 3s. 6d. each; post 8vo, illustrated boards, 2s. each.

Thornicroft's Model.
The Leaden Casket.
Self-Condemned.
That other Person.

Hunt. — Essays by Leigh Hunt.
A Tale for a Chimney Corner, and other Pieces. With Portrait and Introduction by EDMUND OLLIER. Post 8vo, cloth limp, 2s.

Hydrophobia: an Account of M.
PASTEUR's System. Containing a Translation of all his Communications on the Subject, the Technique of his Method, and the latest Statistical Results. By RENAUD SUZOR, M.B., C.M. Edin., and M.D. Paris, Commissioned by the Government of the Colony of Mauritius to study M. PASTEUR's new Treatment in Paris. With 7 Illustrations. Crown 8vo, cloth extra, 6s.

Indoor Paupers. By ONE OF THEM. Crown 8vo, 1s.; cloth, 1s. 6d.

Ingelow. — Fated to be Free : A
Novel. By JEAN INGELOW. Crown 8vo, cloth extra, 3s. 6d.; post 8vo, illustrated boards, 2s.

Irish Wit and Humour, Songs
of. Collected and Edited by A. PERCEVAL GRAVES. Post 8vo, cloth limp, 2s. 6d.

Irving — Tales of a Traveller.
By WASHINGTON IRVING. Post 8vo, cloth limp, 2s.

Jay (Harriett), Novels by:
Post 8vo, illustrated boards, 2s. each.
The Dark Colleen.
The Queen of Connaught.

Janvier. — Practical Keramics
for Students. By CATHERINE A. JANVIER. Crown 8vo, cloth extra, 6s.

Jefferies (Richard), Works by:
Crown 8vo, cloth extra, 6s. each.
The Life of the Fields.
The Open Air.

Nature near London. Crown 8vo, cloth extra, 6s.; post 8vo, cloth limp, 2s. 6d.

Jennings (H. J.), Works by:
Curiosities of Criticism. Post 8vo, cloth limp, 2s. 6d.

Lord Tennyson: A Biographical Sketch. With a Photograph-Portrait. Crown 8vo, cloth extra, 6s.

Jerrold (Tom), Works by:
Post 8vo, 1s. each; cloth, 1s. 6d. each.
The Garden that Paid the Rent.
Household Horticulture: A Gossip about Flowers. Illustrated.
Our Kitchen Garden: The Plants we Grow, and How we Cook Them.

Jesse.—Scenes and Occupa-
tions of a Country Life. By EDWARD
JESSE. Post 8vo, cloth limp, 2s.

Jeux d'Esprit. Collected and
Edited by HENRY S. LEIGH. Post 8vo,
cloth limp, 2s. 6d.

Jones (Wm., F.S.A.), Works by:
Crown 8vo, cloth extra, 7s. 6d. each.
Finger-Ring Lore: Historical, Le-
gendary, and Anecdotal. With over
Two Hundred Illustrations.
Credulities, Past and Present; in-
cluding the Sea and Seamen, Miners,
Talismans, Word and Letter Divina-
tion Exorcising and Blessing of
Animals, Birds, Eggs, Luck, &c.
With an Etched Frontispiece.
**Crowns and Coronations: A History
of Regalia in all Times and Coun-
tries.** With One Hundred Illus-
trations.

Jonson's (Ben) Works. With
Notes Critical and Explanatory, and
a Biographical Memoir by WILLIAM
GIFFORD. Edited by Colonel CUN-
NINGHAM. Three Vols., crown 8vo,
cloth extra, 18s.; or separately, 6s. each.

Josephus, The Complete Works
of. Translated by WHISTON. Containing both "The Antiquities of the
Jews" and "The Wars of the Jews."
Two Vols., 8vo, with 52 Illustrations
and Maps, cloth extra, gilt, 14s.

Kempt.—Pencil and Palette:
Chapters on Art and Artists. By ROBERT
KEMPT. Post 8vo, cloth limp, 2s. 6d.

Kershaw.—Colonial Facts and
Fictions: Humorous Sketches. By
MARK KERSHAW. Post 8vo, illustrated
boards, 2s.; cloth, 2s. 6d.

King (R. Ashe), Novels by:
Crown 8vo, cloth extra, 3s. 6d. each;
post 8vo, illustrated boards, 2s. each.
A Drawn Game.
"The Wearing of the Green."

Kingsley (Henry), Novels by:
Oakshott Castle. Post 8vo, illustrated boards, 2s.
Number Seventeen. Crown 8vo, cloth
extra, 3s. 6d.

Knight.—The Patient's Vade
Mecum: How to get most Benefit
from Medical Advice. By WILLIAM
KNIGHT, M.R.C.S., and EDWARD
KNIGHT, L.R.C.P. Crown 8vo, 1s.;
cloth, 1s. 6d.

Lamb (Charles):
Lamb's Complete Works, in Prose
and Verse, reprinted from the Ori-
ginal Editions, with many Pieces
hitherto unpublished. Edited, with
Notes and Introduction, by R. H.
SHEPHERD. With Two Portraits and
Facsimile of Page of the "Essay on
Roast Pig." Cr. 8vo, cl. extra, 7s. 6d.
The Essays of Elia. Complete Edi-
tion. Post 8vo, cloth extra, 2s.
Poetry for Children, and Prince
Dorus. By CHARLES LAMB. Care-
fully reprinted from unique copies.
Small 8vo, cloth extra, 5s.
Little Essays: Sketches and Charac-
ters. By CHARLES LAMB. Selected
from his Letters by PERCY FITZ-
GERALD. Post 8vo, cloth limp, 2s. 6d.

Lane's Arabian Nights, &c.:
The Thousand and One Nights:
commonly called, in England, "THE
ARABIAN NIGHTS' ENTERTAIN-
MENTS." A New Translation from
the Arabic, with copious Notes, by
EDWARD WILLIAM LANE. Illustrated
by many hundred Engravings on
Wood, from Original Designs by
WM. HARVEY. A New Edition, from
a Copy annotated by the Translator,
edited by his Nephew, EDWARD
STANLEY POOLE. With a Preface by
STANLEY LANE-POOLE. Three Vols.,
demy 8vo, cloth extra, 7s. 6d. each.
Arabian Society in the Middle Ages:
Studies from "The Thousand and
One Nights." By EDWARD WILLIAM
LANE, Author of "The Modern
Egyptians," &c. Edited by STANLEY
LANE-POOLE. Cr. 8vo, cloth extra, 6s.

Lares and Penates; or, The
Background of Life. By FLORENCE
CADDY. Crown 8vo, cloth extra, 6s.

Larwood (Jacob), Works by:
The Story of the London Parks.
With Illustrations. Crown 8vo, cloth
extra, 3s. 6d.

Post 8vo, cloth limp, 2s. 6d. each.
Forensic Anecdotes.
Theatrical Anecdotes.

Life in London; or, The History
of Jerry Hawthorn and Corinthian
Tom. With the whole of CRUIK-
SHANK'S Illustrations, in Colours, after
the Originals. Crown 8vo, cloth extra,
7s. 6d.

Linton (E. Lynn), Works by:
Post 8vo, cloth limp, 2s. 6d. each.
Witch Stories.
The True Story of Joshua Davidson.
Ourselves: Essays on Women.

LINTON (E. LYNN), *continued—*
Crown 8vo, cloth extra, 3s. 6d. each; post 8vo, illustrated boards, 2s. each.
Patricia Kemball.
The Atonement of Leam Dundas.
The World Well Lost.
Under which Lord?
With a Silken Thread.
The Rebel of the Family.
"My Love!" | Ione.

Longfellow:
Crown 8vo, cloth extra, 7s. 6d. each.
Longfellow's Complete Prose Works. Including "Outre Mer," "Hyperion," "Kavanagh," "The Poets and Poetry of Europe," and "Driftwood." With Portrait and Illustrations by VALENTINE BROMLEY.
Longfellow's Poetical Works. Carefully Reprinted from the Original Editions. With numerous fine Illustrations on Steel and Wood.

Long Life, Aids to: A Medical, Dietetic, and General Guide in Health and Disease. By N. E. DAVIES, L.R.C.P. Crown 8vo, 2s.; cloth limp, 2s. 6d.

Lucy.—Gideon Fleyce: A Novel. By HENRY W. LUCY. Crown 8vo, cl. ex., 3s. 6d.; post 8vo, illust. bds., 2s.

Lusiad (The) of Camoens. Translated into English Spenserian Verse by ROBERT FFRENCH DUFF. Demy 8vo, with Fourteen full-page Plates, cloth boards, 18s.

Macalpine. — Teresa Itasca, and other Stories. By AVERY MAC-ALPINE. Crown 8vo, bound in canvas, 2s. 6d.

McCarthy (Justin H., M.P.), Works by:
An Outline of the History of Ireland, from the Earliest Times to the Present Day. Cr. 8vo, 1s.; cloth, 1s. 6d.
Ireland since the Union: Sketches of Irish History from 1798 to 1886. Crown 8vo, cloth extra, 6s.
The Case for Home Rule. Crown 8vo, cloth extra, 5s.
England under Gladstone, 1880-85. Second Edition, revised. Crown 8vo, cloth extra, 6s.
Doom! An Atlantic Episode. Crown 8vo, 1s.; cloth, 1s. 6d.
Our Sensation Novel. Edited by JUSTIN H. MCCARTHY. Crown 8vo, 1s.; cloth, 1s. 6d.
Hafiz in London. Choicely printed. Small 8vo, gold cloth, 3s. 6d.

McCarthy (Justin, M.P.), Works by:
A History of Our Own Times, from the Accession of Queen Victoria to the General Election of 1880. Four Vols. demy 8vo, cloth extra, 12s. each.—Also a POPULAR EDITION, in Four Vols. cr. 8vo, cl. extra, 6s. each. —And a JUBILEE EDITION, with an Appendix of Events to the end of 1886, complete in Two Vols., square 8vo, cloth extra, 7s. 6d. each.
A Short History of Our Own Times. One Vol., crown 8vo, cloth extra, 6s.
History of the Four Georges. Four Vols. demy 8vo, cloth extra, 12s. each.   [Vol. I. *now ready.*

Crown 8vo, cloth extra, 3s. 6d. each; post 8vo, illustrated boards, 2s. each.
Dear Lady Disdain.
The Waterdale Neighbours.
A Fair Saxon.
Miss Misanthrope.
Donna Quixote.
The Comet of a Season.
Maid of Athens.
Camiola: A Girl with a Fortune.

Post 8vo, illustrated boards, 2s. each.
Linley Rochford.
My Enemy's Daughter.

"The Right Honourable:" A Romance of Society and Politics. By JUSTIN MCCARTHY, M.P., and Mrs. CAMPBELL-PRAED. New and Cheaper Edition, crown 8vo, cloth extra, 6s.

MacDonald (George, LL.D.), Works by:
Works of Fancy and Imagination. Pocket Edition, Ten Volumes, in handsome cloth case, 21s. Vol. I. WITHIN AND WITHOUT. THE HIDDEN LIFE.—Vol. 2. THE DISCIPLE. THE GOSPEL WOMEN. A BOOK OF SONNETS. ORGAN SONGS.—Vol. 3. VIOLIN SONGS. SONGS OF THE DAYS AND NIGHTS. A BOOK OF DREAMS. ROADSIDE POEMS. POEMS FOR CHILDREN. Vol. 4. PARABLES. BALLADS. SCOTCH SONGS.—Vols. 5 and 6. PHANTASTES: A Faerie Romance.—Vol. 7. THE PORTENT.— Vol. 8. THE LIGHT PRINCESS. THE GIANT'S HEART. SHADOWS. — Vol. 9. CROSS PURPOSES. THE GOLDEN KEY. THE CARASOYN. LITTLE DAYLIGHT.—Vol. 10. THE CRUEL PAINTER. THE WOW O' RIVVEN. THE CASTLE. THE BROKEN SWORDS. THE GRAY WOLF. UNCLE CORNELIUS.
The Volumes are also sold separately in Grolier-pattern cloth, 2s. 6d. each.

Macdonell.—Quaker Cousins:
A Novel. By AGNES MACDONELL.
Crown 8vo, cloth extra, 3s. 6d.; post
8vo, illustrated boards, 2s.

Macgregor. — Pastimes and
Players. Notes on Popular Games.
By ROBERT MACGREGOR. Post 8vo,
cloth limp, 2s. 6d.

Mackay.—Interludes and Un-
dertones; or, Music at Twilight. By
CHARLES MACKAY, LL.D. Crown 8vo,
cloth extra, 6s.

Maclise Portrait-Gallery (The)
of Illustrious Literary Characters;
with Memoirs—Biographical, Critical,
Bibliographical, and Anecdotal—illus-
trative of the Literature of the former
half of the Present Century. By
WILLIAM BATES, B.A. With 85 Portraits printed on an India Tint. Crown
8vo, cloth extra, 7s. 6d.

Macquoid (Mrs.), Works by:
Square 8vo, cloth extra, 10s. 6d. each.
In the Ardennes. With 50 fine Illus-
trations by THOMAS R. MACQUOID.
Pictures and Legends from Nor-
mandy and Brittany. With numer-
ous Illustrations by THOMAS R.
MACQUOID.
About Yorkshire. With 67 Illustra-
tions by T. R. MACQUOID.

Crown 8vo, cloth extra, 7s. 6d. each.
Through Normandy. With 90 Illus-
trations by T. R. MACQUOID.
Through Brittany. With numerous
Illustrations by T. R. MACQUOID.

Post 8vo, illustrated boards, 2s. each.
The Evil Eye, and other Stories.
Lost Rose.

Magician's Own Book (The):
Performances with Cups and Balls,
Eggs, Hats, Handkerchiefs, &c. All
from actual Experience. Edited by
W. H. CREMER. With 200 Illustrations.
Crown 8vo, cloth extra, 4s. 6d.

Magic Lantern (The), and its
Management: including full Prac-
tical Directions for producing the
Limelight, making Oxygen Gas, and
preparing Lantern Slides. By T. C.
HEPWORTH. With 10 Illustrations.
Crown 8vo, 1s.; cloth, 1s. 6d.

Magna Charta. An exact Facsimile of the Original in the British
Museum, printed on fine plate paper,
3 feet by 2 feet, with Arms and Seals
emblazoned in Gold and Colours. 5s.

Mallock (W. H.), Works by:
The New Republic; or, Culture, Faith
and Philosophy in an English Country
House. Post 8vo, cloth limp, 2s. 6d.;
Cheap Edition, illustrated boards, 2s.
The New Paul and Virginia; or, Posi-
tivism on an Island. Post 8vo, cloth
limp, 2s. 6d.
Poems. Small 4to, in parchment, 8s.
Is Life worth Living? Crown 8vo,
cloth extra, 6s.

Mallory's (Sir Thomas) Mort
d'Arthur: The Stories of King Arthur
and of the Knights of the Round Table.
Edited by B. MONTGOMERIE RANKING.
Post 8vo, cloth limp, 2s.

Mark Twain, Works by:
The Choice Works of Mark Twain.
Revised and Corrected throughout by
the Author. With Life, Portrait, and
numerous Illustrations. Crown 8vo,
cloth extra, 7s. 6d.
The Innocents Abroad; or, The New
Pilgrim's Progress: Being some Ac-
count of the Steamship "Quaker
City's" Pleasure Excursion to
Europe and the Holy Land. With
234 Illustrations. Crown 8vo, cloth
extra, 7s. 6d.—Cheap Edition (under
the title of "MARK TWAIN'S PLEASURE
TRIP"), post 8vo, illust. boards, 2s.
Roughing It, and The Innocents at
Home. With 200 Illustrations by F.
A. FRASER. Cr. 8vo, cl. ex., 7s. 6d.
The Gilded Age. By MARK TWAIN
and CHARLES DUDLEY WARNER.
With 212 Illustrations by T. COPPIN.
Crown 8vo, cloth extra, 7s. 6d.
The Adventures of Tom Sawyer.
With 111 Illustrations. Crown 8vo,
cloth extra, 7s. 6d.—Cheap Edition,
post 8vo, illustrated boards, 2s.
The Prince and the Pauper. With
nearly 200 Illustrations. Crown 8vo,
cloth extra, 7s. 6d.
A Tramp Abroad. With 314 Illusts.
Cr. 8vo, cloth extra, 7s. 6d.—Cheap
Edition, post 8vo, illust. bds., 2s.
The Stolen White Elephant, &c.
Crown 8vo, cloth extra, 6s.; post 8vo,
illustrated boards, 2s.
Life on the Mississippi. With about
300 Original Illustrations. Crown
8vo, cloth extra, 7s. 6d.—Cheap Edition, post 8vo, illustrated boards, 2s.
The Adventures of Huckleberry
Finn. With 174 Illustrations by
E. W. KEMBLE. Crown 8vo, cloth
extra, 7s. 6d.—Cheap Edition, post
8vo, illustrated boards, 2s.

Marlowe's Works. Including
his Translations. Edited, with Notes
and Introductions, by Col. CUN-
NINGHAM. Crown 8vo, cloth extra, 6s.

Marryat (Florence), Novels by:
Crown 8vo, cloth extra, 3s. 6d. each;
post 8vo, illustrated boards, 2s. each.
Open! Sesame! | Written in Fire

Post 8vo, illustrated boards, 2s. each.
A Harvest of Wild Oats.
A Little Stepson.
Fighting the Air.

Massinger's Plays. From the
Text of WILLIAM GIFFORD. Edited
by Col. CUNNINGHAM. Crown 8vo,
cloth extra, 6s.

Masterman.—Half a Dozen
Daughters: A Novel. By J. MASTER-
MAN. Post 8vo, illustrated boards, 2s.

Matthews.—A Secret of the
Sea, &c. By BRANDER MATTHEWS.
Post 8vo, illustrated boards, 2s ; cloth,
2s. 6d.

Mayfair Library, The:
Post 8vo, cloth limp, 2s. 6d. per Volume.
A Journey Round My Room. By
XAVIER DE MAISTRE. Translated
by HENRY ATTWELL.
Quips and Quiddities. Selected by
W. DAVENPORT ADAMS.
The Agony Column of "The Times,"
from 1800 to 1870. Edited, with an
Introduction, by ALICE CLAY.
Melancholy Anatomised: A Popular
Abridgment of "Burton's Anatomy
of Melancholy."
Gastronomy as a Fine Art. By
BRILLAT-SAVARIN.
The Speeches of Charles Dickens.
Literary Frivolities, Fancies, Follies,
and Frolics. By W. T. DOBSON.
Poetical Ingenuities and Eccentrici-
ties. Selected and Edited by W. T.
DOBSON.
The Cupboard Papers. By FIN-BEC.
Original Plays by W. S. GILBERT.
FIRST SERIES. Containing: The
Wicked World — Pygmalion and
Galatea—Charity — The Princess—
The Palace of Truth—Trial by Jury.
Original Plays by W. S. GILBERT.
SECOND SERIES. Containing: Broken
Hearts — Engaged — Sweethearts —
Gretchen—Dan'l Druce—Tom Cobb
—H.M.S. Pinafore — The Sorcerer
—The Pirates of Penzance.
Songs of Irish Wit and Humour.
Collected and Edited by A. PERCEVAL
GRAVES.
Animals and their Masters. By Sir
ARTHUR HELPS.
Social Pressure. By Sir A. HELPS.
Curiosities of Criticism. By HENRY
J. JENNINGS.
The Autocrat of the Breakfast-Table.
By OLIVER WENDELL HOLMES. Il-
lustrated by J. GORDON THOMSON.

MAYFAIR LIBRARY, *continued—*
Pencil and Palette. By ROBERT
KEMPT.
Little Essays: Sketches and Charac-
ters. By CHAS. LAMB. Selected from
his Letters by PERCY FITZGERALD.
Forensic Anecdotes; or, Humour and
Curiosities of the Law and Men of
Law. By JACOB LARWOOD.
Theatrical Anecdotes. By JACOB
LARWOOD.
Joux d'Esprit. Edited by HENRY S.
LEIGH.
True History of Joshua Davidson.
By E. LYNN LINTON.
Witch Stories. By E. LYNN LINTON.
Ourselves: Essays on Women. By
E. LYNN LINTON.
Pastimes and Players. By ROBERT
MACGREGOR.
The New Paul and Virginia. By
W. H. MALLOCK.
New Republic. By W. H. MALLOCK.
Puck on Pegasus. By H. CHOLMONDE-
LEY-PENNELL.
Pegasus Re-Saddled. By H. CHOL-
MONDELEY-PENNELL. Illustrated by
GEORGE DU MAURIER.
Muses of Mayfair. Edited by H.
CHOLMONDELEY-PENNELL.
Thoreau: His Life and Aims. By
H. A. PAGE.
Puniana. By the Hon. HUGH ROWLEY.
More Puniana. By the Hon. HUGH
ROWLEY.
The Philosophy of Handwriting. By
DON FELIX DE SALAMANCA.
By Stream and Sea. By WILLIAM
SENIOR.
Old Stories Re-told. By WALTER
THORNBURY.
Leaves from a Naturalist's Note-
Book. By Dr. ANDREW WILSON.

Mayhew.—London Characters
and the Humorous Side of London
Life. By HENRY MAYHEW. With
numerous Illustrations. Crown 8vo,
cloth extra, 3s. 6d.

Medicine, Family.—One Thou-
sand Medical Maxims and Surgical
Hints, for Infancy, Adult Life, Middle
Age, and Old Age. By N. E. DAVIES,
L.R.C.P. Lond. Cr. 8vo, 1s.; cl., 1s. 6d.

Merry Circle (The): A Book of
New Intellectual Games and Amusements. By CLARA BELLEW. With
numerous Illustrations. Crown 8vo,
cloth extra, 4s. 6d.

Mexican Mustang (On a),
through Texas, from the Gulf to the
Rio Grande. A New Book of American Humour. By ALEX. E. SWEET and
J. ARMOY KNOX, Editors of "Texas
Siftings." With 265 Illusts. Cr. 8vo,
cloth extra, 7s. 6d.

Middlemass (Jean), Novels by:
Post 8vo, illustrated boards, 2s. each.
Touch and Go. | Mr. Dorillion.

Miller. — Physiology for the Young; or, The House of Life: Human Physiology, with its application to the Preservation of Health. For Classes and Popular Reading. With numerous Illusts. By Mrs. F. FENWICK MILLER. Small 8vo, cloth limp, 2s. 6d.

Milton (J. L.), Works by:
Sm. 8vo, 1s. each; cloth ex., 1s. 6d. each.

The Hygiene of the Skin. A Concise Set of Rules for the Management of the Skin; with Directions for Diet, Wines, Soaps, Baths, &c.
The Bath in Diseases of the Skin.
The Laws of Life, and their Relation to Diseases of the Skin.

Molesworth (Mrs.).—Hathercourt Rectory. By Mrs. MOLESWORTH, Author of "The Cuckoo Clock," &c. Cr. 8vo, cl. extra, 4s. 6d.

Moncrieff. — The Abdication; or, Time Tries All. An Historical Drama. By W. D. SCOTT-MONCRIEFF. With Seven Etchings by JOHN PETTIE, R.A., W. Q. ORCHARDSON, R.A., J. MACWHIRTER, A.R.A., COLIN HUNTER, A.R.A., R. MACBETH, A.R.A., and TOM GRAHAM, R.S.A. Large 4to, bound in buckram, 21s.

Murray (D. Christie), Novels by. Crown 8vo, cloth extra, 3s. 6d. each; post 8vo, illustrated boards, 2s. each.
A Life's Atonement. | A Model Father.
Joseph's Coat. | Coals of Fire.
By the Gate of the Sea.
Val Strange. | Hearts.
The Way of the World.
A Bit of Human Nature.
First Person Singular.
Cynic Fortune.

Old Blazer's Hero. With Three Illustrations by A. McCORMICK. Crown 8vo, cloth extra, 6s.
One Traveller Returns. By D. CHRISTIE MURRAY and HENRY HERMAN. Cr. 8vo, cl. ex., 6s. [*Preparing.*

North Italian Folk. By Mrs. COMYNS CARR. Illust. by RANDOLPH CALDECOTT. Sq. 8vo, cl. ex., 7s. 6d.

Novelists. — Half-Hours with the Best Novelists of the Century: Choice Readings from the finest Novels. Edited, with Critical and Biographical Notes, by H. T. MACKENZIE BELL. Crown 8vo, cl. ex., 3s. 6d. [*Preparing.*

Nursery Hints: A Mother's Guide in Health and Disease. By N. E. DAVIES, L.R.C.P. Crown 8vo, 1s.; cloth, 1s. 6d.

O'Connor.—Lord Beaconsfield: A Biography. By T. P. O'CONNOR, M.P. Sixth Edition, with a New Preface, bringing the work down to the Death of Lord Beaconsfield. Crown 8vo, cloth extra, 7s. 6d.

O'Hanlon. — The Unforeseen: A Novel. By ALICE O'HANLON. New and Cheaper Edition. Post 8vo, illustrated boards, 2s.

Oliphant (Mrs.) Novels by:
Whiteladies. With Illustrations by ARTHUR HOPKINS and H. WOODS. Crown 8vo, cloth extra, 3s. 6d.; post 8vo, illustrated boards, 2s.
Crown 8vo, cloth extra, 4s. 6d. each.
The Primrose Path.
The Greatest Heiress in England.

O'Reilly.—Phœbe's Fortunes: A Novel. With Illustrations by HENRY TUCK. Post 8vo, illustrated boards, 2s.

O'Shaughnessy (Arth.), Works by:
Songs of a Worker. Fcap. 8vo, cloth extra, 7s. 6d.
Music and Moonlight. Fcap. 8vo, cloth extra, 7s. 6d.
Lays of France. Cr. 8vo, cl. ex., 10s. 6d.

Ouida, Novels by. Crown 8vo, cloth extra, 5s. each; post 8vo, illustrated boards, 2s. each.
Held in Bondage. | Signa.
Strathmore. | In a Winter City.
Chandos. | Ariadne
Under Two Flags. | Friendship.
Cecil Castlemaine's Gage. | Moths.
| Pipistrello.
Idalia | A Village Commune.
Tricotrin. |
Puck. | Bimbi.
Folle Farine. | In Maremma
Two Little Wooden Shoes. | Wanda.
| Frescoes. [ine.
A Dog of Flanders. | Princess Naprax-
Pascarel. | Othmar.

Wisdom, Wit, and Pathos, selected from the Works of OUIDA by F. SYDNEY MORRIS. Sm. cr. 8vo, cl. ex., 5s.

Parliamentary Elections and Electioneering in the Old Days (A History of). Showing the State of Political Parties and Party Warfare at the Hustings and in the House of Commons from the Stuarts to Queen Victoria. Illustrated from the original Political Squibs, Lampoons, Pictorial Satires, and Popular Caricatures of the Time. By JOSEPH GREGO, Author of "Rowlandson and his Works," "The Life of Gillray," &c. Demy 8vo, cloth extra, with a Frontispiece coloured by hand, and nearly 100 Illustrations, 16s.

Page (H. A.), Works by:
Thoreau: His Life and Aims: A Study. With Portrait. Post 8vo, cl. limp, 2s. 6d.
Lights on the Way: Some Tales within a Tale. By the late J. H. ALEXANDER, B.A. Edited by H. A. PAGE. Crown 8vo, cloth extra, 6s.
Animal Anecdotes. Arranged on a New Principle. Cr. 8vo, cl. extra, 5s.

Pascal's Provincial Letters. A New Translation, with Historical Introduction and Notes, by T. M'CRIE, D.D. Post 8vo, cloth limp, 2s.

Patient's (The) Vade Mecum: How to get most Benefit from Medical Advice. By WILLIAM KNIGHT, M.R.C.S., and EDWARD KNIGHT, L.R.C.P. Crown 8vo, 1s.; cloth, 1s. 6d.

Paul Ferroll:
Post 8vo, illustrated boards, 2s. each.
Paul Ferroll: A Novel.
Why Paul Ferroll Killed his Wife.

Payn (James), Novels by:
Crown 8vo, cloth extra, 3s. 6d. each
post 8vo, illustrated boards, 2s. each.
Lost Sir Massingberd.
The Best of Husbands.
Walter's Word.
Less Black than we're Painted.
By Proxy. | High Spirits.
Under One Roof.
A Confidential Agent.
Some Private Views.
A Grape from a Thorn.
For Cash Only. | From Exile.
The Canon's Ward.
The Talk of the Town.

Post 8vo, illustrated boards, 2s. each.
Kit: A Memory. | Carlyon's Year.
A Perfect Treasure.
Bentinck's Tutor.|Murphy's Master.
What He Cost Her.
Fallen Fortunes. | Halves.
A County Family. | At Her Mercy.
A Woman's Vengeance.
Cecil's Tryst.
The Clyffards of Clyffe.
The Family Scapegrace.
The Foster Brothers.| Found Dead.
Gwendoline's Harvest.
Humorous Stories.
Like Father, Like Son.
A Marine Residence.
Married Beneath Him.
Mirk Abbey. | Not Wooed, but Won.
Two Hundred Pounds Reward.

In Peril and Privation: Stories of Marine Adventure Re-told. A Book for Boys. With numerous Illustrations. Crown 8vo, cloth gilt, 6s.
Holiday Tasks: Being Essays written in Vacation Time. Crown 8vo, cloth extra, 6s.
Glow-Worm Tales. 3 Vols., cr. 8vo.

Paul.—Gentle and Simple. By MARGARET AGNES PAUL. With a Frontispiece by HELEN PATERSON. Cr. 8vo, cloth extra, 3s. 6d.; post 8vo, illustrated boards, 2s.

Pears.—The Present Depression in Trade: Its Causes and Remedies. Being the "Pears" Prize Essays (of One Hundred Guineas). By EDWIN GOADBY and WILLIAM WATT. With an Introductory Paper by Prof. LEONE LEVI, F.S.A., F.S.S. Demy 8vo, 1s.

Pennell (H. Cholmondeley), Works by:
Post 8vo, cloth limp, 2s. 6d. each.
Puck on Pegasus. With Illustrations.
Pegasus Re-Saddled. With Ten full-page Illusts. by G. DU MAURIER.
The Muses of Mayfair. Vers de Société, Selected and Edited by H. C. PENNELL.

Phelps (E. Stuart), Works by:
Post 8vo, 1s. each; cl. limp, 1s. 6d. each.
Beyond the Gates. By the Author of "The Gates Ajar."
An Old Maid's Paradise.
Burglars in Paradise.

Pirkis (Mrs. C. L.), Novels by:
Trooping with Crows. Fcap. 8vo, picture cover, 1s.
Lady Lovelace. Post 8vo, illustrated boards, 2s.   [*Preparing.*

Planché (J. R.), Works by:
The Pursuivant of Arms; or, Heraldry Founded upon Facts. With Coloured Frontispiece and 200 Illustrations. Cr. 8vo, cloth extra, 7s. 6d.
Songs and Poems, from 1819 to 1879. Edited, with an Introduction, by his Daughter, Mrs. MACKARNESS. Crown 8vo, cloth extra, 6s.

Plutarch's Lives of Illustrious Men. Translated from the Greek, with Notes Critical and Historical, and a Life of Plutarch, by JOHN and WILLIAM LANGHORNE. Two Vols., 8vo, cloth extra, with Portraits, 10s. 6d.

Poe (Edgar Allan):—
The Choice Works, in Prose and Poetry, of EDGAR ALLAN POE. With an Introductory Essay by CHARLES BAUDELAIRE, Portrait and Facsimiles. Crown 8vo, cl. extra, 7s. 6d.
The Mystery of Marie Roget, and other Stories. Post 8vo, illust.bds.,2s.

Pope's Poetical Works. Complete in One Vol. Post 8vo, cl. limp, 2s.

Praed (Mrs. Campbell-).—"The Right Honourable:" A Romance of Society and Politics. By Mrs. CAMPBELL-PRAED and JUSTIN MCCARTHY, M.P. Cr. 8vo, cloth extra, 6s.

Price (E. C.), Novels by:
Crown 8vo, cloth extra, 3s. 6d. each; post 8vo, illustrated boards, 2s. each.
Valentina. | The Foreigners.
Mrs. Lancaster's Rival.

Gerald. Post 8vo, illust. boards, 2s.

Princess Olga—Radna; or, The
Great Conspiracy of 1881. By the Princess OLGA. Cr. 8vo, cl. ex., 6s.

Proctor (Richd. A.), Works by:
Flowers of the Sky. With 55 Illusts. Small crown 8vo, cloth extra, 4s. 6d.
Easy Star Lessons. With Star Maps for Every Night in the Year, Drawings of the Constellations, &c. Crown 8vo, cloth extra, 6s.
Familiar Science Studies. Crown 8vo, cloth extra, 7s. 6d.
Saturn and its System. New and Revised Edition, with 13 Steel Plates. Demy 8vo, cloth extra, 10s. 6d.
The Great Pyramid: Observatory, Tomb, and Temple. With Illustrations. Crown 8vo, cloth extra, 6s.
Mysteries of Time and Space. With Illusts. Cr. 8vo, cloth extra, 7s. 6d.
The Universe of Suns, and other Science Gleanings. With numerous Illusts. Cr. 8vo, cloth extra, 7s. 6d.
Wages and Wants of Science Workers. Crown 8vo, 1s. 6d.

Rabelais' Works. Faithfully
Translated from the French, with variorum Notes, and numerous characteristic Illustrations by GUSTAVE DORÉ. Crown 8vo, cloth extra, 7s. 6d.

Rambosson.—Popular Astro-
nomy. By J. RAMBOSSON, Laureate of the Institute of France. Translated by C. B. PITMAN. Crown 8vo, cloth gilt, numerous Illusts., and a beautifully executed Chart of Spectra, 7s. 6d.

Reade (Charles), Novels by:
Cr. 8vo, cloth extra, illustrated, 3s. 6d. each; post 8vo, illust. bds., 2s. each.
Peg Woffington. Illustrated by S. L. FILDES, A.R.A.
Christie Johnstone. Illustrated by WILLIAM SMALL.
It is Never Too Late to Mend. Illustrated by G. J. PINWELL.
The Course of True Love Never did run Smooth. Illustrated by HELEN PATERSON.
The Autobiography of a Thief; Jack of all Trades; and James Lambert. Illustrated by MATT STRETCH.
Love me Little, Love me Long. Illustrated by M. ELLEN EDWARDS.
The Double Marriage. Illust. by Sir JOHN GILBERT, R.A., and C. KEENE.
The Cloister and the Hearth. Illustrated by CHARLES KEENE.
Hard Cash. Illust. by F. W. LAWSON.

READE (CHARLES), continued—
Griffith Gaunt. Illustrated by S. L. FILDES, A.R.A., and WM. SMALL.
Foul Play. Illust. by DU MAURIER.
Put Yourself in His Place. Illustrated by ROBERT BARNES.
A Terrible Temptation. Illustrated by EDW. HUGHES and A. W. COOPER.
The Wandering Heir. Illustrated by H. PATERSON, S. L. FILDES, A.R.A., C. GREEN, and H. WOODS, A.R.A.
A Simpleton. Illustrated by KATE CRAUFORD. [COULDERY.
A Woman-Hater. Illust. by THOS.
Singleheart and Doubleface: A Matter-of-fact Romance. Illustrated by P. MACNAB.
Good Stories of Men and other Animals. Illustrated by E. A. ABBEY, PERCY MACQUOID, and JOSEPH NASH.
The Jilt, and other Stories. Illustrated by JOSEPH NASH.
Readiana. With a Steel-plate Portrait of CHARLES READE.

Reader's Handbook (The) of
Allusions, References, Plots, and Stories. By the Rev. Dr. BREWER. Fifth Edition, revised throughout, with a New Appendix, containing a COMPLETE ENGLISH BIBLIOGRAPHY. Cr. 8vo, 1,400 pages, cloth extra, 7s. 6d.

Red Spider: A Romance. By
the Author of "John Herring," &c. Two Vols., crown 8vo.

Rice (Portrait of James).—
Specially etched by DANIEL A. WEHRSCHMIDT for the New Library Edition of BESANT and RICE's Novels. A few Proofs before Letters have been taken on Japanese paper, size 15¾ × 10 in. Price 5s. each.

Richardson. — A Ministry of
Health, and other Papers. By BENJAMIN WARD RICHARDSON, M.D., &c. Crown 8vo, cloth extra, 6s.

Riddell (Mrs. J. H.), Novels by:
Crown 8vo, cloth extra, 3s. 6d. each; post 8vo, illustrated boards, 2s. each.
Her Mother's Darling.
The Prince of Wales's Garden Party
Weird Stories.

Post 8vo, illustrated boards, 2s. each.
The Uninhabited House.
Fairy Water.
The Mystery in Palace Gardens.

Rimmer (Alfred), Works by:
Square 8vo, cloth gilt, 10s. 6d. each.
Our Old Country Towns. With over 50 Illustrations.
Rambles Round Eton and Harrow. With 50 Illustrations.
About England with Dickens. With 58 Illustrations by ALFRED RIMMER and C. A. VANDERHOOF.

Robinson Crusoe: A beautiful
reproduction of Major's Edition, with
37 Woodcuts and Two Steel Plates by
GEORGE CRUIKSHANK, choicely printed.
Crown 8vo, cloth extra, 7s. 6d.

Robinson (F. W.), Novels by:
Crown 8vo, cloth extra, 3s. 6d. each ;
post 8vo, illustrated boards, 2s. each.
Women are Strange.
The Hands of Justice.

Robinson (Phil), Works by:
Crown 8vo, cloth extra, 7s. 6d. each.
The Poets' Birds.
The Poets' Beasts.
The Poets and Nature: Reptiles,
Fishes and Insects. [*Preparing.*

Rochefoucauld's Maxims and
Moral Reflections. With Notes, and
an Introductory Essay by SAINTE-
BEUVE. Post 8vo, cloth limp, 2s.

Roll of Battle Abbey, The; or,
A List of the Principal Warriors who
came over from Normandy with William the Conqueror, and Settled in
this Country, A.D. 1066–7. With the
principal Arms emblazoned in Gold
and Colours. Handsomely printed, 5s.

Rowley (Hon. Hugh), Works by:
Post 8vo, cloth limp, 2s. 6d. each.
Puniana: Riddles and Jokes. With
numerous Illustrations.
More Puniana. Profusely Illustrated.

Runciman (James), Stories by:
Post 8vo, illustrated boards, 2s. each
cloth limp, 2s. 6d each.
Skippers and Shellbacks.
Grace Balmaign's Sweetheart.
Schools and Scholars.

Russell (W. Clark), Works by:
Crown 8vo, cloth extra, 6s. each; post
8vo, illustrated boards, 2s. each.
Round the Galley-Fire.
On the Fo'k'sle Head.
In the Middle Watch.
Crown 8vo, cloth extra, 6s. each.
A Voyage to the Cape.
A Book for the Hammock.
The Frozen Pirate, the New Serial
Novel by W. CLARK RUSSELL, Author
of "The Wreck of the *Grosvenor*,"
began in "Belgravia" for July, and
will be continued till January next.
One Shilling, Monthly. Illustrated.

Sala.—Gaslight and Daylight.
By GEORGE AUGUSTUS SALA. Post
8vo, illustrated boards, 2s.

Sanson.—Seven Generations
of Executioners: Memoirs of the
Sanson Family (1688 to 1847). Edited
by HENRY SANSON. Cr.8vo, cl.ex. 3s. 6d.

Saunders (John), Novels by:
Crown 8vo, cloth extra, 3s. 6d. each ;
post 8vo, illustrated boards, 2s. each.
Bound to the Wheel
Guy Waterman.|Lion in the Path.
The Two Dreamers.
One Against the World. Post 8vo,
illustrated boards, 2s.

Saunders (Katharine), Novels
by. Cr. 8vo, cloth extra, 3s. 6d. each;
post 8vo, illustrated boards, 2s. each.
Joan Merryweather.
Margaret and Elizabeth.
The High Mills.
Heart Salvage. | Sebastian.
Gideon's Rock.
Crown 8vo, cloth extra, 3s. 6d.

Science Gossip: An Illustrated
Medium of Interchange for Students
and Lovers of Nature. Edited by J. E.
TAYLOR, F.L.S., &c. Devoted to Geo-
logy, Botany, Physiology, Chemistry,
Zoology, Microscopy, Telescopy, Phy-
siography, &c. Price 4d. Monthly; or
5s. per year, post free. Vols. I. to
XIV. may be had at 7s. 6d. each; and
Vols. XV. to XXII. (1886), at 5s. each.
Cases for Binding, 1s. 6d. each.

Scott (Sir Walter), Poems by:
Marmion. With over 100 new Illusts.
by leading Artists. Sm.4to,cl.ex..10s.
The Lay of the Last Minstrel. With
over 100 new Illustrations by leading
Artists. Sm.4to, cl. ex., 16s.

"Secret Out" Series, The:
Cr. 8vo, cl. ex., Illusts., 4s. 6d. each.
The Secret Out: One Thousand
Tricks with Cards, and other Re-
creations; with Entertaining Experi-
ments in Drawing-room or "White
Magic." By W. H. CREMER. 300 Illusts.
The Art of Amusing: A Collection of
Graceful Arts,Games,Tricks,Puzzles,
and Charades By FRANK BELLEW.
With 300 Illustrations.
Hanky-Panky: Very Easy Tricks,
Very Difficult Tricks, White Magic
Sleight of Hand. Edited by W. H.
CREMER. With 200 Illustrations.
The Merry Circle: A Book of New
Intellectual Games and Amusements.
By CLARA BELLEW. Many Illusts.
Magician's Own Book: Performances
with Cups and Balls, Eggs, Hats,
Handkerchiefs, &c. All from actual
Experience. Edited by W. H. CRE-
MER. 200 Illustrations.

Senior.—By Stream and Sea.
By W. SENIOR. Post 8vo, cl.limp, 2s.6d.

Seven Sagas (The) of Prehis-
toric Man. By JAMES H. STODDART,
Author of "The Village Life." Crown
8vo, cloth extra, 6s.

SWINBURNE'S (A. C.) WORKS, *continued—*
Songs of the Springtides. Cr. 8vo, 6s.
Studies in Song. Crown 8vo, 7s.
Mary Stuart : A Tragedy. Cr. 8vo, 8s.
Tristram of Lyoncsse, and other Poems. Crown 8vo, 9s.
A Century of Roundels. Small 4to' 8s.
A Midsummer Holiday, and other Poems. Crown 8vo, 7s.
Marino Faliero : A Tragedy. Cr.8vo,6s.
A Study of Victor Hugo. Cr. 8vo, 6s.
Miscellanies. Crown 8vo, 12s.
Locrine : A Tragedy. Crown 8vo, 6s.

Symonds.—Wine, Women, and
Song: Mediæval Latin Students' Songs. Now first translated into English Verse, with Essay by J. ADDINGTON SYMONDS. Small 8vo, parchment, 6s.

Syntax's (Dr.) Three Tours :
In Search of the Picturesque, in Search of Consolation, and in Search of a Wife. With the whole of ROWLANDSON's droll page Illustrations in Colours and a Life of the Author by J. C. HOTTEN. Med. 8vo, cloth extra, 7s. 6d.

Taine's History of English
Literature. Translated by HENRY VAN LAUN. Four Vols., small 8vo, cloth boards, 30s.—POPULAR EDITION, Two Vols., crown 8vo, cloth extra, 15s.

Taylor's (Bayard) Diversions
of the Echo Club: Burlesques of Modern Writers. Post 8vo, cl. limp, 2s.

Taylor (Dr. J. E., F.L.S.), Works
by. Crown 8vo, cloth ex., 7s. 6d. each.
The Sagacity and Morality of Plants: A Sketch of the Life and Conduct of the Vegetable Kingdom. Coloured Frontispiece and 100 Illust.
Our Common British Fossils, and Where to Find Them: A Handbook for Students. With 331 Illustrations.

Taylor's (Tom) Historical
Dramas: "Clancarty," "Jeanne Darc," "'Twixt Axe and Crown," "The Fool's Revenge," "Arkwright's Wife," "Anne Boleyn," "Plot and Passion." One Vol., cr. 8vo, cloth extra, 7s. 6d.
*** The Plays may also be had separately, at 1s. each.

Tennyson (Lord): A Biogra-
phical Sketch. By H. J. JENNINGS. With a Photograph-Portrait. Crown 8vo, cloth extra, 6s.

Thackerayana: Notes and Anec-
dotes. Illustrated by Hundreds of Sketches by WILLIAM MAKEPEACE THACKERAY, depicting Humorous Incidents in his School-life, and Favourite Characters in the books of his every-day reading. With Coloured Frontispiece. Cr. 8vo, cl. extra, 7s. 6d.

Thomas (Bertha), Novels by :
Crown 8vo, cloth extra, 3s. 6d. each
post 8vo, illustrated boards, 2s. each.
Cressida. | Proud Maisie.
The Violin-Player.

Thomas (M.).—A Fight for Life :
A Novel. By W. MOY THOMAS. Post 8vo, illustrated boards, 2s.

Thomson's Seasons and Castle
of Indolence. With a Biographical and Critical Introduction by ALLAN CUNNINGHAM, and over 50 fine Illustrations on Steel and Wood. Crown 8vo, cloth extra, gilt edges, 7s. 6d.

Thornbury (Walter), Works by
Haunted London. Edited by EDWARD WALFORD, M.A. With Illustrations by F. W. FAIRHOLT, F.S.A. Crown 8vo, cloth extra, 7s. 6d.
The Life and Correspondence of J. M. W. Turner. Founded upon Letters and Papers furnished by his Friends and fellow Academicians. With numerous Illusts. in Colours, facsimiled from Turner's Original Drawings. Cr. 8vo, cl. extra, 7s. 6d.
Old Stories Re-told. Post 8vo, cloth limp, 2s. 6d.
Tales for the Marines. Post 8vo, illustrated boards, 2s.

Timbs (John), Works by :
Crown 8vo, cloth extra, 7s. 6d. each.
The History of Clubs and Club Life in London. With Anecdotes of its Famous Coffee-houses, Hostelries, and Taverns. With many Illusts.
English Eccentrics and Eccentricities: Stories of Wealth and Fashion, Delusions, Impostures, and Fanatic Missions, Strange Sights and Sporting Scenes, Eccentric Artists, Theatrical Folk, Men of Letters, &c. With nearly 50 Illusts.

Trollope (Anthony), Novels by:
Crown 8vo, cloth extra, 3s. 6d. each ;
post 8vo, illustrated boards, 2s. each.
The Way We Live Now.
Kept in the Dark.
Frau Frohmann. | Marion Fay.
Mr. Scarborough's Family.
The Land-Leaguers.
Post 8vo, illustrated boards, 2s. each.
The Golden Lion of Granpere.
John Caldigate. | American Senator

Trollope (Frances E.), Novels by
Crown 8vo, cloth extra, 3s. 6d. each ;
post 8vo, illustrated boards, 2s. each.
Like Ships upon the Sea.
Mabel's Progress. | Anne Furness.

Trollope (T. A.).—Diamond Cut
Diamond, and other Stories. By T. ADOLPHUS TROLLOPE. Post 8vo, illustrated boards, 2s.

Trowbridge.—Farnell's Folly :
A Novel. By J. T. TROWBRIDGE. Post
8vo, illustrated boards, 2s.

Turgenieff. — Stories from
Foreign Novelists. By IVAN TURGE-
NIEFF, and others. Cr. 8vo, cloth extra,
3s. 6d.; post 8vo, illustrated boards, 2s.

Tytler (C. C. Fraser-).—Mistress Judith: A Novel. By C. C.
FRASER-TYTLER. Cr. 8vo, cloth extra,
3s. 6d.; post 8vo, illust. boards, 2s.

Tytler (Sarah), Novels by :
Crown 8vo, cloth extra, 3s. 6d. each ;
post 8vo, illustrated boards, 2s. each.
What She Came Through.
The Bride's Pass.
Saint Mungo's City.
Beauty and the Beast.
Noblesse Oblige.
Lady Bell.

Crown 8vo, cloth extra, 3s. 6d. each.
Citoyenne Jacqueline.   Illustrated
by A. B. HOUGHTON.
The Huguenot Family. With Illusts.
Buried Diamonds.

Disappeared. With Six Illustrations
by P. MACNAB. Crown 8vo, cloth
extra, 6s.

Van Laun.—History of French
Literature. By H. VAN LAUN. Three
Vols., demy 8vo, cl. bds., 7s. 6d. each.

Villari. — A Double Bond : A
Story. By LINDA VILLARI. Fcap.
8vo, picture cover, 1s.

Walford (Edw., M.A.),Works by :
The County Families of the United
Kingdom. Containing Notices of
the Descent, Birth, Marriage, Educa-
tion, &c., of more than 12000, dis-
tinguished Heads of Families, their
Heirs Apparent or Presumptive, the
Offices they hold or have held, their
Town and Country Addresses, Clubs,
&c. Twenty-seventh Annual Edi-
tion, for 1887, cloth gilt, 50s.
The Shilling Peerage (1887). Con-
taining an Alphabetical List of the
House of Lords, Dates of Creation,
Lists of Scotch and Irish Peers,
Addresses, &c. 32mo, cloth, 1s.
Published annually.
The Shilling Baronetage (1887).
Containing an Alphabetical List of
the Baronets of the United Kingdom,
short Biographical Notices, Dates
of Creation, Addresses, &c. 32mo,
cloth, 1s.
The Shilling Knightage (1887). Con-
taining an Alphabetical List of the
Knights of the United Kingdom,
short Biographical Notices, Dates of
Creation, Addresses,&c. 32mo,cl.,1s.

WALFORD's (EDW.) WORKS, continued—
The Shilling House of Commons
(1887). Containing a List of all the
Members of Parliament, their Town
and Country Addresses, &c.   New
Edition, embodying the results of
the recent General Election. 32mo,
cloth, 1s. Published annually.
The Complete Peerage, Baronetage, Knightage, and House of
Commons (1887). In One Volume,
royal 32mo, cloth extra, gilt edges, 5s.

Haunted London.   By WALTER
THORNBURY. Edited by EDWARD
WALFORD, M.A. With Illustrations
by F. W. FAIRHOLT, F.S.A. Crown
8vo, cloth extra, 7s. 6d.

Walton and Cotton's Complete
Angler; or, The Contemplative Man's
Recreation; being a Discourse of
Rivers, Fishponds, Fish and Fishing,
written by IZAAK WALTON; and In-
structions how to Angle for a Trout or
Grayling in a clear Stream, by CHARLES
COTTON. With Original Memoirs and
Notes by Sir HARRIS NICOLAS, and
61 Copperplate Illustrations. Large
crown 8vo, cloth antique, 7s. 6d.

Walt Whitman, Poems by.
Selected and edited, with an Introduction, by WILLIAM M. ROSSETTI. A
New Edition, with a Steel Plate Portrait. Crown 8vo, printed on hand-
made paper and bound in buckram, 6s.

Wanderer's Library, The :
Crown 8vo, cloth extra, 3s. 6d. each.
Wanderings In Patagonia; or, Life
among the Ostrich-Hunters.   By
JULIUS BEERBOHM. Illustrated.
Camp Notes: Stories of Sport and
Adventure in Asia, Africa, and
America. By FREDERICK BOYLE.
Savage Life. By FREDERICK BOYLE.
Merrie England in the Olden Time.
By GEORGE DANIEL. With Illustra-
tions by ROBT. CRUIKSHANK.
Circus Life and Circus Celebrities.
By THOMAS FROST.
The Lives of the Conjurers. By
THOMAS FROST.
The Old Showmen and the Old
London Fairs. By THOMAS FROST.
Low-Life Deeps. An Account of the
Strange Fish to be found there. By
JAMES GREENWOOD.
The Wilds of London. By JAMES
GREENWOOD.
Tunis: The Land and the People.
By the Chevalier de HESSE-WAR-
TEGG. With 22 Illustrations.
The Life and Adventures of a Cheap
Jack. By One of the Fraternity.
Edited by CHARLES HINDLEY.
The World Behind the Scenes. By
PERCY FITZGERALD.

PICCADILLY NOVELS, *continued—*
BY CHARLES GIBBON.
Robin Gray.
What will the World Say?
In Honour Bound.
Queen of the Meadow.
The Flower of the Forest.
A Heart's Problem.
The Braes of Yarrow.
The Golden Shaft.
Fancy Free.
Of High Degree.
Loving a Dream.
A Hard Knot.

BY THOMAS HARDY.
Under the Greenwood Tree.

BY JULIAN HAWTHORNE.
Garth.
Ellice Quentin.
Sebastian Strome.
Prince Saroni's Wife.
Dust.
Fortune's Fool.
Beatrix Randolph.
Miss Cadogna.
Love—or a Name.

BY SIR A. HELPS.
Ivan de Biron.

BY MRS. ALFRED HUNT.
Thornicroft's Model.
The Leaden Casket.
Self-Condemned.
That other Person.

BY JEAN INGELOW.
Fated to be Free.

BY R. ASHE KING.
A Drawn Game.
"The Wearing of the Green."

BY HENRY KINGSLEY.
Number Seventeen.

BY E. LYNN LINTON.
Patricia Kemball.
Atonement of Leam Dundas.
The World Well Lost.
Under which Lord?
With a Silken Thread.
The Rebel of the Family
"My Love!" | Ione.

BY HENRY W. LUCY.
Gideon Fleyce.

BY JUSTIN McCARTHY.
The Waterdale Neighbours.
A Fair Saxon.
Dear Lady Disdain.
Miss Misanthrope.
Donna Quixote.
The Comet of a Season.
Maid of Athens.
Camiola.

BY MRS. MACDONELL
Quaker Cousins.

PICCADILLY NOVELS, *continued—*
BY FLORENCE MARRYAT.
Open! Sesame! | Written in Fire.

BY D. CHRISTIE MURRAY.
Life's Atonement. | Coals of Fire.
Joseph's Coat. | Val Strange.
A Model Father. | Hearts.
By the Gate of the Sea
The Way of the World.
A Bit of Human Nature.
First Person Singular.
Cynic Fortune.

BY MRS. OLIPHANT.
Whiteladies.

BY MARGARET A. PAUL.
Gentle and Simple.

BY JAMES PAYN.
Lost Sir Massing- | A Confidential
  berd. | Agent.
Best of Husbands | A Grape from a
Walter's Word. | Thorn.
Less Black than | For Cash Only.
  We're Painted.| Some Private
By Proxy | Views.
High Spirits. | The   Canon's
Under One Roof.| Ward
From Exile. | Talk of the Town.

BY E. C. PRICE.
Valentina. | The Foreigners.
Mrs. Lancaster's Rival.

BY CHARLES READE.
It is Never Too Late to Mend.
Hard Cash.
Peg Woffington.
Christie Johnstone.
Griffith Gaunt. | Foul Play.
The Double Marriage.
Love Me Little, Love Me Long.
The Cloister and the Hearth.
The Course of True Love.
The Autobiography of a Thief.
Put Yourself in His Place.
A Terrible Temptation.
The Wandering Heir. | A Simpleton
A Woman-Hater. | Readiana.
Singleheart and Doubleface.
The Jilt.
Good Stories of Men and other
Animals.

BY MRS. J. H. RIDDELL.
Her Mother's Darling.
Prince of Wales's Garden-Party.
Weird Stories.

BY F. W. ROBINSON.
Women are Strange.
The Hands of Justice.

BY JOHN SAUNDERS.
Bound to the Wheel.
Guy Waterman.
Two Dreamers.
The Lion in the Path.

PICCADILLY NOVELS, *continued—*

BY KATHARINE SAUNDERS.
Joan Merryweather.
Margaret and Elizabeth.
Gideon's Rock. | Heart Salvage.
The High Mills. | Sebastian.

BY T. W. SPEIGHT.
The Mysteries of Heron Dyke.

BY R. A. STERNDALE.
The Afghan Knife.

BY BERTHA THOMAS.
Proud Maisie. | Cressida.
The Violin-Player.

BY ANTHONY TROLLOPE.
The Way we Live Now.
Frau Frohmann. | Marion Fay.
Kept in the Dark.
Mr. Scarborough's Family.
The Land-Leaguers.

PICCADILLY NOVELS, *continued—*

BY FRANCES E. TROLLOPE.
Like Ships upon the Sea.
Anne Furness.
Mabel's Progress.

BY IVAN TURGENIEFF, &c.
Stories from Foreign Novelists.

BY SARAH TYTLER.
What She Came Through.
The Bride's Pass.
Saint Mungo's City.
Beauty and the Beast.
Noblesse Oblige.
Citoyenne Jacqueline.
The Huguenot Family.
Lady Bell.
Buried Diamonds.

BY C. C. FRASER-TYTLER.
Mistress Judith.

BY J. S. WINTER.
Regimental Legends.

CHEAP EDITIONS OF POPULAR NOVELS.
Post 8vo, illustrated boards, 2s. each.

BY EDMOND ABOUT.
The Fellah.

BY HAMILTON AÏDÉ.
Carr of Carrlyon. | Confidences.

BY MRS. ALEXANDER.
Maid, Wife, or Widow?
Valerie's Fate.

BY GRANT ALLEN.
Strange Stories.
Philistia.
Babylon.

BY SHELSLEY BEAUCHAMP.
Grantley Grange.

BY W. BESANT & JAMES RICE.
Ready-Money Mortiboy.
With Harp and Crown.
This Son of Vulcan. | My Little Girl.
The Case of Mr. Lucraft.
The Golden Butterfly.
By Celia's Arbour.
The Monks of Thelema.
'Twas in Trafalgar's Bay.
The Seamy Side.
The Ten Years' Tenant.
The Chaplain of the Fleet.

BY WALTER BESANT.
All Sorts and Conditions of Men.
The Captains' Room.
All in a Garden Fair.
Dorothy Forster.
Uncle Jack

BY FREDERICK BOYLE.
Camp Notes. | Savage Life.
Chronicles of No-man's Land.

BY BRET HARTE.
An Heiress of Red Dog.
The Luck of Roaring Camp.
Californian Stories.
Gabriel Conroy. | Flip.
Maruja.

BY ROBERT BUCHANAN.
The Shadow of | The Martyrdom
the Sword. | of Madeline.
A Child of Nature. | Annan Water.
God and the Man. | The New Abelard.
Love Me for Ever. | Matt.
Foxglove Manor. |
The Master of the Mine.

BY MRS. BURNETT.
Surly Tim.

BY HALL CAINE.
The Shadow of a Crime.

BY MRS. LOVETT CAMERON
Deceivers Ever. | Juliet's Guardian

BY MACLAREN COBBAN.
The Cure of Souls.

BY C. ALLSTON COLLINS.
The Bar Sinister.

BY WILKIE COLLINS.
Antonina. | Queen of Hearts.
Basil. | My Miscellanies.
Hide and Seek. | Woman in White.
The Dead Secret. | The Moonstone.

WILKIE COLLINS, *continued.*

Man and Wife.	Haunted Hotel.
Poor Miss Finch.	The Fallen Leaves.
Miss or Mrs. ?	Jezebel's Daughter
New Magdalen.	The Black Robe.
The Frozen Deep.	Heart and Science
Law and the Lady.	"I Say No."
The Two Destinies	The Evil Genius.

BY MORTIMER COLLINS.

Sweet Anne Page.	From Midnight to
Transmigration.	Midnight.
A Fight with Fortune.	

MORTIMER & FRANCES COLLINS.

Sweet and Twenty.	Frances.

Blacksmith and Scholar
The Village Comedy.
You Play me False.

BY DUTTON COOK.

Leo.	Paul Foster's Daughter.

BY C. EGBERT CRADDOCK.
The Prophet of the Great Smoky Mountains.

BY WILLIAM CYPLES.
Hearts of Gold.

BY ALPHONSE DAUDET.
The Evangelist; or, Port Salvation.

BY JAMES DE MILLE.
A Castle in Spain.

BY J. LEITH DERWENT.
Our Lady of Tears. | Circe's Lovers.

BY CHARLES DICKENS.

Sketches by Boz.	Oliver Twist.
Pickwick Papers.	Nicholas Nickleby

BY MRS. ANNIE EDWARDES.
A Point of Honour. | Archie Lovell.

BY M. BETHAM-EDWARDS.

Felicia.	Kitty.

BY EDWARD EGGLESTON.
Roxy.

BY PERCY FITZGERALD.

Bella Donna.	Never Forgotten.

The Second Mrs. Tillotson.
Polly.
Seventy-five Brooke Street.
The Lady of Brantome.

BY ALBANY DE FONBLANQUE.
Filthy Lucre.

BY R. E. FRANCILLON.

Olympia.	Queen Cophetua.
One by One.	A Real Queen.

Prefaced by Sir H. BARTLE FRERE.
Pandurang Hari.

BY HAIN FRISWELL.
One of Two

BY EDWARD GARRETT.
The Capel Girls.

BY CHARLES GIBBON.

Robin Gray.	The Flower of the
For Lack of Gold.	Forest.
What will the	Braes of Yarrow.
World Say ?	The Golden Shaft.
In Honour Bound.	Of High Degree.
In Love and War.	Fancy Free.
For the King.	Mead and Stream.
In Pastures Green	Loving a Dream.
Queen of the Mea-	A Hard Knot.
dow.	Heart's Delight.
A Heart's Problem	

BY WILLIAM GILBERT.
Dr. Austin's Guests
The Wizard of the Mountain.
James Duke.

BY JAMES GREENWOOD.
Dick Temple.

BY JOHN HABBERTON.
Brueton's Bayou. | Country Luck.

BY ANDREW HALLIDAY.
Every-Day Papers.

BY LADY DUFFUS HARDY.
Paul Wynter's Sacrifice.

BY THOMAS HARDY.
Under the Greenwood Tree.

BY J. BERWICK HARWOOD.
The Tenth Earl.

BY JULIAN HAWTHORNE.

Garth.	Sebastian Strome
Ellice Quentin.	Dust.

Prince Saroni's Wife.

Fortune's Fool.	Beatrix Randolph.

BY SIR ARTHUR HELPS.
Ivan de Biron.

BY MRS. CASHEL HOEY.
The Lover's Creed.

BY TOM HOOD.
A Golden Heart.

BY MRS. GEORGE HOOPER.
The House of Raby.

BY TIGHE HOPKINS.
'Twixt Love and Duty.

BY MRS. ALFRED HUNT.
Thornicroft's Model.
The Leaden Casket.
Self-Condemned.

BY JEAN INGELOW.
Fated to be Free.

BY HARRIETT JAY.
The Dark Colleen.
The Queen of Connaught.

BY MARK KERSHAW.
Colonial Facts and Fictions.

BY R. ASHE KING.
A Drawn Game.
"The Wearing of the Green."

BY HENRY KINGSLEY.
Oakshott Castle.

BY E. LYNN LINTON.
Patricia Kemball.
The Atonement of Leam Dundas

CHEAP POPULAR NOVELS, *continued—*

E. LYNN LINTON, *continued—*

The World Well Lost.
Under which Lord?
With a Silken Thread.
The Rebel of the Family.
"My Love." | Ione.

BY HENRY W. LUCY.

Gideon Fleyce.

BY JUSTIN McCARTHY.

Dear Lady Disdain | Miss Misanthrope
The Waterdale | Donna Quixote.
Neighbours. | The Comet of a
My Enemy's | Season.
Daughter. | Maid of Athens.
A Fair Saxon. | Camiola.
Linley Rochford. |

BY MRS. MACDONELL.

Quaker Cousins.

BY KATHARINE S. MACQUOID.

The Evil Eye. | Lost Rose.

BY W. H. MALLOCK.

The New Republic.

BY FLORENCE MARRYAT.

Open! Sesame | A Little Stepson.
A Harvest of Wild | Fighting the Air.
Oats. | Written in Fire.

BY J. MASTERMAN.

Half-a-dozen Daughters.

BY BRANDER MATTHEWS.

A Secret of the Sea.

BY JEAN MIDDLEMASS.

Touch and Go. | Mr. Dorillion.

BY D. CHRISTIE MURRAY.

A Life's Atonement | Hearts.
A Model Father. | Way of the World.
Joseph's Coat. | A Bit of Human
Coals of Fire. | Nature.
By the Gate of the | First Person Sin-
Sea. | gular.
Val Strange. | Cynic Fortune.

BY ALICE O'HANLON.

The Unforeseen.

BY MRS. OLIPHANT.

Whiteladies.

BY MRS. ROBERT O'REILLY.

Phœbe's Fortunes.

BY OUIDA.

Held in Bondage. | Two Little Wooden
Strathmore. | Shoes.
Chandos. | In a Winter City.
Under Two Flags. | Ariadne.
Idalia. | Friendship.
Cecil Castle- | Moths.
maine's Gage. | Pipistrello.
Tricotrin. | A Village Com-
Puck. | mune.
Folle Farine. | Bimbi.
A Dog of Flanders. | Wanda.
Pascarel. | Frescoes.
Signa. [Ine. | In Maremma.
Princess Naprax- | Othmar.

CHEAP POPULAR NOVELS, *continued—*

BY MARGARET AGNES PAUL.

Gentle and Simple.

BY JAMES PAYN.

Lost Sir Massing- | Like Father, Like
berd. | Son.
A Perfect Trea- | Marine Residence.
sure. | Married Beneath
Bentinck's Tutor. | Him.
Murphy's Master. | Mirk Abbey.
A County Family. | Not Wooed, but
At Her Mercy. | Won.
A Woman's Ven- | Less Black than
geance. | We're Painted.
Cecil's Tryst. | By Proxy.
Clyffards of Clyffe | Under One Roof.
The Family Scape- | High Spirits.
grace. | Carlyon's Year.
Foster Brothers. | A Confidential
Found Dead. | Agent.
Best of Husbands. | Some Private
Walter's Word. | Views.
Halves. | From Exile.
Fallen Fortunes. | A Grape from a
What He Cost Her | Thorn.
Humorous Stories | For Cash Only.
Gwendoline's Har- | Kit: A Memory.
vest. | The Canon's Ward
£200 Reward. | Talk of the Town.

BY MRS. PIRKIS.

Lady Lovelace.

BY EDGAR A. POE.

The Mystery of Marie Roget.

BY E. C. PRICE.

Valentina. | The Foreigners.
Mrs. Lancaster's Rival.
Gerald.

BY CHARLES READE.

It Is Never Too Late to Mend.
Hard Cash. | Peg Woffington.
Christie Johnstone.
Griffith Gaunt.
Put Yourself in His Place.
The Double Marriage.
Love Me Little, Love Me Long.
Foul Play.
The Cloister and the Hearth
The Course of True Love.
Autobiography of a Thief.
A Terrible Temptation.
The Wandering Heir.
A Simpleton. | A Woman-Hater
Readiana. | The Jilt.
Singleheart and Doubleface.
Good Stories of Men and other
Animals.

BY MRS. J. H. RIDDELL.

Her Mother's Darling.
Prince of Wales's Garden Party.
Weird Stories. | Fairy Water.
The Uninhabited House.
The Mystery in Palace Gardens.

BY F. W. ROBINSON,

Women are Strange.
The Hands of Justice.

CHEAP POPULAR NOVELS, *continued*—

BY JAMES RUNCIMAN.
Skippers and Shellbacks.
Grace Balmaign's Sweetheart.
Schools and Scholars.

BY W. CLARK RUSSELL.
Round the Galley Fire.
On the Fo'k'sle Head.
In the Middle Watch.

BY BAYLE ST. JOHN.
A Levantine Family

BY GEORGE AUGUSTUS SALA.
Gaslight and Daylight.

BY JOHN SAUNDERS.
Bound to the Wheel.
One Against the World.
Guy Waterman.
The Lion in the Path.
Two Dreamers.

BY KATHARINE SAUNDERS.
Joan Merryweather.
Margaret and Elizabeth.
The High Mills.
Heart Salvage. | Sebastian.

BY GEORGE R. SIMS.
Rogues and Vagabonds.
The Ring o' Bells.
Mary Jane's Memoirs.

BY ARTHUR SKETCHLEY.
A Match in the Dark.

BY T. W. SPEIGHT.
The Mysteries of Heron Dyke.

BY R. A. STERNDALE.
The Afghan Knife.

BY R. LOUIS STEVENSON.
New Arabian Nights. | Prince Otto.

BY BERTHA THOMAS.
Cressida. | Proud Maisie.
The Violin-Player.

BY W. MOY THOMAS.
A Fight for Life.

BY WALTER THORNBURY.
Tales for the Marines.

BY T. ADOLPHUS TROLLOPE.
Diamond Cut Diamond.

BY ANTHONY TROLLOPE.
The Way We Live Now.
The American Senator.
Frau Frohmann.
Marion Fay.
Kept in the Dark.
Mr. Scarborough's Family.
The Land-Leaguers.
The Golden Lion of Granpere.
John Caldigate.

By FRANCES ELEANOR TROLLOPE
Like Ships upon the Sea.
Anne Furness. | Mabel's Progress.

BY J. T. TROWBRIDGE.
Farnell's Folly.

BY IVAN TURGENIEFF, &c.
Stories from Foreign Novelists.

CHEAP POPULAR NOVELS, *continued*—

BY MARK TWAIN.
Tom Sawyer.
A Pleasure Trip on the Continent of Europe.
A Tramp Abroad.
The Stolen White Elephant.
Huckleberry Finn.
Life on the Mississippi.

BY C. C. FRASER-TYTLER.
Mistress Judith.

BY SARAH TYTLER.
What She Came Through.
The Bride's Pass.
Saint Mungo's City.
Beauty and the Beast.

BY J. S. WINTER.
Cavalry Life. | Regimental Legends.

BY LADY WOOD.
Sabina.

BY EDMUND YATES.
Castaway. | The Forlorn Hope.
Land at Last.

ANONYMOUS.
Paul Ferroll.
Why Paul Ferroll Killed his Wife.

POPULAR SHILLING BOOKS.
Jeff Briggs's Love Story. By BRET HARTE.
The Twins of Table Mountain. By BRET HARTE.
Mrs. Gainsborough's Diamonds. By JULIAN HAWTHORNE.
Kathleen Mavourneen. By Author of "That Lass o' Lowrie's."
Lindsay's Luck. By the Author of "That Lass o' Lowrie's."
Pretty Polly Pemberton. By the Author of "That Lass o' Lowrie's."
Trooping with Crows. By Mrs. PIRKIS.
The Professor's Wife. By LEONARD GRAHAM.
A Double Bond. By LINDA VILLARI.
Esther's Glove. By R. E. FRANCILLON.
The Garden that Paid the Rent. By TOM JERROLD.
Curly. By JOHN COLEMAN. Illustrated by J. C. DOLLMAN.
Beyond the Gates. By E. S. PHELPS.
An Old Maid's Paradise. By E. S. PHELPS.
Burglars in Paradise. By E.S.PHELPS.
Doom: An Atlantic Episode. By JUSTIN H. MacCARTHY, M.P.
Our Sensation Novel. Edited by JUSTIN H. MacCARTHY, M.P.
A Barren Title. By T. W. SPEIGHT.
Wife or No Wife? By T. W. SPEIGHT.
How the Poor Live. By G. R. SIMS.
A Day's Tour. By PERCY FITZGERALD.
The Silverado Squatters. By R. LOUIS STEVENSON.

www.ingramcontent.com/pod-product-compliance
Lightning Source LLC
Chambersburg PA
CBHW030631030726
47497CB00006B/1732